THE LAST GOOD WAR

A World War II Novel

by

CHARLES J. BRAUNER

© Copyright 2003 by Charles J. Brauner. All rights reserved.
No part of the publication may be reproduced or transmitted in any form or by any means, electronic or mechanical, including photocopy, recording or any information storage and retrieval system, without permission in writing from the publisher.

Printed in Canada.

Disclaimer

This book is a work of fiction. The names, characters, places, and events are either drawn from the author's imagination or used fictionally to give credence to the story. Any resemblance to actual persons living or dead is entirely coincidental.

The cover was designed and painted by the author, Charles J. Brauner. (CjB)

National Library of Canada Cataloguing in Publication

Brauner, Charles J.
  The last good war / Charles J. Brauner.
ISBN 1-4120-0388-1
  1. World War, 1939-1945—Aerial operations, Canadian—Fiction.
  I. Title.
PS8553.R362L38 2003   C813'.6   C2003-902819-4
PR9199.4.B728L38 2003

TRAFFORD

This book was published on-demand in cooperation with Trafford Publishing.
On-demand publishing is a unique process and service of making a book available for retail sale to the public taking advantage of on-demand manufacturing and Internet marketing. **On-demand publishing** includes promotions, retail sales, manufacturing, order fulfilment, accounting and collecting royalties on behalf of the author.

Suite 6E, 2333 Government St., Victoria, B.C. V8T 4P4, CANADA
Phone   250-383-6864   Toll-free 1-888-232-4444 (Canada & US)
Fax   250-383-6804   E-mail   sales@trafford.com
Website www.trafford.com   TRAFFORD PUBLISHING IS A DIVISION OF TRAFFORD HOLDINGS LTD.
Trafford Catalogue #03-0757   www.trafford.com/robots/03-0757.html

Dedication

To my father **Charles Brauner**, Ensign, Small Ships Branch, Army Transport Service, buried in the U.S. National Cemetery located in the Punch Bowl, Oahu, Hawaii.

To my cousin **Martin Henry Mann**, Gunnery Sergeant, U.S. Marine Corps who made six island invasions during the war in the Pacific.

To my friend **Max Wolfgang Boysen**, Aviation Radioman's Mate 3/c who flew in Curtiss Helldivers during World War II.

And to all those who served with honor.

Homage to Sailors Lost at Sea

Hard past Deadman's Shoal
Hear the shrilldeer shriek
Of the tufted shipwreck shrike
Who bears the drowned sailor's soul
Aloft in a horn-hooked beak
Curved to thread God's lofty pike
With a kiss
That sends the lost mariner's cry
Echoing through Eternity.

CjB

CHAPTER ONE

Total war
Between implacable foes
Always boils down
To a test of character.

As soon as the Japanese carrier planes sank the American Pacific battleship fleet at Pearl Harbor, Carson Braddock and Max Bryson became eager to leave their homes in Canada and enlisted in the United States Navy. At sixteen years of age minus a month, Carson was dark, quick-witted, and volatile. Fully six weeks younger, Max was fair-skinned, diligent, and sensitive. Both boys were quiet, athletic, bright, verbal, and confident of their actions.

As cousins, the consuming force in their lives was to aid the efforts of Carson's father serving with the Australians in New Guinea. The September 1942 telegram of regret announcing his death in action drove them to act. The tactics were simple: skip their tenth grade high school classes and hitchhike ninety miles south from Vancouver, British Columbia to Seattle, Washington. There they presented their doctored Canadian birth certificates along with forged letters of permission to enlist, and tried hard to look seventeen.

Having skipped lunch the boys munched on a large tin of Ritz crackers simply because they were not available anywhere in Vancouver. Dressed in blue blazers, white shirts, gray pants, argyle socks, and well-polished black shoes, they sat in the U.S. Navy recruiting office with their hair tousled and their collars and striped ties open at the neck. *Formal dress and a casual manner*, Carson Braddock reminded himself silently. *Confidence with no show of arrogance or disrespect. That's how Americans want to see*

Canadians. Max took in the portly build and flushed face of the senior recruiting officer and sized him up in the only terms he knew. *Middle-aged and built a lot like Uncle Carson,* he mused to himself on a cautionary note. *With a nose for bull-shit that would put a bird dog to shame.*

The forty-five year old Chief Petty Officer was wearing dress blues and the dark double-breasted jacket hid his paunch. His chevrons and hash marks were in "good conduct" gold. The service stripes alone gave his sleeve more gold braid than an admiral wore. For an hour he marched them through the physical and then smiled when they gave him their well-rehearsed pitch.

"We know that seventeen is too young for pilot training," Carson Braddock confessed. "So we want to become rear-seat gunners in dive-bombers flying off aircraft carriers."

"Since we have built models of just about every plane that flies," Max Bryson explained, "aircraft recognition should be a snap."

It was a crisp, clear, and forceful presentation. But the eager glow that softened their youthful cheeks and the innocence in their eyes made the battle seasoned chief petty officer hesitate. Despite the order to fill his quota before returning to sea duty, he had to give the lads one last chance to back out before signing each of them up for a hitch in the regular Navy.

"The Navy's new V-Six Aircrew Training Program can sure use a couple more good men," the grizzled chief gunner's mate allowed. "But what do you think about facing down a pair of enemy machine-guns backed up by a brace of twenty millimeter wing cannons when all you've got in the rear seat of your Douglas Dauntless is a pair of thirty-caliber pea shooters?"

The question forced both boys to take notice of the silver aircrew wings that Chief Gunner's Mate Lawrence K. Walsh wore above his battle ribbons. Although he seemed much too old and fleshy for the young man's war in the air, the cousins looked him over again with renewed respect. The eyes were steady, the hands were callused from hard work, and the CPO's shoulders had the spread and set of a seasoned brawler. He was not a man to spar with or to try to brush aside. Even so, they dared not depart from their carefully researched reply.

"The shortest life expectancy in the world," Carson chirped. "One full minute under enemy guns."

"But then there's the bright side," Max ventured. "With twin Browning machine-guns in the new Curtiss Helldiver and twenty-four-hundred rounds per barrel we will have two whole minutes of firepower."

The joint reply had just the right mixture of precise information and raw nerve to be audacious without being arrogant. Their easy yet respectful manner, the bright look of expectation on their faces, and the grace with which they moved their hands as they spoke all brought back a flicker of pain for the twins he had lost with the battleship Arizona.

"You'll do," Chief Gunner's Mate Larry Walsh declared. "Here's your dinner allowance and a buck extra. The train leaves right after supper. But mark my words. If you can't show me a receipt for a telegram to your parents you'll be on my special-work-detail all the way down to your Memphis Boot Camp. I shit you not."

He knows we are underage, Max thought. *But he's letting us join up anyway.*

That's what I call a sharp son-of-a-bitch, Carson reasoned without words. *If we lack the guts to tell our folks we don't have any business being here.*

Both cousins saw important things in a remarkably similar light. Nevertheless, Carson usually probed beneath the surface in search of some lesson buried just out of sight. Slight though it was, that, and Carson's left-handedness, amounted to the only major difference between them. It was what gave Carson the edge when it came to leadership. Still, it remained a difference that neither of them noticed and only their parents suspected.

The telegram was the hardest part of their enlistment. The twenty-two-word apology underscored the rashness of their decision. *Forgive me, Mom*, ran unstated throughout the whole text. But the pain it generated lingered even after it was sent. Neither boy had ever, knowingly, inflicted such a hurt on the ones he loved most. Nor was it a torment that they could bear in silence.

"It's a piercing twinge that flares up until I can hardly stand it and then subsides for no good reason," Carson confessed on the train to the new Naval Air Technical Training Center outside Memphis, Tennessee. "It's like a long yet flexible hat pin driven deep into my heart."

Carson's was an agony made all the more cruel by his mother's terrible loss. Written in a simple code embedded in the second character of each word, his father's letters had kept her informed of his trials taking Aussie coast watchers up the Fly River, deep into the jungles of New Guinea. Now her letters were returning every day stamped "Deceased, return to sender." As only sons, Young Carson and Little Max were almost as aware of the strain that their run-away enlistment was putting on the two families as they were of the terrible accomplishments of the enemy. Yet the rigors of boot camp and navy life left them little time to think of home.

"You call this the sunny south," Carson complained as he jumped out of the sack on the first morning. "Shit, our Eskimos have warmer sunrises in the Arctic."

Without warning a brawny six footer from Mississippi punched him in the chest and knocked him back against the triple-decker bunk. Immediately Max moved forward to his cousin's defense. A second blow drove half the breath out of Carson's lungs. Even so, he waved his cousin away. Rearing back, Carson Braddock hauled off with a roundhouse that caught Sonny-Jay Cantrell in the ribs. It wasn't a damaging blow but it took his antagonist by surprise.

"I'll be a white negra," the southerner said. "Is that all a Canuck will take?"

"You're fuckin A, Reb," Carson replied. "What about you?"

Dancing to his right Carson landed a powerful left on Mississippi's jaw. "Fight! Fight!" rang through the barracks like a call to arms. Content with a draw the southerner strolled off to the showers with Carson and Max following on his heels. After that no one challenged the Canadians until they were flying off the aircraft carrier Brandywine in the South Pacific.

From the Solomon Islands to the China Sea they battled against enemy war ships, fighter planes, and medium bombers right up to the coast of Japan. And each combat mission was a dance with death as the invisible partner. The attack they made on the Japanese ships reinforcing Rabaul cost the lives of combat aircrewman

Sonny-Jay Cantrell and his pilot. When their damaged Douglas Dauntless skip bombed a Mutsuki Class destroyer it was caught in the explosion that sent the gunship to the bottom. The twin engine Mitsubishi Ki-46 Dinah that Max shot down over the Philippine Sea used its upward firing 37 millimeter cannon to disable their Dauntless. Their fiery crash landing aboard the Brandywine killed the pilot and sent Max to sick bay with facial burns and three broken ribs. And the single engine Nakajima Ki-27 Nate making a kamikaze attack on the Brandywine rammed its fixed landing gear through Carson's cockpit before he blew it apart with his .30 caliber machine-guns. The cuts and concussion he got from the tire and metal wheel-pants kept Carson off the flight line for a week. So by the time they each had four kills the cousins were battle toughened eighteen-year-olds totally committed to the invasion of Japan. But war is full of surprises. Yet even in late summer 1945 neither the two combat seasoned Canadians nor the entire Allied armed forces had any idea of what lay in store.

CHAPTER TWO

The fighter pilot's hand-chase
Holds a slice of history
Men are obliged to watch
Because war
Is the sideshow of Destiny.

In the purple morning light of early August 1945, the approach of dawn swept the gray sea off the coast of Japan like a weak beacon skimming pebbled slate. American sailors on watch scanned the swells and troughs with night glasses. Seasoned lookouts used their sensitive peripheral vision to search for the tiny feather of foam a submarine's periscope trails in its wake. Half hidden in the fading night, the three attack groups that made up Task Force Fifty-eight went into action.

In each group, the minesweepers, the destroyers, the lean cruisers, and the broad-beamed battleships drew their protective rings in tight around the vulnerable aircraft carriers. Moving swiftly, the flattops swung into the wind. The single engine planes were set at odd angles all across the USS Brandywine's flight deck as they unfolded their wings. Belching exhaust and warming up their motors, the deck load of fighters and bombers aboard shook like a swarm of nervous hornets driving off the ocean spray's damp chill.

"Prepare to launch," Squadron leader Lieutenant Commander Gregory Hawkins told the deck-master from the cockpit of his dive-bomber. "And make sure my Helldivers take off from a rising bow."

Seated eight feet behind the pilot, the middle-aged radio operator in the rear cockpit of the squadron leader's dive-bomber looked up from adjusting the tension on his sending key as Greg Hawkins finished. Clean shaven, fleshy in his leather flight helmet, and peering out beneath dark goggles set above bushy eyebrows, the chief aviation radioman's mate fixed the young ensign acting as deck-master with a glare hard enough to shatter glass.

"If even one of our planes leaves the deck as the bow plunges down into a trough," Chief Chester Flannigan warned, "I will personally have you keel hauled stark naked in a shark infested bay. I shit you not—Sir."

The seasoned twenty-year-old ensign grinned knowingly back at the chief. Nevertheless, he eyed the waves with care as he withdrew to his signal platform. Manually, the plane handlers turned the aircraft into the wind and lined them up for take-off. The wave of a white flag started a radial engine Grumman Avenger charging up the deck with ever increasing speed. Having the greatest range, the three-man torpedo bombers took off first.

At the bow, the heavily laden TBF Avenger rushed off into the night with a dip and an engine growl that underlined its struggle to stay airborne. Slowly, the almost black aircraft rose above the invisible union of a purple sea and the violet sky. Only then did the dark wings and glass greenhouse with its tucked down ball turret flash back a muted signal of success.

With the hidden sun defining and then melting the horizon, the rest of the torpedo planes and all of the dive-bombers took to the air. Each single engine Curtiss Helldiver rolled down the deck on a dip that gradually changed into a rising bow as the huge vessel plunged through an oncoming ground swell. That slight rise thrust the overloaded dive-bomber into the air with the added lift of a stiff springboard. Even so, every dive-bomber sank on the brink of a stall. Only its powerful Wright Cyclone engine and howling Hamilton propeller blades hauled it up out of the boundary layer of heavy air that carpeted the sea.

Finally, last of all, the high-speed fighter planes with their fuel-thirsty engines and smaller gas tanks finished rising from the flight deck. Before they retracted their landing gear, the Grumman F6Fs looked like long-legged vultures leaving their lair. The noise of their engines blended into a monotonous throb as the several squadrons of orbiting planes climbed up into a pale sky that showered them with invisible light.

Ominous in silhouette, the Grumman Hellcats shed a bit of their menace as the paintings of elongated nudes emblazoned on their cowlings stood out in bright Technicolor. Climbing up to join them, the young radiomen in the trailing flight of dive-bombers surveyed the fighter planes flying top-cover with professional disdain.

"What do you think?" Aviation Radioman Second Class Max Bryson inquired over the squadron's limited range voice frequency. "Does the bare breasted broad on the cowling reflect the fighter pilot's prowess or his intellect?"

"Well, that's easy enough to tell," his cousin, rear seat radio-gunner ARM 2/C Carson Braddock replied from an accompanying Helldiver. "Whenever the Lord is serious about the separation of mind from body the victim talks and walks like a movie star."

All through the squadron, idle chatter and flagrant breeches of radio discipline masked the tension that the raid generated. As the opening phase of Operation Downfall, the overall plan for the invasion of Japan, the attack on the anchorage at Kure marked a major escalation in the Fifth Fleet's efforts to silence the enemy's last line of naval defense.

There, just across the bay from Hiroshima, the Japanese battleship Nagato swung at anchor while the battlewagons Haruna, Ise, and Hyuga were tucked away in deep coves. With only Nagato actually afloat, the other capital ships were fixed targets resting on a shallow bottom. Still, their guns remained a menace to anything navigating close to the coast as it sailed the Inland Sea. Indeed, each one was a fortress of firepower that filled the morning sky with a fusillade of anti-aircraft fire as the American carrier planes swept in across the bay. Still climbing and last to commit, the deadly dive-bombers had a commanding view of the assault.

"Even without the combat air patrol we left behind to protect our carrier," Carson Braddock observed, "there must be over sixty planes from the Brandywine involved."

"And nearly a hundred from the Enterprise and the

Independence," Max added.

The Japanese harbor was a tight crescent of well traveled water edged by mountains that rose almost straight up from the beach. Yet the wide mouth of the bay was deep enough for the Nagato to anchor within a hundred yards of a shoreline littered with a jumble of service facilities. The loading piers, dry docks, repair yards, storage tanks, and sheet metal sheds rose up the hillsides of the sheltered anchorage behind a tangle of barricades that bristled with guns. The massive firepower and the incredibly steep terrain were enough to make even the most seasoned fliers nervous.

To put a crimp in the enemy anti-aircraft fire, the attacking Grumman fighter planes strafed the forty-millimeter gun platforms with rockets and machine-gun fire. As they pulled up, they dropped their external fuel tanks and two hundred fifty-pound bombs on the heavy guns nestled in the foothills. The explosions and the return anti-aircraft fire raised a curtain of sand and smoke that half hid the mountains in a blue and gray haze. Despite the powder-curtain, however, the Navy Hellcat struck by a four-inch shell cut a swath of fire through the heavy battle smoke as it shed a wing and smashed into the mountain. The bright burst of yellow flame and the great ball of black smoke that rose from the crash site wrenched the gut of every man aloft. Yet each phase of the assault continued to unfold along well-established lines without a break in the radio chatter.

The flights of torpedo bombers following half a mile behind the fighter planes bored in through that swirling smoke shield just a few feet above the water. Each stubby Grumman Avenger carried a radio operator in its belly compartment as well as a pilot and a top turret gunner at opposite ends of the long glass greenhouse that stretched the full width of the wing. Instead of torpedoes, however, each TBF Avenger carried an overload of high-explosive bombs. Driving in at two hundred forty knots, the formation of "Turkeys" skimmed the waves. The slipstream from their noisy propellers pressed shallow troughs in the water. Accustomed to both the hazards and the deep concentration the assault demanded, however, the seasoned aircrew only intensified its banter as they bore down on the Nagato.

"You can't beat barreling-in deck high on an anchored battlewagon," the middle-aged enlisted pilot flying the leading Avenger declared. "It's almost as good as slipping it to a hungry broad from behind with your hands full of tits."

"If you don't mind dodging tracers," the aging Chief Gunner's Mate Larry Walsh contended. "But I'll grant you this. It's a damned sight better than air-sea rescue."

The mindless chatter kept the crewmen in touch as they penetrated the killing zone. By half blotting-out the unavoidable dangers that engulfed them it actually intensified their concentration and improved their battle task performance. Even so, however, the enemy's counter-thrusts were everywhere. The anti-aircraft fire from the battlewagon rushed past the midnight-blue wings and cream colored underbelly of the TBF with the flap and flutter of long streamers in a wind tunnel. Deftly, the single engine Grumman Avenger darted in under the cannon fire from the battleship's heavy guns. Chilled, bathed in sweat, and alert to every rasp and shudder of the aircraft, the young radio-gunner seated in the belly compartment felt an unwanted nervous sneer creeping into his voice.

"Talk about your generosity," ARM3/C Barry Chapman scoffed. "Just about anything beats landing a float plane held together with library paste and bailing wire right in the Jap's back yard."

The huge cannon shells that roared over their heads rattled the fragile greenhouse. Facing backward, Chief Larry Walsh swung his Sperry ball turret from side to side and riddled Japanese gunnery barges with his fifty-caliber machine-gun as the plane left them behind. Through his sights he caught a glimpse of a blown up Japanese gunner stiffening in mid-air as he took a burst of hot slugs in his chest. Seated in the belly with a thirty-caliber Browning between his legs, the radioman sprayed anything they passed over. Lacking a gunsight, Barry Chapman's eyes lingered on the bearded old man he riddles as the poor devil dove from his elevated fishing platform. But not even the sight of that innocent victim could take his mind off his own danger.

"Don't push in too close to shore, Skipper," Barry warned. "The mountains looming up on either side of us look like they climb away into a two mile high slab of horned alligator hide."

Suddenly, the dark blue Grumman Avenger rose up in a steep climb and banked sharply across the face of the mountain. The heavy anti-aircraft fire exploding all around it shook the wings and peppered the tail surfaces with shrapnel.

"BOMBS AWAY," Chief Enlisted Pilot Peter Cramer shouted. "HOLD ON TO THOSE BOOZE SODDEN, GUT-WRENCHING, FUCKED-UP STOMACHS."

Straining hard as it skimmed the pointed treetops of a less than vertical evergreen forest, the battered Grumman Avenger rattled like a paper bag holding peanuts. Below, and only a bit behind the escaping aircraft, the straight sides of the cylindrical bombs hit the brittle top layer of the water at almost two hundred eighty miles an hour. All four of them bounced along the surface of the sheltered bay like two rows of skillfully skipped stones. In their final leap they rose just enough to strike the Nagato high above the torpedo bulge and hit the lighter armor that shields the crew-deck. Aided by staggered detonation, the two bombs with delayed action fuses penetrated the battleship's citadel.

The five-hundred pounder exploded in the battleship's main galley and wiped out the rescue team waiting for orders. Concussion tore the steel structure apart and the incredible heat set the entire mess hall on fire. Japanese sailors stacking benches and rolling out fire hoses were blown apart by a blast hot enough to scorch their limbs in mid-air. But the thousand pound bomb was worse. It skidded into the sickbay like a greased hippopotamus and erupted with a force that blew out every bulkhead. The blast killed all the patients and the ship's entire medical staff. Doctors, pharmacist mates, male nurses, influenza victims, and men recovering from surgery all perished from shock waves that burst their lungs and sucked their hearts dry. As the dead collapsed, burned, writhed, and crumpled, a great surge of heat ignited some powder bags in the magazine below the forward gun-turret. A series of secondary explosion blew open the undogged hatches on the main deck and sent thick arms of flame shooting high above the ship's clean-lined pagoda. Black ash and dark smoke shrouded the exposed gun crews in the gray mist that settled on the weather deck.

Each wave of torpedo planes that followed added high explosive bombs to the destruction on the beach or close to shore. The torrent of five-hundred pounders smashed into docks, clobbered sheds, blew up barges, set a loaded freighter on fire, sank a mine sweeper, and reduced a harbor tug to splinters. The thousand pounders uprooted piers, blew tin roofs off repair sheds, and knocked the windows and walls out of barracks, office buildings, and machine shops. But the most spectacular destruction took place in isolation.

The heavy bomb that struck the ammunition ship unloading in a narrow cove sent the bridge of the decimated vessel hurtling up into the air atop a brilliant black and yellow fireball. Battered, stunned, and blistered with burn-boils but still conscious and moving about, the officers and ratings inside coughed and choked on the acrid cordite smoke as they hurtled to their death. All around the bay, the harbor facilities were ablaze with pockets of devastation. Seen from the dive-bombers orbiting high above, the destruction looked complete.

"God-damn," Carson Braddock commented. "Those Turkeys sure lay volcanic eggs."

Three miles above that ash-strewn inferno, the cold air was still and the sky was clear as the dive-bombers moved into position for their assault. In the early morning sunlight the straight leading edge and tapered wing of each Curtiss Helldiver sent a champagne-glass shaped shadow speeding up the heavily treed mountain slopes as three of the four flights of dive-bombers tightened their formation for a swift peel-off.

"As the dive unwinds you start skimming the mountainside at ten thousand feet and its two miles straight down to sea level from there," Squadron Leader Gregory Hawkins warned. "Watch out for tall trees and any outcropping of bare rock."

Waiting a moment for the advice to sink in, Chief Flannigan in the rear seat of the squadron leader's Helldiver spit in his palm and extinguished his cigar in the moisture. As he flipped the butt out of the open cockpit he pressed the throat mike attached to his oxygen mask to make sure that his warning reached his squadron mates loud and clear.

"The hot shot who comes away with pine branches in his bomb bay doors will lose a month's flight pay," Chief Aviation Radioman's Mate Chester Flannigan threatened. "I shit you not."

At sea level the narrow inlets ran up between the separate mountain ranges like sky blue felt spread between the extended fingers of a gnarled hand. The mixture of yellow sunlight and dark green shadow dappled the ridgeback crests below with a seamless intensity that gave the mountains the appearance of a huge camouflage net. And the forest green marked with patches of yellow alder leaves and rusted larch branches made the battle blue dive-bombers all but invisible from above.

"Our Marines flying top-cover report that there are no enemy aircraft within fifty-miles," Squadron leader Hawkins broadcast. "So let's get some hits."

"Irregardless," Chief Flannigan added. "Each rear-seat gunner will quarter scan the sky above and behind like it was a virgin's snatch hiding a dose of the crabs. I sh…."

Chief Flannigan's routine oaths were too frequent and vehement for the young aircrewmen to resist. Together, a chorus of voices cut him off in a cadence and timbre that mocked his own.

"I SHIT YOU NOT," the fifteen aviation radiomen doing double-duty as aerial gunners bellowed. "AND THAT'S THE NAKED TRUTH."

The gag was rhythmic, well practiced, and familiar. It drew almost no comment. And even though Chester Flannigan waited it out with the skilled timing of a stand-up comic milking a belly laugh, he acted annoyed.

"Belay the chatter," the chief ordered. "It's battle alert from here right down to the deck. So get those cockpits straightened away. Keep a tight ass hole. And for Christ's sake check-six."

Automatically, every rear seat gunner made a swift but penetrating scan through the six o'clock position that swung around in a thirty-degree cone that circled the tail of his aircraft. The lack of anything to report gave the pilots assurance that there were no enemy planes moving into firing position.

Confident, each of the first three flights of dive-bombers swung inland to take up a position above a different shallow bottomed cove tucked deep in the steep mountains that lined the harbor. As a four-plane formation crested the ridge all eyes peered down at a scuttled capital ship tied up to a dock like an overloaded steel canoe. Instantly, the whole flight of Helldivers came under light and heavy enemy cannon fire.

A flurry of one-inch shells rose to meet them and mark their speed and precise direction. Black puffs from three-inch shells blossomed above and below to bracket their altitude. Five-inch anti-aircraft shells spiraled up to their flight level for effect. Audible bursts that erupted beneath the wings rocked the blue dive-bombers like angry hands on a cradle.

"Christ," Max Bryson commented. "They're throwin' up enough tonnage to beat our bomb load five to one."

An explosion just ahead of Carson's banking dive-bomber sent the sizzle of hot steel rushing through the propeller arc and along the slipstream. The shredded smoke filled his cockpit with the bitter tang of cordite. Regardless of the hazard and discomfort, however, both Canadian rear-seat gunners concentrated on the final preparations for the dive.

"With gunnery like that," Carson Braddock observed, "the bastards don't need the proximity fuse."

Suddenly, a Japanese four-inch shell blew the cowling off a Helldiver in the leading flight as it dove into a narrow gorge. The wounded pilot slumped forward and struggled with the controls. The battered dive-bomber banked hard as the pilot pulled the plane up into a steep stall. Slowly, she flopped over on to her back, dove down, rolled right side up, and fell off into a violent spin. The fatally injured pilot smeared blood all over the inside of his cockpit canopy as he fought to gain control and unload his bombs. The five-hundred-pound bombs spilled away from the plane like pebbles from a wagon wheel. Knifing down, they exploded among the trees as the damaged wingtip began to fold.

"MAY DAY! MAY DAY!" the radio-gunner in the rear seat broadcast. "This crate is coming apart like a peeled banana!"

In slow motion, a nylon parachute blossomed from the rear seat. Caught in the spin and the churn of the slipstream, the canopy snagged on the tail fin and wrapped the rudder and the elevators in white cloth. Wild centrifugal force tore the helpless gunner out of his cockpit and spun him around at the end of the shroud lines in a wide and accelerating arc. Shedding cockpit covers and torn wing panels, the doomed plane dropped far into the steep and incredibly narrow valley. As the fliers above watched, the parachute's long nylon cords whipped the young airman into the face of a cliff just before the plane crashed and exploded. Crushed like a fly on a windscreen, the inert body of Chris Foreman from Gila Bend, Arizona, clung to the sheer granite wall as flames and smoke engulfed it.

"Their luck ran out," Chief Flannigan declared in a somber voice over the squadron frequency. "Now let's all get back to work."

Released from the spell of the crash, the two Canadian radio-gunners flying in the squadron leader's formation prepared for their dive by following a fixed routine. Expertly, Carson Braddock and Max Bryson cranked open their cockpit covers and braced their bodies against the icy slipstream that swirled around them. The stout stay wires that held their machine-guns in place were easy to unhook. As soon as the twin-barreled weapons were swung outboard, a few pumps on a steel handle lowered the turtleback shelter fared into the tailfin down and out of the way. With gloved hands they secured the smoke bombs in their sheet metal racks on the floor, smoothed out the folded ammunition belts running up from the feed cans, charged both thirty-caliber machine-guns, and fired off test busts. Swiftly, the cordite in the gun-smoke bit into their sinuses like raw ammonia on a winter day.

"Make sure your inflatable life raft is secure in the overhead tube," Max Bryson advised. "You don't want it sliding into the back of your head in a sharp pull out."

Facing backward, the rear-seat gunners remained on almost continuous lookout as they completed their cockpit duties. From fifteen thousand feet the sky above was a brittle blue bereft of clouds and enemy aircraft. Ignoring the continuous burst of anti-aircraft shells, each gunner turned from side to side in order to scan to the right and the left, above, and below. Their trained eyes caught, registered, and quickly looked past every friendly plane aloft. Circling in a wide arc, the four planes in the squadron leader's flight kept tabs on the rest of the Curtiss dive-bombers as they moved up to their dive points. Busy, alert, and on guard, the cousins felt the tension mount. Bright, keen, and bristling with nervous energy, the young men pinned their trust on technical ability and fast reflexes.

Both Canadian rear-seat gunners were bundled in reddish-brown leather flight jackets. They wore white silk scarves to keep their necks from chaffing as a result of the almost continuous sector scans their gunnery demanded. With their machine-guns balanced against the slipstream, they pulled their yellow cowhide gloves tight on their hands. A few adjustments fitted the green Polaroid goggles more comfortably to their faces and eyes.

At eighteen, Max Bryson was pale skinned and freckled but the fine lines that open cockpit flying had etched around his mouth added a grim and brittle intensity to his blue eyes. Each time he chinned his machine-guns and worked out an imaginary lead in the iron sight mounted between the two gun barrels the thought of avenging his uncle's death hovered nearby. Just a wingspan away, eighteen-year-old Carson Braddock had dark and unruly hair that never stayed completely hidden beneath his leather helmet. Nor did the anguish and pain of the loss of his father stay locked up inside his head. Although he never spoke of it, the care he took in bore sighting his weapons and reinforcing his Scarff ring for the maximum concentration of his gunfire reflected Big Carson's wish to see him excel. Despite a casual look, his full lips and slender nose took on a menacing edge as soon as he turned serious.

"Boost your oxygen intake for a few minutes," Carson Braddock recommended. "There's no sense having your stomach juices up in your throat just because we have to go down backwards to cover our rear-ends in the dive."

The Curtiss SB2C-5E Helldiver was three inches short of a fifty foot wing span. She weighed just over eight tons on take-off. The flat nose, long greenhouse, and rounded fin and rudder made the stiff landing hook that stuck out behind her tail wheel look like an afterthought. The "Beast" was driven by a nineteen hundred horsepower Wright Cyclone engine that gave it a cruising speed just two miles an hour slower than that of the navy's top fighter plane, the Grumman Hellcat. The pilot sat high above the leading edge of the wing embedded mid-way down the plane's fuselage. Being atop the plane's center of gravity, he suffered fewer Gs during a pull out than the man in the back seat.

"Scanning this unbroken blue sky is like staring hard in a dream," Carson ventured. "With nothing to focus upon it soon starts to hurt."

The Helldiver's rear-seat cockpit had a Plexiglas cover that opened forward. The enclosure half sheltered the radio-gunner's ANARC 13 pre-tuned radio and the orange screen of his radarscope even when the cockpit was open. Around him there was a chest high steel ring that allowed his swivel mounted machine-guns to travel forward as far as his arms could push them against the stiff slipstream. In action, he operated a pair of hand-held thirty caliber Browning machine-guns. The rudder and the horizontal stabilizer both stood in the way of shooting directly astern. So it required intense concentration to keep from shooting your tail off. But the worst part was the pull out. The G force always drained away Carson's consciousness for a second or two.

"I still get a knot in my stomach," Max confessed, "tighter than a monkey's paw."

Anticipating the pain and stress of the blackout already, Carson and Max locked their hands on the gun grips so they could open fire on any available target even before the mist cleared from their brains. Poised and ready, well in advance of the peel off that started the dive, each gunner's entire body was as tense as a leaf spring under a heavy load. And all the while, they twisted, tilted, and turned their heads slightly to keep their eyes from focusing on a fixed point in empty space. Sky-lock was the aerial gunner's most common failing since it dulled and even deadened the vision for short periods. So the cousins regularly pinched their necks and tapped their goggles to fend off the lure of that restful blank stare and reported the slightest irregularity.

"Skipper," Carson Braddock warned. "I'd swear there's metal glinting in the sunlight at angels twenty-five some thirty miles astern."

"Our Vought Corsair fighter-cover tops out at angels twenty three," Max Bryson advised. "And whatever it is ain't big enough to show up brighter than static snow on radar. So it's nothing as large as a B-29 or even a Jap Betty."

The warning of a possible bogey that was some six minutes flying time away was an unwelcome distraction. Still in tight formation, the young ensign at the controls of Max's dive-bomber gently fish-tailed their Helldiver through a mushy bank and turn that signaled his concern to his fellow pilots as he replied to the Canadian gunners.

"I'll be damned," Carson's twenty-two year old pilot commented. "If you guys had any better eyesight you'd see the Lord in the sunrise."

"My guess is that it's a lone Army Airforce P-38 on a re-con mission," Max's pilot replied. "But keep an eye on it until it's our turn to dive."

The eleven remaining planes in the three forward flights peeled off high above the Japanese battleships. Like a shark rolling to bite, the bank into a steep dive flashed the fish-belly white on each Helldiver's underside. As they dropped away in two-thousand-foot intervals they bore straight into smoking streams of anti-aircraft fire that the targeted battleships threw aloft.

The eight batteries of five-inch twin mounts on the Haruna sent up shells staggered to burst along the flight's line of descent. A shell that blew up beneath the starboard wing of the third Helldiver flipped it over like a flapjack and dumped it into the almost vertical tree line. The crippled aircraft took the tops off a dozen hemlocks before it shed its wings and exploded, killing Chubby Ward from Cannon Beach, Oregon, and his pilot.

Straining against wide open dive brakes, the four Helldivers plummeting down on the Ise faced four batteries of one-inch cannons and a steady stream of machine-gun fire. The cannon shells were red hot and trailing tracer smoke that earned them the nickname of flaming onions. The small arms fire rose up and spread outward like the spray from a fire hose. At eight thousand feet the leading plane carrying Jimmy-jack Quaid out of Bunkie, Louisiana, in the rear seat was hit. All the way down she shed thin strips of aluminum and plexiglass that turned her slipstream into a flying junkyard. The flame and smoke trailed a long line of scrap as she augured into the water just aft of the battlewagon.

The flight of four sturdy American aircraft racing their own shadows down the mountainside that sheltered the Hyuga managed to dodge anti-aircraft fire until they reached the vertical cliff that shielded the battlewagon. For a moment, the stricken plane and the bomb that fell from its belly traveled together like doomed companions. Then the Helldiver started the strained curve of her pull-out and the bomb dove for the target.

"There goes Gunter Dietrich," Carson lamented. "His mother in Bird-in-Hand, Pennsylvania, will get a telegram for sure."

Before she could get out of range Helldiver number seventy-three was caught in the crossfire from the battleship's five-inch guns and a dozen of her one-inch cannons. Direct hits and near misses ventilated the wings and tail surfaces with holes and tore off chunks of the elevators and rudder. Unable to level out or pull up, the Helldiver skimmed over the surface of the water until it dipped a wing and cartwheeled through three full turns. Kicking up spray like a runaway water wheel, she fell apart and sank in half a dozen pieces marked by white splashes. The toll was terrible but the battle damage inflicted by the bomb Gunter's pilot dropped was awesome as well.

A mile behind the wreckage their thousand-pound bomb pierced the steel deck of the Hyuga, penetrated the lower decks, and erupted inside the armor plated citadel. Contained within sixteen-inch thick hull plates, the explosion blew out bulkheads like they were made of cardboard. For a hundred feet the blast crushed work crews and rescue teams to a pulp. The pressure of the blast stove in her forward magazine and a fireball touched off twenty tons of ammunition that rose with such force it wrapped another Helldiver in its fire cloud. The secondary explosions tilted the ship's upright pagoda over the side and sent shock waves through the hull that made the water all around the battlewagon erupt in a froth of mud-strewn foam. Despite the results, however, losses took precedence.

"I count four planes shot down and seven direct hits on the

battlewagons," Carson Braddock reported as his pilot hovered over the dive point. "The Haruna is listing twenty degrees to port. And the Ise will take longer to float then the Arizona."

The loss of twenty-five percent of the squadron with the attack still in progress was a staggering blow. To have it all inflicted by anti-aircraft fire and an unexpected explosion when there wasn't even an enemy plane in sight was almost unthinkable. To fight off the thought Chief Petty Officer Flannigan redirected everyone's attention to the chaos down below.

"Judging from the smoke and flames billowing and flashing from the Hyuga's ten story high pagoda," Chester Flannigan exulted, "I'd say it's barbecue time in officer's country."

Grief was a poison that had no place in battle. Spontaneous abuse and vituperative scorn was the antidote. As a leftover ripple of the original shock wave generated by the enemy's surprise attack on Pearl Harbor it traveled well across the Pacific Ocean. No matter how much damage the U.S. Navy inflicted on the Japanese Imperial Fleet it was never quite enough. But the two Canadians did not need the treatment. As seasoned enlisted men second only to Chief Petty Officer Flannigan, Carson Braddock and Max Bryson went on high alert against an attack from above.

CHAPTER THREE

The ultimate high wire act
Is aerial combat
Where avenging angels
Wrestle to the death
Without a net.

Intense anti-aircraft fire burst all around Squadron Leader Greg Hawkins' Helldivers. Five-inch shells, dozens of flaming onions, and barrages of forty-millimeter cannon fire pockmarked the sky above and behind the four-plane flight. The thin streaks of black smoke that flashed past the open cockpits carried ash that darkened the fliers' faces. The pungent odor of spent gunpowder made Max's nose run. Lightly masked and sniffling, Carson cupped his hands over his earphones and pressed them hard against his head. Beset by the drone of the engine and the incessant rattle of the airframe, he was determined to catch every word of the incoming message.

"DIVE LEADER. DIVE LEADER. WATCH OUT," the top-cover commander urged from twenty-three thousand feet. "Three bogies are descending on your pregnant falcons from out of the sun."

The plain language message put the dive-bombers on instant battle alert. Engines revved, wings dipped, and eyes scanned the heavens even as fresh orders were being issued.

"Helldivers move into diamond defense," Gregory Hawkins ordered. "Pilots prepare for evasive action."

"Gunners concentrate on incoming aircraft," Chet Flannigan advised. "Remember, the Zero's wing guns are usually set to converge at six hundred feet in front of his propeller. That gives you the advantage for the first quarter mile that the yellow bastard is in range."

The American squadron leader forged ahead straight and level. The two nearest Helldivers went into a shallow dive and then rose up—off and just behind—the Skipper's wings. The last plane put on a burst of speed and eased into the tail end of the diamond. Within easy sight of each other, the tail-gunners scanned the dogfight overhead and tracked through the frozen vapor trails around the sun. Positioned on the outer edges of the diamond, the two Canadian gunners had a head-on view of the attacking enemy aircraft. Without conscious effort they both switched to battle time where things happened so fast it made time seem to slow to a crawl.

"Re-think your sight picture fast," Carson Braddock ordered. "The square air-intake for the oil cooler protruding beneath the circular cowling marks these babies as Franks not Zeros."

Dropping like winged artillery shells, the three Japanese fighter planes dove straight for the diamond formation at well over four hundred miles an hour. The rear-seat defenders hunched behind their hand held machine-guns and fixed the low wing enemy attackers atop the outer ring of their circular gunsights. Warnings flashed back and forth across the airwaves with the speed of light.

"That means they've got twice the fire power," Max Bryson reported. "And a top-speed that's thirty knots faster."

As the wingspan of the overtaking aircraft spread beyond the width of the iron-sight it came into range. Each radio-gunner opened fire with a three second burst.

"If that ain't bad enough," Carson added, "the latest model has a pair of twenty millimeter cannons shooting parallel along the nose of the fuselage. So you can kiss that closing range-advantage good bye."

Grouped close together, the paired bursts of eight thirty-caliber machine-guns sent hundreds of rounds tearing into the leading Frank's nose, wings, and belly. Hits tore strips of metal off the enemy's cowling and the underside of his wings. The flames that burst from the Japanese leader's engine left a trail of black smoke in his wake. Steadily, the defensive machine-gun fire stiffened and converged on the leading attacker in a deadly hail of hot slugs at eight hundred feet. Even so, the Frank's cannons and machine-guns remained silent.

"BREAK RIGHT. BREAK RIGHT," Carson Braddock shouted to his pilot over the intercom. "The fuckers are out of ammunition and bent on a sure kill."

"THEY'RE GONNA RAM," Max Bryson yelled to his pilot. "BREAK LEFT. BREAK LEFT."

The two outside Helldivers peeled away from the diamond formation in opposite directions. In moments the Japanese fighter planes closed the gap. Hosed with machine-gun fire at point blank range, the leading Frank plunged into the rear dive-bomber like an angry hawk falling on an owl in flight. The chop and crunch of the enemy's propeller slicing through the trailing Helldiver's rear cockpit rose above the speed-screams of the aircraft like the growl of a chainsaw outshouting the wind.

The smoking engine of the Japanese fighter plane buried itself in the dive-bomber's wing and stayed there as the Frank's fuselage and wings twisted and struggled to break away. Initially, the two planes spun around and around, tangled in each other's wreckage. Gaining speed, they fell away tied tightly in a twisted plume of black smoke.

But the mid-air collision and fatal plunge of the defense diamond's tail-end Charlie only intensified the efforts of the squadron leader's remaining dive-bombers. Using long five-second bursts, Lieutenant Commander Hawkins's rear-seat gunner pumped a pulsing stream of machine-gun fire into the Japanese fighter plane closing in on his tail.

"Come and get it, Tojo," Chief Chester Flannigan shouted into the chug of his own guns. "This is your passport to Hell."

Alerted by the break away on each side, twenty-eight year old Lieutenant Commander Gregory Hawkins rammed the control stick forward and nosed his Helldiver over into a vertical dive. In the rear seat, Chief Petty Officer Chet Flannigan rose to his feet and squeezed off another burst point blank at the menacing enemy fighter plane.

At the age of forty-two the flab on his arms shook and his legs trembled. Still, his intense stream of bullets ripped open the Frank's firewall. Smoking tracers cut the Japanese pilot up with terrible wounds as his plane closed in for the kill. The speeding enemy fighter plane curled its steel propeller to a stuttering halt as it smashed into the Helldiver's belly and tore it apart. The Frank's massive radial engine ripped through the open bomb bay doors, dislodged the thousand pound bomb, and split the Helldiver's gas tank apart as the Japanese aircraft exploded. The eruption broke the American dive-bomber in half and sent the pilot's nose section and the gunner's tail-end cartwheeling away in opposite directions. Shattered, the smoking fragments of the Japanese plane fluttered down toward the water.

"God damn," Carson Braddock mumbled, "Those Kamikaze fuckers mean business."

The fate of Greg Hawkins and Chet Flannigan was made clear by the absence of movement in either piece of wreckage. The separate sections of their Helldiver skidded through a flat spin and slid off into a spiral that seemed reluctant to descend. Each sheet of wrinkled aluminum that tore away added to the anguish of the survivors and yet the loss of their doomed comrades had to be suppressed.

"It ain't over yet," Max Bryson replied. "Number three son is still on the prowl."

Despite the danger from the missing Kamikaze fighter plane, the two Canadian gunners had difficulty looking away from their stricken comrades. The wreckage of all four aircraft continued to burn as the pieces tumbled down toward the smoke shrouded bay three miles below. Yet again, there were no parachutes. But the growl of the attacker's engine drew their eyes to the threat approaching from behind the blind spot their tall tail fin created. Still, before they could bring their guns to bear, the third Japanese Frank streaked past them in a steep dive and rushed down toward the wreck-strewn harbor.

"He's got the skull and crossbones insignia of a pirate on his rudder," Max declared. "That makes him part of the Fifty-eighth Shimbu-tai."

To save precious seconds the cousins spoke to each other over the short range inter-squadron frequency as if they controlled the dive-bombers. Fully in tune with their aircrewmen, the pilots in the front seats translated thought into action.

"That fucking Army squadron is based right here just outside Hiroshima." Carson replied. "If we keep our perforated brakes closed we can overtake the bastards in a drawn out dive."

Skillfully, the cousins' pilots wrung the heavy Helldivers through a tight bank and descending twist that left the gunners hanging from their seat belts as the planes came together. Stress bends on the wings and the elevators dimpled the panels between the ribs and sent tiny rays of orange sunlight bouncing off the battle blue aluminum. The two dive-bombers were so close their wings overlapped as they headed down after the lone Nakajima Ki-84 streaking for home.

The Frank's dark green fuselage and almost thirty-seven foot wingspan moved above the current ripples that swirled across the bay like a metal locust skimming a pond. Every few seconds the plane sent back white puffs of engine exhaust as the pilot leaned out the fuel mixture and fine tuned the throttle to increase his speed. Hunched forward against his shoulder straps, the twenty-six year old fighter pilot coaxed his aircraft to top performance with the gentle tones of encouragement that a skilled mechanic showers on his favorite machine.

"Plunge like a living waterfall," Pilot Officer Shinichi Yamagato proclaimed inside the closed cockpit of the Nakajima Hurricane, "then turn and devour."

The seasoned Japanese flier used his improvised rear-view mirror to keep a close watch on the Helldivers chasing him. Even as he stretched his dive and lost a little speed he remained convinced that he could out run them. His lithe body and knowing hands urged the machine to exceed its design limit with pumping squirms and loving caresses. Fear was not a factor even though the intended victim had become the aggressor. Gaining on his enemy Carson Braddock did some coaxing of his own.

"That's it, Tojo," Carson insisted. "Just keep dropping into thicker air and see who slows down faster."

Anxious to overtake the enemy fighter plane and never idle, the tail gunners in the pursuing dive-bombers tucked their machine-guns away and cranked up the retracted rear hood until it fit snug against the tail fin. Then they wound their cockpit covers shut to streamline the airflow. Slowly, the airspeed indicator edged past the red-line at four hundred miles an hour and trembled against the peg. Vibrations rattled the airframe so hard the mixture of spent cartridge casings and bronze belt-clips strewn all over the cockpit floor bounced like metal jumping beans. The noise was loud and both radiomen pressed their earphones against their heads to hear the incoming voice message broadcast in the clear.

"Helldivers abandon pursuit and return to target area," the senior bombing leader ordered. "I say again, abandon pursuit. Hiroshima is off limits. Acknowledge. Over."

Unwilling to obey, the two battle blue Helldivers dropped down over the bay like angry hawks. Fired-up by losses tinged with guilt, the pilots and the radio-gunners ignored the message in a collective silence that doubled the tension. Soaked in sweat, the Canadians in the rear seats re-laid the ammunition belts in the feeder cans and charged each Browning thirty-caliber machine-gun with a sharp tug on the arming rod. Even though their guns were tucked away under the collapsible "turtle back" hood, each man was calculating his attack as they neared their combined assault point. Frank or Zero, Carson told himself, one is much like the other when approached from above and behind.

Give me a concentrated burst at point-blank range every time, Carson mused to himself. *As the geisha said to the temple priest.*

Shivering through his assault ritual, Carson studied the olive grey-green camouflage and the beige underside of the descending enemy aircraft. The wings stuck straight out from the sleek fuselage. The stretched aluminum skin trembled until the rivet heads shook like beads of sweat on the body of a record breaking athlete. *She's a beauty*, he told himself. *Spare, trim, and deadly.*

Overtaking the enemy at last, the Helldiver slipped into the blind spot below and behind the Nakajima Ki 84. Carson prepared to attack. He cranked open his cockpit canopy, worked the paired machine-guns out into the slipstream, and hand-pumped the lever that retracted the turtle back hood that had sheltered the guns.

"I gotcha now, Babe," he crooned into the slipstream that swirled around his open cockpit. "Like slipping it to a virgin on a hayride."

Warm low altitude currents swirled around the cockpit. The cutting odor of acid swept in on the smoke from the anti-aircraft shells exploding all around them. But neither rear-seat gunner took notice.

"You got two minutes to live," Max speculated. "Like a dragon fly in a hurricane."

Each plane rocked and bounced as it rushed through the bubbles of air that rose from the streets and the rooftops of the city below. Even at five thousand feet, the warmth and odor of Hiroshima filled the air with a mixture of industrial and human waste further contaminated by gun smoke. Undeterred by the friendly fire, the Frank charged across town and headed for its home field. Locked into escape-tempo the Japanese pilot saw and felt every event stretch and twist in dream time.

Off to one side and slightly out of range below the enemy aircraft, Max Bryson opened his cockpit cover and swung his guns out into firing position. As soon as both gunners were ready, they waved to each other and their thumbs-up gesture served as a signal for the other's pilots to lighten the load.

"Heads up," Max called out to the citizens below. "We're sending a few blockbusters your way."

Hold your fire until you can count the rivets on the enemy's fuselage, Max reminded himself. *We don't want to scare this yellow-belly off.*

The sudden release of the thousand pound bomb-load made each Helldiver bob up in the airstream like a cork. Alert to the jump, the gunners cheeked their grips and worked their iron sights down until they had the Frank on the edge of the three-inch outer ring.

"I've got a bead on the main fuel tank directly above where his retractable wheels come together," Carson Braddock reported. "One burst and the lousy fucker's got a crotch full of flaming gasoline."

Swiftly, the wingspan of the enemy fighter plane spread out to the full diameter of the iron ring and the rear-seat gunners found themselves within range. Practiced and disciplined, they each clocked off an imaginary three-second burst before opening fire on the enemy plane that was slowly floating in just above them. During that silent count-down both men moved back into battle-time where everything danced in rapid motion.

Max's initial burst tore off the landing flap on the starboard wing, brought down the wheel strut on that side, and weakened the main spar. Smoking, shedding metal, and rolling over gently, the Frank steepened its dive and the damaged wing shook with the rapid flutter of a taut sail in a cyclone.

"Either that Nip is a rotten pilot or he's dead," Max Bryson observed. "No turns. No banks. No loops. No evasive action what-so-ever."

"He deserves top marks for the way he nursed every ounce of speed out of that baby," Carson allowed. "But I'd bet he's never been up against anything more maneuverable than a B-29."

Carson's opening rounds cut the oil line and ruptured the main gas tank. The flames that engulfed the engine and poured into the cockpit were accompanied by a thick stream of black smoke that streaked back along the belly of the stricken plane and blossomed into a dark plume that tumbled out behind. Shooting together, the two gunners caught the Japanese plane in a crossfire that riddled it with holes before it dropped out of range.

"Bright as a Roman candle," Carson commented. "On automatic pilot."

The moment the rear seat guns fell silent, the pilots carried out a slow roll that swung their Helldivers over the descending enemy aircraft and leveled off beneath the Frank's unprotected belly. A sharp skid and a swift sideslip drifted the dive-bombers closer in toward the enemy aircraft. Chinning their guns and gauging the lead for a deflection shot, the two cousins compared notes as the Frank slid into range.

"This is weird," Carson Braddock declared over the VHF frequency. "As soon as the two targets came together it was as if I couldn't miss."

Instinctively, Max knew what his cousin meant. There were always two targets. The imagined one was your weapon's point of maximum destruction that your eyes projected almost a thousand feet out into the empty sky. The more tangible target was the flight path of the enemy aircraft extended to where that plane will be a full two seconds from now. The trick was to see them both at the same time and put one smack on top of the other before firing a three-second burst.

Even as he made a mental affirmation, the enemy fighter plane slid along the cross hairs of Max's ring-sight and drifted back into the point of destruction nine hundred feet beyond his guns. Expertly, he locked his chin into the cup his hand made against the grip and thumbed the trigger. The sighting, the tight chinning to keep a constant sight base, and the movement of the weapon as an extension of his forward vision were all automatic. The rapid jolts that the bucking weapon delivered to his jaw blurred his vision but his mind kept the enemy plane and the arc of the smoking tracers almost together. *Gotcha now, you bastard*, Max muttered to himself. *Sayonara.*

Since the tracer bullets fell slightly short of the invisible unencumbered rounds traveling between them, the perfect sight picture was always slightly out of focus. The instinctively timed bursts pounded the Frank's eighteen-cylinder radial engine and shattered the canopy that enclosed the burning pilot. Just above Max's hot tracers, the rip-saw devastation from Carson's guns took hold and the damaged wing peeled away. The combined fire power of four machine-guns hammering the enemy with eighty rounds every second made the aircraft disintegrate in mid-air. The flaming wreckage left a trail of black smoke that traced its fall like a wide stick of soft charcoal.

"If the only good Jap is a dead one," Carson proposed, "that kamikaze pilot is a candidate for sainthood."

The abusive bravado poured out from the exhilaration of victory. Momentarily it masked the inner turmoil of the kill. At the final stage, each stream of lead that poured from the twin thirty-caliber machine-guns was as hot and fluid as blood spurting from a ruptured artery. The gunner's lifeblood poured into the enemy aircraft like a noxious fluid destroying the alien creature by direct transfusion. For a few seconds, Carson was attached to that dying machine and the struggle drained him of all compassion. Sweating, aching, and churning with the nausea of destruction he sank down into his bucket seat and slumped over the guns. In that brief moment of terrible exhaustion a small measure of his being changed. Each time it happened the effects were unnoticeable, except for a tightening of the worry lines at the corners of his eyes. And those were inflicted by the thought that burned in his brain. *In these few seconds I have become a killer yet again. Surely, I am marked with the stain that will never fade out entirely.* Then the pensive instant passed and Carson returned to his surroundings with renewed immediacy.

Released from the punishing vortex of battle-time, both gunners became aware of the anti-aircraft fire bursting all around them. The black smoke, the sour taste of gunpowder, and the snap of shrapnel piercing their metal wings came into focus all at once. Carson's chest heaved and Max's stomach churned as their pilots whipped the dive-bombers over into steep banks and dove their planes to give the Japanese gunners on the ground harder targets to hit.

Not far below, the crash of the enemy fighter plane added to the explosions set off by the four quarter ton bombs that ruined an entire city block of downtown Hiroshima. The bombs had blown up a lacquer, tar, and paint factory and the flames were ravishing all the nearby office buildings and warehouses. But the anti-aircraft fire from surrounding roof tops was too thick and accurate for a closer look.

"Make a map of the city," Carson directed. "Let's see if we can chart the layout of their defenses."

A burst above and ahead of Max's Helldiver cracked the bulletproof glass in front of his pilot's cockpit and shattered the side panes. Uninjured, the pilot banked hard and swung away to dodge the next burst and keep the two dive-bombers far enough apart to make them separate targets.

"I've got the downtown core," Max reported. "You take the industrial corridor that leads down to the waterfront."

Skimming across the rooftops at high speed, the dive-bombers banked and swerved to go around tall buildings in their path and flew between belching smokestacks like a pair of chimney swifts. Despite their violent evasive action however, a barrage of forty millimeter cannon shells raked Carson's Helldiver. A series of small explosions tore away long sections of the dive brakes and the landing flaps on the trailing edge of the wings. Damaged but not crippled, the plane dropped its tail just enough for the increased incidence to give the wings slightly added lift.

"You mark down the heavy stuff," Carson suggested. "I'll keep track of where the light cannon rounds and the concentrated machine-gun fire is coming from."

"Roger that," Max replied. "For whatever good it will do."

Still moving in unison, the two dive-bombers swooped down over the sea port section of town and hurried across the harbor to the comparative safety of the wide outer bay. Traveling at top speed, they hugged the rippled surface like cormorants. Seeking safety in nearness the two damaged Helldivers drew so close together their wings overlapped. It was a relief to be alone over the well traveled waters of the Inland Sea. To save fuel the pilots throttled back and climbed slowly as they crossed the shoreline of Shikaku. The neatly stepped rice paddies that twisted up the green landscape gave the steep mountains a softness that stressed how well they shielded the tiny fishing villages from the ravages of the open Pacific Ocean. Entranced by the beauty of the scenery, the rear-seat gunners alternated their tasks. While one carried out a sector scan the other gathered up the spent cartridge casings rattling around beneath his feet. Once they cleared the highest ridge Carson and Max were able to receive the Morse code message being sent by their bombing raid's senior target master. It took them each a few minutes to decode the five letter groups and convert the message into plain language.

"Urgent. Urgent. To the two Helldivers returning from the unauthorized strike on Hiroshima. On landing the pilots will be confined to quarters pending a summary court martial. The radio-gunners will pack their gear and prepare to fly to the island of Tinian within the hour. Do not acknowledge this message. I say again: Do not acknowledge. Out."

In a quick glance across the wing's length of air space between them, the cousins flashed a solemn thumbs up signal that confirmed full understanding. With the message copied, decoded, and found to be clear, each radioman related it to his pilot through the intercom. Slowly, Carson Braddock peeled the yellow rawhide gloves off his hands and used his moist palms to warm his cheeks. *What can they do to us on Tinian,* he wondered, *that they can't do aboard the Brandywine?*

CHAPTER FOUR

Modern weaponry
In the hands of fanatics
Is a recipe
For genocide

Tinian is a small volcanic island in the Marianas some fifteen hundred miles due south of Tokyo. The American Marines who waded ashore at Carolinas Point and Saharon Bay took the island in a week. Even so, the final mop-up was full of fierce skirmishes. Nevertheless, the steep hills that rose to golden crests beneath billowing clouds offered the hard working Sea-Bees relief from the vast expanse of bright ocean all around. The rich foliage soothed the eyes of exhausted aircrews returning from long missions over Japan. Even the gutted landing crafts and the shattered palm trees along the beach were muted by the translucent green that danced in the waves off shore. Still, the heavy surf that pulverized seashells and carried the bits all along the coast where they fell like streaks of white chalk on the black sand hinted of hazards near at hand. But nothing softened the glare of the paired, parallel, two-mile long cement runways that stretched to the water's edge. Indeed, the huge silver four-engine bombers that were dispersed along the airstrip added to it. The long untapered fuselages of the parked B-29s shimmering in the heat gave off the glassy glow of a desert mirage. Yet all that vanished at sunset soon after the two Canadian aircrewmen from the Brandywine arrived. Their brisk hand salutes were returned by the young Army Airforce Colonel and the middle aged Navy Captain who greeted them. The officers wasted no time on preliminaries while leading them into a nearby Quonset hut.

"You bombed Hiroshima," the Colonel declared. "Against

explicit orders to the contrary."

The charge was as bald as it was true. Instinctively, the cousins knew that they had to quibble if they were to find any room to maneuver. Fatigue added an extra edge to the hint of insubordination their dirty clothing harbored. The grime on their dungarees and the acrid fumes seeping from their blue chambray shirts gave them the look and smell of hard-rock miners.

"No sir," ARM2/C Carson Braddock insisted. "We merely dove through its air space and lightened our load to nail the survivor of the kamikaze flight that wiped out a couple of our buddies along with our skipper and the squadron's chief petty officer."

The traces of weapons oil and cordite that hung in the folds of their blue dungarees brought the smell of combat into the room. Even so Carson's aggressive defense startled the seasoned naval officer. As the man in charge, however, Colonel Tibbets bent his head in patient expectation of some follow up. Airman ARM2/C Bryson supplied it.

"Show me an Army fighter pilot who wouldn't have done the same, sir," Max Bryson ventured, "and I'll bet that you would not want to fly with him."

The colonel shook his head and nodded an airman's agreement before looking to his colleague. The battle seasoned Navy Captain William Pastor smiled as the door to the top-secret planning room closed. Instantly, the aircrewmen uncovered and folded their crushed white sailor's caps until they looked like cloth croissants. A quick thrust tucked them beneath their belts and left their hands free.

"Stand at," fifty year old Captain William 'Deke' Pastor prefaced, "EASE."

The crisp planting of their feet eighteen inches apart and the slap of their hands clasping a wrist behind their backs rang out as a stamp and a clap that circled the room. Not yet properly bathed and rested, the traces of anti-aircraft soot on Carson's cheeks and brows made the thin lines on his lean face into deeply etched pencil marks. The heat, the body odor, and the sweat trickling down the sailors' spines turned the traces of battle odor rancid. The arched steel shed was a huge oven. And the only relief to the eyes was the hundreds of photographs assembled into a large map on the corrugated walls. Recognizing it as a typical briefing map for a bombing raid over Japan the cousins took it under professional scrutiny.

"That's a pastiche of aerial recon shots of Hiroshima," Max observed. "They must have been taken from over twenty thousand feet more than a month ago."

"Unfortunately," Carson added, "the city is honeycombed with new defense fortifications that can only be spotted from below five thousand feet."

The hand drawn maps the sailors took out of their pockets showed unmarked anti-aircraft emplacements in the city's downtown core that provoked keen interest. Seeing their chance, Carson and Max picked up sticks of red and yellow chalk and went to the map. Quick yet working with care, they circled a dozen heavy anti-aircraft gun revetments in the industrial district and twice as many forty-millimeter cannon platforms in the dock area. For a closer look the gray haired navy captain took out his horn-rimmed glasses and studied the additions to the wall map. Sensing his service comrades' fatigue, William 'Deacon' Pastor rubbed his weather beaten cheeks, took off his eyeglasses, and softened his voice.

"You men have had an exhausting trip on top of a rugged combat mission," the navy captain declared. "Why don't you clean up, go to chow, and get some rest? We will see you on the flight line shortly after midnight."

Like all enlisted men, the cousins had learned the value of silence under hostile scrutiny. Feeling drained and anxious to leave, they waited until the colonel spoke his piece.

"I beg your pardon, Captain," Colonel Paul Tibbets protested. "We can't take these men along. They lack security clearance."

"It is really quite simple, Colonel," 'Deke' Pastor said. "These men know too much to be left behind. Especially with the press sniffing around for details. And you've seen their maps. We don't have anyone else with their up-to-date grasp of Hiroshima's fortifications."

The colonel was only half the age of the Navy captain, but the decision was his and they all knew it. As he weighed the matter, his bloodless lips and pale cheeks gave his expressionless face the vacant look of an unfinished portrait. Then, suddenly, the color returned and he broke out in a gentle smile.

"Welcome aboard, Navy," Colonel Paul Tibbets declared. "Take off is oh two hundred hours. Don't be late."

The sailors squared their caps across their foreheads, saluted, and left. Just getting out of the Quonset hut without having charges laid against them was a relief. In the mess hall they rustled up some Spam-and-eggs from the late-duty cook. Their bunks were bare mattresses spread out on the fire escape landing of the Sea-Bee barracks. Sleep arrived as instantaneous oblivion. Suddenly, the barracks watch warden was waking them in time to wash up before reporting to the flight line. As he left he gave them some sobering news.

"I don't want to alarm you," the chief carpenter's mate whispered. "But you ought to know that your senior naval officer is carrying a cyanide capsule for every man on the flight."

"Don't worry about us, Chief," Carson said, mustering his bravado. "That's just in case one of us gets close enough to Hirohito to spike his tea."

But the joke did nothing to lighten the anxiety. Even so, it shrank to insignificance as they stepped outside and walked into a night brilliantly illuminated by three one-million-candle-power floodlights.

"Close-up" Max grumbled, "those beams pack a luminous shock wave."

The anti-aircraft searchlights used for night loading made the seven B-29s warming up look like giant neon tubes. The fuel trucks pumping eight thousand gallons into each of the four back-up planes were engulfed in fumes of hundred-octane gasoline that had them shimmering on the edge of invisibility. Throughout the fueling the three separate aircrews slated to carry out the mission kept their jaws slack so the vibrations of the engines did not make their teeth chatter. At peak test power, with a wingspan of one hundred forty-one feet and a fuselage almost a hundred feet long, the fully loaded B-29s were seventy-ton leviathans straining at their brakes. The fuss and strain of securing the unarmed atomic bomb put the crew of the lone strike aircraft on edge.

"Careful men," Navy Captain Deke Pastor warned. "That baby you're putting to bed weighs close to five tons."

Dressed in clean dungarees and work shirts covered by their cordovan colored navy flight jackets, the two sailors climbed aboard the Enola Gay and stretched out on the double-decker bunks in the rear pressurized compartment. Around them, the regular crewmen finished off their checklists and settled into their take-off positions. As usual, the pilot's chat with the control tower was piped throughout the aircraft.

"Dimples Eight Two to North Tinian Tower," Colonel Paul Tibbets stated. "I need taxi-out and take-off instructions."

"Dimples Eight Two from North Tinian Tower," the traffic controller replied. "Take off to the east on runway A for Able."

With its lights out, the silver B-29 moved away from the ground crew and the camera detail under her own power. The surge of the engines and rush of acceleration gave each of the fourteen men on board the feeling of plunging headlong into a dark abyss.

"How come we are the only one carrying a bomb?" Max Bryson inquired as the overloaded B-29 picked up speed. "Don't they trust the other guys?"

"Even though we call our nine thousand pound egg Little Boy," the Air Force belly gunner declared, "one is all we need."

The boast put the newcomers on guard. Flying in an unfamiliar bomber and having no proper battle station gave the two cousins a mild case of the jitters.

"It seems more like a virgin's maiden-head to me," Carson Braddock quipped. "One is all you've got."

Overloaded by fifteen thousand pounds, the massive B-29 thundered down the runway like a railroad tank car. As it passed the two-mile marker the flares lined up along the last three hundred yards of the airstrip began to flash by in a blur. At one hundred eighty miles an hour the Enola Gay was racing over rough cement just a stone's throw from the water.

"Son of a bitch," Carson swore. "He's used up the runway and now he's crossing the fuckin' beach."

The bumps faded just as the land gave way to the black sand that stretched down to the sea. The smooth flow of the plane through the ocean spray told the crew they were airborne. The strain of lifting so much dead weight on thin silver wings made the main spars groan like elephants shifting timber. Noisily, the plane climbed out over the dark sea. Inside, the eleven man regular crew continued to cringe as the grinding of the bolts and rivets worked through the entire airframe.

"God damn," Max Carson said. "That was closer than a circumcision done by a blind Rabbi."

At five hundred feet the perilously loaded aircraft shook itself out from head to tail like a dog drying its coat. Fully wrung out, she steadied into normal flight. Only the bright stars overhead and the fingers of flame flashing out of the exhaust tubes relieved the total darkness. In the compact pressure cabins the remote control turret gunners settled down for the long flight to enemy airspace. With nothing better to do, the sailors looked out through the observation bubble and checked on the two accompanying B-29s some three miles away. As tiny dark patches that occasionally blocked out a few stars and replaced them with yellow flickers of engine exhaust they held no interest. So the sailors retired to their bunks to catch up on lost sleep.

Once the Enola Gay passed through four thousand feet the co-pilot throttled back the engines and dampened the in-board motors by pitting the pulse of the other two against them. It kept the plane from shuddering through periodic power surges. As the flight wore on and the plane began a more gradual climb, the air inside the pressurized compartments grew chilly and stale. Even so, Carson and Max slept until they were shaken into near wakefulness.

"Come with me," Captain Pastor ordered. "I need your help in the bomb-bay."

"Captain, we are radio operators," Carson protested. "We don't know anything about bombs."

"Hell, I've never set off anything bigger than a cherry-bomb," Max declared. "Unless you count the stick of dynamite that blew up Old Man Hogan's outhouse."

Bundled in the warmth of their fleece lined flight jackets, the two sailors shivered until their bodies woke up and their fatigue subsided. The borrowed sheepskin boots, the cowhide gloves, and the goggle helmets they wore left only the front of their faces exposed.

"Rest easy, men," the captain advised. "I will be guiding your hands and fingers every step of the way."

As the prostitute said to the college of cardinals, Carson thought with a wry smirk and a quiet chuckle that made his cousin give a sympathetic snort. Puzzled, the two Canadians tightened their scarves around their necks and followed the naval officer toward the unpressurized bomb bay.

"We loaded the bomb unfused," Captain Deke Pastor explained, "so that if we crashed on take-off we wouldn't blow Tinian off the map."

"The crew told us you cut your hands up pretty badly," Carson said, "practicing the in-flight re-arming procedure all night without any gloves."

Captain Pastor nodded assent as they descended the bomb bay entrance ladder. In the roseate glow of the high altitude morning, the frosty air that swept across the catwalk of the cavernous compartment cut through the worn denim dungarees the sailors wore. Their calves and thighs were numb in minutes.

"Everybody knows you've got the drill down cold," Max indicated. "So what's the trouble?"

The question put Deke Pastor on the spot. As the Navy's top specialist in nuclear weapons, the gray haired senior officer was supposed to be self-sufficient when it came to fusing the bomb. It hurt him even to think of the stupidity that had created a difficulty he could not handle all by himself. And since it was urgent to finish the job while they could work in the unpressurized bomb bay without oxygen he had no choice but to reveal the bare bones of the problem.

"As I was about to finish wiring the low altitude detonator my glasses fell off and vanished beneath the bomb casing," Deke Pastor confessed. "I didn't think to bring an extra pair. So I need your eyes and hands to complete the final connection."

The mixture of graphite and frozen blood that was congealed on Deke Pastor's fingers gave the captain's hands the stringy look of death. Oversized, even for the Enola Gay's bomb bay, the world's first atom bomb hung from the shackles like a suspended hippopotamus. Cradled in its harness and capped by the small canister that would open automatically and release the parachute designed to slow and steady its descent, "Little Boy" seemed strangely alone.

"Christ," Max Bryson remarked. "It looks like a miniature submarine."

Max and Carson left their cowhide gunnery gloves on as they fingered the fuse mechanism under the captain's expert guidance. The detonator in the tail was designed to drive the plunger down through the full length of the weapon the moment it got near enough to the earth for the atomic explosion to spread its force out in an inverted cone that would do maximum damage. The wires linking the electric exploder to the altitude pressure gauge were color coded to minimize the chance of error.

"The blue and the yellow wires want to be connected to the right and the left bottom terminals," Captain Deke Pastor declared. "Respectively."

"Check," Carson replied and made the connections. "Blue on my right. Yellow to my left."

"That is correct," Deke Pastor affirmed. "In ordinance, left and right always refer to your hands as you face the weapon, unless otherwise specified."

Even with the outer doors closed, the roar of the Enola Gay's four massive engines and the throb of her propellers invaded the steel ribbed bomb bay. Shaken until their chests ached, the Navy men shouted like sandhogs on jackhammers to make themselves heard.

"Double check," Max confirmed. "All connections as directed—safe, solid, and secure."

"Now unscrew the three green plugs," Captain Deke Pastor ordered. "And replace them with red ones."

"The safety fuses are out," Carson reported. "And the live ones are in place."

"We are in business," Max declared. "The electrical connection is complete. She is armed."

Unlike battle time, the moment gave all three men an opportunity to reflect. The two enlisted men studied the huge bomb casing in ignorance. Their only knowledge of Uranium 235 came from a daily afternoon radio program called Captain Midnight. Still, the simple fact that it hung there all alone was impressive. The naval officer saw it in the full knowledge of its awesome power, however. And his appreciation for the very immensity of it, as well as the help given, drove him to divulge top secret information.

"That's the equivalent of twenty thousand tons of TNT," Deke Pastor announced. "Alive and set to explode the moment her tiny drag-chute lowers her down to eight hundred feet above the center of the city."

"Ooooo-eeee," Max wheezed. "That's more tonnage than our carrier based dive-bombers have dropped in the whole God-damned war."

Amazed, Carson Braddock fastened up the faceplate that covered the center of the tail section where the fins crossed and gave the screwdriver back to the captain. Max Bryson rubbed the grease smudges off the parachute canister. Together, they gave the weapon a final pat and waited to be dismissed.

"Thank you, men. You have been a tremendous help," the anxious officer stated. "If you don't mind, I would like to keep this a Navy secret for the moment. The colonel and the crew have enough on their minds right now."

Nodding assent, the sailors left the captain behind with his tools and his wiring diagrams. They moved like moles through the long pressurized tunnel that brought them out in the forward compartment of the B-29. Emerging in bright sunlight, they unzipped their flight jackets and took a careful look around. Numbed by the steady drone of the engines they wiggled their jaws and cracked their inner ears to open them to speech.

"Talk about a God's eye view," Carson declared. "This is fantastic."

Standing on the upper deck of the glassed in cabin they felt as if they were in the command car of a blimp. The circular nose of the plane was covered in tinted glass that gave them panoramic coverage of the sky and the curved horizon. Busy and efficient, the pilot, the co-pilot, and the flight engineer concentrated on their final performance check while the navigator and the radar operator fed target co-ordinates and wind direction to the bombardier as the Enola Gay climbed to bombing altitude.

Viewed from thirty thousand feet the coast of southern Honshu was a pale blue expanse of shallow water edging along sandy shores and great stretches of tree lined cliffs. The bright sky, and the curved line of approaching landscape visible through the glassed in nose, turned the cockpit into a bubble gliding over the edge of the earth.

"Hiroshima dead ahead in clear view," Colonel Paul Tibbets announced. "On course. On time. On target. Good show. Out."

Enchanted, Carson and Max settled into unoccupied landing seats next to the crew's tiny galley. They felt the drag as the bomb-bay doors swung open. Everyone tensed as the industrial city nestled in the hills beyond the bay started to slide beneath the nose of the plane.

"We are about a mile above the height their best anti-aircraft guns can reach, Colonel," Max explained. "Besides, they don't have the proximity fuse."

"Even so," Carson added, "below twenty thousand feet they're on top of you like Gangbusters."

The crew fell silent as the Enola Gay approached the drop-point. The pilots, the technicians, and the gunners all increased their concentration as the two accompanying B-29s extended their separation from the Enola Gay.

"The good news is that the Japs won't bother to send fighter planes up this high," Max declared. "Not for what looks like a reconnaissance flight or a three plane nuisance raid."

As soon as the others were fifty miles behind, the accompanying aircraft turned away from Hiroshima. Going in alone, the Boeing Superfortress trembled with power as the crew checked out every new vibration that rattled through the airframe as well as each precaution that sprang to mind.

"Make sure you've got your dark glasses on," the navigator, Lieutenant Dutch Van Kirk, advised as he handed the cousins theirs.

"And don't even think of staring at the explosion."

The Enola Gay was a hollow shell of mechanical noise when the bombardier took control for the run on the target. Hunched over his Norden bombsight, Major Tom Larabee steered the plane so that the cross-hairs of the sight left the seven tributaries of the Ota River behind and settled on the four-hundred-foot-span of the Aioi Bridge that stretched across the Honkawa and the Motoyasu rivers.

"Mark down the date as eight-fifteen A.M. August sixth nineteen forty-five," Bombardier Tom Larabee declared. "Remember Pearl Harbor. Bombs away."

The release of nine thousand pounds of dead weight sent the Enola Gay leaping up in a sudden climb that Colonel Tibbets fashioned into a steep bank and swerving turn. The silver B-29 swung away from the city center and swept out toward the bay like a huge kite cut loose from its string in a stiff breeze.

"I can see it, colonel," the tail gunner reported. "The stabilizing parachute is open and she is falling fast, straight, and normal."

"STOP WATCHING THE GOD DAMNED THING AND GET YOUR DARK GLASSES ON, SERGEANT," the bombardier ordered. "Even with that small restraining chute deployed she will still explode in one minute and fifty-three seconds. The light will make you blind before you can blink."

Shrinking and twisting as it fell, the atomic bomb looked no more menacing than the thick stem on a white daisy cast off a high cliff. Still, the shallow arc of her traverse and the relentless penetration of her six-mile fall turned suspense into agony.

"If you can find it in your heart," Deke Pastor said as he emerged from the tunnel, "say a prayer for the people down there."

Watched in fitful glances, the small white parachute shrank as it fell and steadied its mammoth load. Transfixed, the bombardier noted the nuclear weapon's drift toward the T-shaped bridge that spanned the city's two rivers. The whole airframe shuddered as the Enola Gay's four engines erupted with a throaty roar and the plane swung into a violent evasive maneuver. The sudden vertical bank and climbing turn put ground zero behind them. Simultaneously, the regular crew braced for the shock wave that would overtake them moments after the giant explosion flashed its unearthly light into every corner of the aircraft. Instinctively, Carson and Max wrapped their arms and legs around the ladder that led to the tunnel going aft and waited for a fierce body blow. The pilot and the co-pilot held the control yoke in an iron grip in case the wave's impact tumbled the plane about or damaged the flight surfaces. The bombardier, the navigator, the radar operator, and the flight engineer huddled over their instruments to protect them from flying debris. The gunners in their fire control stations covered their dark goggles with their hands to protect their vision further. And as the plane leveled off and sped out over the bay the pilot broke with their standard routine.

"Jesus Christ, practice is one thing," Colonel Paul Tibbets protested. "But I can't do any blind-flying today."

With a sweep of his hand the pilot tore the dark goggles off and threw them away. Everyone else kept his eyes sheltered and his body braced as the Enola Gay sped out high over the bright blue bay and headed for the Inland Sea. Everyone, that is, except Captain Deke Pastor who sat hunched against the entrance to the connecting tunnel holding his leather helmet in his hand.

"Your goggles, Captain," the radio operator warned. "You're not wearing your dark glasses."

"You can forget that." Deke Pastor declared. "We are more than three minutes into the drop. The bomb is on the ground. She's a dud."

The verdict swept around the command compartment like a death notice. The dry and slightly caustic pressurized air gave the rattle and shakes of the airframe a brittleness that no one had noticed before. In a mental flash, dread turned to denial.

"Maybe it's a hang-fire fuse," co-pilot Captain Robert Lewis proposed. "It could be doing a slow burn."

"That's right," Lieutenant Dutch Van Kirk insisted. "Over Europe we dropped delayed-action mavericks in every bomb load. Some five minutes after impact all Hell broke loose."

"Impossible," Major Tom Larabee declared. "Little Boy has a split second to reach critical mass or it's all over. Dead forever."

The bombardier's pronouncement fell on the crew with the

finality of a guilty verdict from the bench. There was no appeal. So, despite the steady roar of the B-29s four powerful engines and the creak and rattle of the airframe, the plane droned on in the deathly silence of abject failure. Tinian and a board of inquiry were fifteen hundred miles due South. And no one knew that better than the Deacon, Navy Captain William 'Deke' Pastor.

CHAPTER FIVE

*The absolute nature
Of success and failure
In aerial combat
Makes it warfare's last refuge
Of individualism.*

The Enola Gay slowed and settled into a steady cruising speed at thirty-two thousand feet. Everything was masked in a light blue haze as she crossed over the rocky islands that stood out like garnets embedded in the Inland Sea. Unsure and unprepared for failure, the rest of the men took off their dark goggles. Those with a rear view looked back at the glistening city nestled in the mountains that rimmed the bay. The gloom of the mission and their wasted training filled the Enola Gay with despair. And few felt it more than the men who had to make the bad news official.

"Sparks," Colonel Paul W. Tibbets said to his radioman, "transmit the signal we prayed that we would never have to send. 'Little Boy delivered stillborn.' I say again: 'Stillborn.'"

The sergeant encoded the message and tapped out the five letter groups in Morse code. A short reply acknowledged receipt and the decoded contents were reported to the pilot. For minutes the entire crew flew on in hollow silence. As the city of Hiroshima shrank to just a thin scratch on the coast line far astern, the unlisted passengers found their voices.

"Is that it?" Naval Combat Aircrewman Carson Braddock demanded. "Is that all we do—just say sorry and run?"

"Somebody is gonna want to know what happened," ARM2/C Max Bryson insisted. "And they are going to want precise details in no uncertain terms."

No one else said a word. Captain Deke Pastor nodded his agreement and stood up to lean against the mouth of the tunnel. In the cockpit, the pilot's hands and feet sent almost imperceptible tremors out through the controls. The vibrations transmitted to the wing tips and the tail surfaces made the giant aircraft shudder ever so lightly with his indecision.

"It's no skin off my ass," Carson declared. "But it seems to me we gotta go back."

"And that means low, down, and dirty," Max concluded. "You can't see nothin' but city blocks and wide streets from up here."

Gently, the Enola Gay dipped a sun-drenched wing and turned on the almost motionless tip until the quiet city of Hiroshima lay dead-ahead on the pilot's broad windscreen. As they approached, the green parks and the red-tile roofs that covered the crowded bungalows all stood out as havens of refuge in a city of weathered wood and beige bricks. The tin-roofed factories and corrugated iron warehouses spread away from the grimy industrial core along a network of crooked streets.

"What are you doing, Skipper?" the second Airforce radio operator demanded. "We already left our calling card."

"He's taking us back for some close-up pictures of Ground Zero," the bombardier replied. "Headquarters will be frantic for information about the disposal of the bomb. A few good snap shots might even impress the board of inquiry."

The explanation was crisp, cool, and correct. No one else questioned the need for another pass or doubted the danger it entailed. Yet there were choices ahead known only to the sailors on board.

"If you take her in below ten thousand feet, colonel," Carson Braddock warned. "They will throw everything they've got at us—including their peach baskets."

"We need on-the-spot details of the bomb's location and present condition," the co-pilot explained. "The closer the better."

The reason was cogent and the decision was sound. Even so, the battle seasoned sailors wanted to reduce the risk involved.

"Then send the other two planes in as decoys," Max Bryson advised. "They can draw off some of the ground fire."

"Sorry, they have civilian observers aboard," the flight engineer reported. "And nuclear scientists are much too valuable to risk on a hedge-hopping mission over enemy terrain."

"Once more we are expendable," Max mumbled. "I hope you guys like peaches."

The grumbles turned the mood throughout the aircraft to dark desolation. Caught up in it and keenly aware that the fault might be his, the senior naval officer gave voice to the feelings that surged through the crew.

"On a mission like this, one failure is already a disaster," Captain Deke Pastor insisted. "Either we get good pictures or we might as well not go back. We haven't got that much more to lose."

Silently, the captain took the tiny metal container from his pocket and passed out a small cyanide capsule to each member of the crew. Carson looked at Max before he made his decision. Both cousins refused to accept a pill.

"Of course, you know what this means," Deke Pastor said softly. "If it looks like we're going down I will have to shoot you both."

"That's one way to keep a secret," Max Bryson replied. "But I wouldn't bank on it."

Under Carson Braddock's direction, Colonel Tibbets swung the rapidly descending B-29 wide of the city so it could turn back out of sight and make a safer inland approach. Racing along at just under four hundred miles an hour, the huge bomber rocked and shook from the heat rising off the mountains as it came around in a steeply banked turn.

"This four engine Boeing may not be a dive bomber," Max Bryson allowed, "but I haven't felt like this since ten of us rode down the Grouse Mountain ski jump standing up on a six man toboggan."

The speeding Superfortress skimmed in just above the mountains that wrapped around the city in a half crown. She followed the slope of the foothills down over the suburbs and roared across the poorly defended residential district at rooftop height. Max Bryson scanned ahead and pointed out the parks and the playing fields where the anti-aircraft guns were concentrated. Together, the two naval aircrewmen showed the pilot and the co-pilot the safest crooked path toward the city center.

"Careful now," Carson advised. "There's a gun battery in every school yard."

"Watch out for anything that looks like a glade of trees or a yard full of bushes," Max warned. "The bastards shoot right through their own camouflage nets."

The huge shadow of the bomber raced across the red-tile roofs and the cobble stone streets. With each bank and swerve it shrank and swelled like an ever-changing inkblot as every man aboard adjusted himself to the swift onset of battle time.

The anti-aircraft shells that burst all around the Enola Gay littered the plane's flight path with lethal puffs of black smoke ahead and behind. The heavy guns spread throughout the rail yard tracked the B-29 with deadly fire that pierced the wing repeatedly and opened up holes in the fuselage. The explosions and the concussion from near misses sent the plane lurching toward the well-protected industrial district before anyone was ready. Sweating and grinding his teeth, Colonel Paul Tibbets fought hard to control the skid. He raised the starboard wing just in time to clear a smokestack that loomed up out of nowhere. The machine-guns on the ground caught the struggling aircraft in a crossfire that traveled with it for half a mile.

"I am hit and hurt," the belly turret gunner reported from his fire control station. "I think I'm gonna pass out."

"I'll look after that," Max volunteered and started into the tunnel leading aft. "We will need all our fire power when their fighter planes find us."

The tracers from twenty and forty millimeter cannons mounted on rooftops and platforms wrapped the Enola Gay in smoke trails that unfolded like charcoal party-streamers. The return fire from the plane's four remote control gun turrets chewed up the ground targets with short but deadly bursts.

"Keep clear of those barrage balloons," Carson warned. "Their cable skirts protect the power stations and the main government buildings."

As they raced down the river, a shower of machine-gun bullets and rifle slugs fired from armed barges punctured the wings and the metal fuselage with the ping and high pitched squeal of popping rivets. Undeterred, the bomb-aimer searched out the designated impact zone despite the crash and clatter of spent metal whirling around his nose-compartment.

"The weapon is intact on a main thoroughfare," Bombardier Tom Larabee reported. "The parachute that lowered it down to a semi-soft landing is still attached."

"I see it," the co-pilot confirmed. "A man and a woman are standing nearby and warning the crowd to move back."

"I don't care if Hirohito's horse is pissing on it," Captain Deke Pastor growled. "Have you got the God-damned unexploded bomb on film?"

"Roger, Captain, "the red-bearded bombardier replied. "You should be able to read the fucker's serial number from these shots."

"All right," navigator Dutch Van Kirk declared. "Let's head for the barn."

Immediately, Colonel Tibbets swung the damaged Superfortress over the downtown hospital and followed Carson's guidance to the stockyards and the shantytown that surrounded it. The plane skimmed the thatched roofs of the inner city hovels so close a dusty trail of twigs and straw rose in its wake. But the warehouses nearby bristled with guns that ranged in from both sides. Shrapnel from an overhead burst tore through the forward control compartment and bloodied the flight engineer. The heavy anti-aircraft shell that exploded under the wing tore the cowling off an engine and tipped the bomber over into a steep bank.

"Fire in the left inboard engine," the twenty-three year old co-pilot reported. "The propeller is winding up like a run-away windmill."

"Shut it down," Colonel Tibbets ordered. "And piss hard and long on that raging inferno."

Co-pilot Captain Bob Lewis cut off the fuel supply to the burning engine and triggered the fire-bottle that smothered the flames in foam. Trailing a thin line of black smoke, the B-29 leveled off above the docks. Light cannon fire from the shipyards shattered her plexiglass nose with dozens of rounds that exploded like a string of firecrackers and filled the control compartment with smoke and flying slivers of hot steel.

"Aiyeee," Major Larabee screamed. "I'm scalped."

The bombardier grabbed his leather helmet and held his head in both hands as blood from a massive scalp wound oozed out through his fingers. Moving quickly, Carson Braddock dropped down into the battered nose compartment and threw his flight jacket over the wounded man's upraised arms and shoulders as a makeshift shelter to shield his head from the howling wind. Even then, the stream of cold air rushing in through the shattered canopy tore at the dressing he wound around the bombardier's cracked skull. Yet Larabee was not the only one in pain.

"My legs. Oh God, my legs," the co-pilot yelled. "The bones are on fire from the inside."

With the help of the wounded radio operator, Carson dragged the crippled co-pilot out of his seat and gave him a shot of morphine. The agony from the young officer's torn up legs made the man kick and thrash so hard it took an extra dose of the painkiller to knock him out. As he faded into deep unconsciousness, the navigator slid into the co-pilot's chair and doctored his own facial lacerations.

"Are you sure this is the best way out?" Dutch Van Kirk inquired. "We are taking a Hell of a beating."

"Christ no, Lieutenant. There might well be a dozen better ways," Carson confessed. "But down on the deck with a tub like this we've got no choice. The longer we take to clear the city the better chance their fighter planes have to find us. Heading out over the bay and through Bungo Strait at break-neck speed makes it an over water trip all the way home."

The Enola Gay thundered across the docks and drew heavy gunfire from every armed merchant ship in the harbor. Shrapnel and bullets riddled the flight engineer's instrument panels and cut the radio operator down as he hunched over the radarscope. Suddenly, a five-inch shell burst just above the nose of the bomber and drove it down with a crack that split the fuselage.

"Son of a bitch," the top turret gunner moaned from his aiming seat. "That lousy Jap shell just broke my arm."

"I've got him," Captain Deke Pastor announced. "He needs a tourniquet and a splint."

As soon as the aiming seat was cleared, Carson Braddock climbed up into the remote control sighting blister. He ran the four fifty-caliber machine-guns through a full traverse. Mounted over and under as well as side-by-side, the compact quad sent out a stream of hot lead that gave the forward top turret the punch of an automated battering ram. The hand grips that moved the guns in unison and the foot pedals that tightened the sight reticle gave him trouble until he opened fire on a cargo ship.

"Whooo-eeee," Carson shouted. "These fifties pump lead like a Jack-hammer quartet."

Carson's tracers curved aft and dropped into the bridge of an armed oil tanker. The hot rounds sent two Japanese sailors diving overboard as the bomber swung out to sea. Another burst toppled the mast of a wooden mine sweeper and scattered her guncrew.

"Save your ammo, Lefty," Max advised. "We've got company dropping in at five o'clock high."

"A pair of bandits, Skipper," tail gunner Sergeant Bob Barron reported. "But I would swear they were ours if there wasn't an orange rising sun on the side of each fuselage."

The Japanese interceptors banked sharply and swung around in a tight pursuit curve that brought them in above and behind the bomber. The enemy planes closed the gap between themselves and the speeding B-29 at just under two miles a minute. As they brought their wing guns to bear the fighters slid sideward in the gunsights of the men who were tracking them.

"These are Tonys made by Kawasaki," Carson Braddock reported. "The water cooled in-line engine and the large airscoop for the radiator toward the trailing edge of the wing makes them easy to mistake for North American P-51 Mustangs."

"Oh, shit," Max Bryson complained. "These fuckers are Ki-61 type one b with thirty-millimeter cannons in their wings."

Sighting by remote control, Max and Carson opened fire with their dorsal and ventral turrets in unison. The tail gunner joined in and added the slow and heavy thump of his twenty-millimeter cannons to the staccato rapping of the machine-gun barrage. The coordinated assault struck the leading Japanese fighter plane head-on and rocked it from side to side as it struggled to stay on course.

Hits behind the engine and all along the fuselage sent showers of shredded metal tumbling back into the Tony's darkening slipstream. Suddenly, the Japanese pilot threw the sleek fighter plane into a tight snap-roll and continued to close the range."

"God-damn," Max remarked. "Don't these yellow bastards know how to shoot anymore? Even the Army pilots are running on kamikaze time."

Almost instantly, the huge Superfortress began to slip and slide around as if it were out of control. Colonel Tibbets kicked hard right rudder and worked the wheel until the B-29 dipped a wing into a banking skid. The Enola Gay lurched heavily and slid off into a five hundred-foot dip.

"Make violent corkscrew turns, Skipper," Carson Braddock directed. "These sons-a-bitches are fixin' to run us down."

A swing in the other direction and a sudden power boost made the smoke trailing from the dead engine curl. In its effort to follow, the Japanese fighter plane dipped and spun with the awkward grace of a crippled dancer writhing in a fatal embrace.

"Shag ass, Skipper," the tail gunner shouted. "This monkey's playing for keeps."

The heavy bomber spit gunfire from half-a-dozen fifty-caliber machine-guns as the mottled green fighter plane made a desperate lunge. Paul Tibbets stamped on the foot pedal and swung the three-story high rudder of the B-29 out from under the grind of the Tony's propeller. Hit by a wall of bullets, the disintegrating Japanese interceptor plunged down in a blur of dappled greens. Its sturdy wing sliced into the tail-gunner's compartment and snapped off flush with the fighter plane's fuselage. Tumbling out of control, the mangled enemy aircraft spun down into the sea below. Its crash ignited a momentary fireball that spurted up and collapsed atop the same ocean wave.

"There's one chrysanthemum that didn't float," the navigator announced from the co-pilot's seat. "But the son-of-a-bitch sure could fly."

"Let's hope he's the only one," Max interjected. "Half our port elevator is missing and there's no more tail gunner."

Shock generated a momentary silence throughout the plane.

Even those who could not see behind their stations turned to look aft.

"Are you sure?" Colonel Tibbets inquired. "He might be unconscious or the intercom could be knocked out."

"Sorry, Skipper. No such luck," Carson disclosed. "That Jap Tony wiped out the entire tail gunner compartment in one tremendous shark bite."

The collision had shoved the crippled B-29 into a flat skid that opened her flank to the second assailant. Banked and launched on a wing-over, the Japanese interceptor shuddered as the bomber's guns converged on her. The Enola Gay dropped a wing and rolled into a vertical bank at the start of a tight pylon turn five hundred feet above the water. A hundred yards away, the Tony opened fire with the machine-guns mounted behind the cowling and the two thirty-millimeter cannons protruding from its wings. The unseen shells from the blazing guns disturbed the air through a wide arc that curved in toward the bomber like a reaper's sickle.

"Brace yourselves," Carson warned. "We're in for a nasty hail storm."

The Tony's heavy cannon-fire ripped through the command compartment with sledge hammer force that tore out chunks of plexiglass and chopped up the instrument panels. Bullets, shrapnel, shreds of hot steel, and slivers of glass all burst in upon the new co-pilot and left his lifeless body limp in a bath of blood. The torrent of debris that tore across the cockpit cut up the colonel's legs just moments before the Japanese airplane crashed in through the bomb bay doors.

The propeller of the enemy fighter plane chewed up the cavernous bomb bay and the force of the crash embedded the Tony's engine into the rear bulkhead of the bomber's forward cabin. The impact tossed the injured aircrewmen around like bandaged rag dolls.

A sudden buck and lurch of the fuselage knocked Captain Pastor down and tore the Superfort's powerful radio transmitter off its bolts and away from the cabin wall. The heavy transmitter rose up in the air and toppled forward on its side. All its weight came down on the corner that landed on Captain Deke Pastor's chest.

The clatter contained a snap with a crunch and the loud crack of bones that denied the captain further breath. Choked with a mouth full of blood, the senior naval officer coughed in a massive body thrust that snapped his head up and back then drove it down—hard. The involuntary spasm spread the gore from his mouth all across his pale blue and lifeless face.

Further aft, the damage to the aircraft was even worse. Anchored only by its engine, the Japanese fighter plane swung down and forward until its wing sheered off the propeller blade of the remaining inboard engine. The sound of the runaway twenty-two hundred horsepower engine thundered through the cabin like a freight train in a tunnel.

"Somebody shut down that inside engine before she shakes this crate to bits," Colonel Paul Tibbets ordered. "And while you're at it, give me full emergency powers on both outer engines."

"Sorry Skipper, you're on your own," Carson Braddock advised. "Dutch's tour of duty is over."

Swathed in blood below the waist, Colonel Paul Tibbets twisted the flight yoke, kicked the rudder pedals, and leaned over to switch off the run away motor and advance the throttles on the outboard engines. The strain deepened the lines across his forehead and moistened the swollen pouches beneath his eyes. The sweat that darkened his khaki shirt across the shoulders ran down his chest in narrow streams.

Battered, bent, and floundering through the air, the severely damaged B-29 groaned, shivered, and rattled as if in pain. The exposed wreckage of the kamikaze hanging from her belly made her look like a stricken sperm whale struggling to get rid of a dead calf. Badly strained, the Enola Gay leveled off a hundred feet above the water and the colonel found the strength to switch fuel tanks and boost the power of the remaining engines another few notches. Even so, the plane hovered on the brink of a stall. The overworked outboard engines screamed as they struggled to lift the weight of the Japanese fighter plane embedded in the bomb bay.

"Get somebody up here to bandage my legs," Colonel Tibbets ordered. "If I lose much more blood I won't have the strength to keep this baby from slipping into the drink."

"Why not set her down while she is still under control?" Max inquired. "Who knows when that Jap plane we're carrying might explode?"

"A bad idea," Carson declared. "With the nose blown open, the belly gutted, and that kamikaze's wing hanging down like a keel we wouldn't have a chance."

The smoke from the smoldering remains of the enemy plane poured from the Enola Gay's belly like black ink. Panting hard and twisted with pain, Colonel Tibbets wrestled with the damaged controls as the plane began to sink closer to the water.

"Hold on fellas," the pilot warned. "It's all or nothing. Here goes."

Easing up on the control column, the colonel let the Enola Gay sink toward the waves. The moment the wing of the enemy plane began to slice through the odd sea swell, the pilot jerked both usable throttles back a few notches and then rammed them forward as far as they would go. The outboard engines coughed, lost revs, surged, and roared with restored power.

"AAAYYEEE!" Carson shouted. "Ride her cowboy."

For just a moment, the Enola Gay staggered in mid-air. The wing tips bent up as the overloaded Superfort sank almost ten feet with its tail down and then swept ahead. With a groan and the squeal of twisting metal the Tony's extended wing sank deep below the surface where the Japanese fighter plane's landing gear slid open. Instantly, the suspended wing slammed into an oncoming wave. A great shudder swept through the fuselage and fluttered the wings of the B-29 as the two airplanes pulled apart.

Yanked loose, the crumpled interceptor tumbled across a shallow ocean trough and disintegrated against an advancing wall of water. Freed just as if she had dropped a six thousand pound bomb, the Enola Gay lurched upward and rose two hundred feet above the regular turquoise swells. Even so, the sudden reprieve left no room for comfort.

"Easy does it, Skipper," Max Bryson advised over the intercom. "You've got a damaged tail fin, an unhinged rudder, and a chewed up elevator all flapping like sails in a hurricane."

"The shell holes are letting sea and sky shine in all over the fuselage," Carson Braddock disclosed. "It looks like the chewing gum holding this crate together is stretched pretty thin."

"Roger. I read you loud and clear," Colonel Tibbets affirmed. "But I'm gonna need some help before I bleed to death."

The pilot eased off on the throttle and fine-tuned the mixture to take some of the strain off the overworked engines. Even so, the wind rushing in through the shattered nose section made it hard to breathe in the cockpit. Unable to bandage the wounded turret gunner in the rear compartment, Max dragged him through the partially collapsed connecting tunnel and propped him up against the galley wall. With Carson treating the pilot's injuries and Max checking out the wounded, the forward cabin looked like a flying ambulance.

"Chart us a course to Iwo Jima," Colonel Tibbets requested. "That should cut the return trip in half."

The demand forced Carson Braddock to snatch a hurried look at the compass, take note of the air speed indicator, and glance at the watch he wore on the inside of his wrist. Without leaving the pilot's side, he ran his eyes across the blood stained map hanging from the navigator's tiny chart table. A lightning glance at the yellow line tracing the emergency route to the nearest island marked in red gave him what he needed to know.

"South by a quarter East," Carson estimated. "We should be there in time for lunch."

The sailor's swift dead reckoning and salty compass reading left the pilot confused and annoyed. Wounded, weak, and pale from loss of blood, the colonel focused his remaining energy in a blast of white heat that sparkled with impatience.

"Don't give me any of that Navy lingo, sailor," Paul Tibbets complained. "This plane flies by Army rules."

The outburst pumped blood through the pilot's arteries and oxygen into his brain. Momentarily revived he made full sense of the other sailor's corrections.

"Judging from the wind ripples striping the surface I'd say we're slicing through an eight knot cross-wind," Max declared. "You'd better hold a compass heading of 179 degrees, Skipper."

"That's better," Paul Tibbets sighed. "Now all this tired old chassis needs is a transfusion."

Working quickly, Carson and Max pulled the blood soaked body of Captain Deke Pastor out from under the overturned radio console and wrapped his corpse in the nylon canopy of a damaged parachute. Between bandage checks on the wounded, Max and Carson took turns feeding Colonel Tibbets cups of hot coffee and shielding him from the steady blast of wind that whistled through the cabin. In their spare time they worked on the transmitter. In less than an hour they had the radio operating well enough to raise the landing strip on Iwo Jima.

"Iwo Control. Iwo Control. This is Dimples Eighty-two," Carson Braddock broadcast. "We will need ambulances on the runway when we land. And you will want at least two doctors standing by in surgery."

"Have a chaplain out there to give last rights," Max added. "And get the graves detail ready to handle body parts."

Gently, the lumbering heavy bomber slipped off an even keel and began a slow slide toward the water. The changing rush of air inside the cabin and the steeply tilted horizon alerted the naval aircrewmen.

"WAKE UP, SKIPPER," Max shouted. "YOU'RE LOSING IT."

"Raise the right wing and ease the stick back, Colonel," Carson directed. "Now boost the engines so she bottoms out under power."

Colonel Tibbets caught the hazardous descent a bare fifty feet above the waves. He leveled the aircraft with the sloppy movements of a drunk struggling to regain his balance. As the plane floundered in a vain effort to gain altitude, Carson and Max removed the dead navigator from the co-pilot's seat and propped him up against the shattered flight engineer's panel. Chatting briskly and offering simple suggestions for trimming the aircraft, they brought the colonel out of his stupor.

"Revive the co-pilot," Colonel Tibbets ordered. "I'm not going to make it."

"You'd have a better chance of waking a black bear up in the middle of hibernation," Max Bryson declared. "It took two shots of morphine to deaden his pain."

Calmly, Aviation Radioman Second Class Carson Braddock

slipped into the co-pilot's seat and placed his hands and feet on the controls. Carson used a feather touch to follow each push of the rudder bar, every shift of the control column, and the slightest turn of the wheel that moved the ailerons out on the wing tips. Hearing no complaints, he tightened his grip and increased the pressure by stages. At some point, the Colonel's movements became touch-signals that Carson put into firm and forceful action. Under their joint efforts the Enola Gay climbed to five thousand feet and leveled off.

"You have done this before, sailor," Colonel Paul Tibbets observed. "More than once."

"Yes sir," Carson Braddock replied. "This is how my pilot taught me to fly back when we had a joy-stick and rudder bars in the rear cockpit of the old Douglas Dauntless."

Haggard and worn, the thirty-two year old Colonel let the frown and the strain of intense concentration fade from his blood starved face. The flesh on his cheeks sagged and the wrinkles deepened into slack folds as he sank down into his seat. Slowly, the tension driving his body melted into flesh-searing fatigue and he aged visibly.

"He did a damned fine job, son," the colonel declared. "I know a lot of seasoned pilots who would sooner bail out than try to fly a crippled B-29 on two engines."

"Thank you, sir," Carson returned. "But you're the one who is flying her. I just supply the muscle."

"Relax and save your strength, Skipper," Max advised. "We will need you in good shape when it comes time to land this derelict."

Exhaustion forced the colonel to do as he was told. From wheel to rudder control and then on to throttle and altimeter checks, he gradually turned most of the level flying over to his new found co-pilot. All around him, the shattered instruments, the shredded cockpit, the smashed plexiglass, and the devastated bombardier's compartment came into focus. Aghast, he stared at each of the dead and the wounded and saw them for the first time.

"Oh my God," Colonel Tibbets moaned. "This isn't the Enola Gay. It's a flying hearse."

Energized by shock and grief, the colonel took over the controls and flew the B-29 with demonic strength that took minutes to fade. Slowly, he forced himself to relax until he barely hinted at the movements with a delicate touch. For a while the team of comatose pilot and robotic co-pilot flew the plane with the awkwardness of a poorly matched pair in a sack race. Then suddenly, their companion's loud announcement of a potential crisis put both pilots at odds and sent the plane skidding across the sky.

"Holy Christ!" Max Bryson exploded. "Where's the fucking camera?"

Max's hasty search through the debris littering the bombardier's compartment turned up the sturdy aerial camera. It was battered but intact alongside the wreckage of the Norden bombsight.

"One more fright like that," the Skipper declared, "and we're all fish bait."

Relieved, Colonel Tibbets and Carson Braddock settled down to regaining better control over the wallowing bomber. In time, the pilot found that he could initiate a throttle movement and Carson would carry it out. A nod or a gesture was all it took to change fuel tanks or set the flaps. Despite their well refined teamwork, however, the thick column of air pouring in through the shattered nose canopy made it harder and harder for them to look out through the cracked Plexiglas as the hours passed. Eventually, the jagged edges and the shattered panes crumpled the meeting of the sky and the sea into a ragged and twisted horizon that promised to make their landing a difficult maneuver.

"It might be easier to bring her in on instruments," Carson observed. "If we still had some instruments."

The frail display of wit helped soften the cries and the heavy breathing of the wounded. Their needs kept Max on a continuous round of bandage checks and warm chats. Those still conscious studied the bent girders and the large holes that encircled their stations and wondered how the Enola Gay continued to hold together. Feeling much like a steward on a flight into the after-life, Max made his way back to the cockpit just to check up on their chances of making it down in one piece.

"Anything you want, Skipper?" Max Bryson inquired. "Water? More coffee? A shot of medicinal alcohol? Rita Hayworth's phone number?"

His gentle touch of mirth brought a weak smile that lightened the load for a moment. Drained, numb, and fighting off blurred vision, the colonel gave in to the agony that tortured his brain.

"What I want," Colonel Paul W. Tibbets replied, "is a plausible account of why that atom bomb failed to explode. Without it, the top brass will have my ass for lunch. I shit you not."

Battered, scorched, and broken beyond repair, the Enola Gay crabbed across the tightly rippled sea toward Iwo Jima. The gutted B-29 fluttered its damaged rudder and elevator surfaces like worn out signal flags as it carried the dead and the wounded toward that tiny island in the Pacific Ocean.

Checking their descent against the shadow that the sun laid down on the smooth surface of the sea both pilots watched the dark silhouette skim in over lime green shallows. With the landing gear retracted the plane's flight path evened out enough to give them a semi-controlled approach. The sudden rush of yellow water and the sight of waves breaking over the outer reef told Carson it was time to stiffen his grip on the yoke and the throttle. At two hundred miles an hour the Enola Gay crabbed in low over the gentle surf that broke on the coral strewn beach and skimmed toward Iwo-Jima's North-South runway.

"Crank her back gently," Colonel Paul Tibbets ordered. "Ease off on the throttles."

Coming in at high speed, the battered tail fin, the loose rudder, and the shorn elevator flapped like battle pennants. The blast of hot air rushing in through the smoke scorched bomb bay, the torn up fuselage, and the shattered nose made their swift passage over the beach an agony of endurance. Shedding loose parts, she streaked in just above the cement runway at the front end of a thick cable of black smoke.

"Pull the control column back hard," Colonel Tibbets advised. "And chop the power."

"Roger, Skipper," Carson confirmed. "If she flares out any flatter we'll skip right across the whole fucking island."

"HOLD THAT STICK TIGHT, SAILOR," Paul Tibbets shouted. "An extra second of control when we hit can make all the difference."

The slight curve just aft of the bomb bay touched down first and the jolt slammed the fuselage forward into the cement with a harsh screech. The engine nacelles of the dead inboard motors and the propeller-tips of the outer engines touched down together. The scrape and grind kicked up a rooster tail of sparks as high as the Superfort's gigantic tail fin.

In the cockpit the sudden drag threw both pilots forward against their shoulder straps and seat belts. Using all his strength, Carson struggled to hold on to the yoke as it jerked forward and slammed back against his chest with the force of a well swung baseball bat.

"If we make it," Carson grunted, "I want you to give—that Nip we shot down——to the tail gunner."

"Bob... Bob... Bob would like that," Paul stammered. "He will go into the book as an ace."

"He more than earned it," Max confirmed. "The hard way."

Strapped in, muscles tense as twisted hemp, and watching the ground speed-by at almost one-hundred-forty miles an hour, the three cockpit companions braced hard as the ruined airframe sagged onto the runway. The crumble and crunching growl of thick metal rasping across concrete was accompanied by a white cloud of friction smoke that spread out from the crushed bomb bay. With no wheels to reduce the friction the wings surrendered their load quickly. Propellers, nacelles, engines, flaps, and outer wing panels all gave way until the entire airframe sagged to the ground as limp as the body parts of a dead heron. Even then, however, the loosely tied together wreckage of the Superfortress careened along the cement like a runaway tank car on ice. The swerves and twists of the Enola Gay threw loose Plexiglas, crumpled fuselage panels, and the plane's large rudder off as it slid to a halt. Wrapped in black smoke, pungent fumes, and cockpit debris, the fliers fumbled with their snarled safety straps as they fought to regain their scrambled vision.

"Nice landing, sir," Carson Braddock offered. "I never thought we would get down in even a half dozen pieces."

"Flying in four engine bombers isn't as dull as I thought," Max Bryson declared. "But I'll still be glad to get back to the safety of a simple dive bomber."

"Don't hold your breath, mate," Colonel Paul W. Tibbets advised. "Since you two are the only survivors fit to travel, my guess is that papers will be cut within the hour to fly you lads and the photographs straight to Headquarters at Pearl."

For a while, all three men sat in silence as they wound down from battle time. The lingering throb of the stilled engines, the leftover clamor of aerial combat, and the din of the crash landing hung in their heads as a deafening numbness that made them feel as if they were still in motion. Eventually, the blare of the emergency rescue vehicles racing down the Enola Gay's mile-long skid mark penetrated their stupor. In their semi-deaf ears, the distant sirens of the fire trucks and the ambulances rose to a high pitch and then faded away. Over and over again the screeches reappeared, as soft as the chirps of barn swallows after a thunderstorm.

CHAPTER SIX

Most of history is fiction
Since so little of experience
Is ever recorded.

Oahu was the only industrialized island in the Hawaiian chain and Honolulu was a city glutted with war work as well as servicemen in transit. The factory smoke mixed with the late summer heat to lay down a coat of grime that soiled a white shirt in an hour. The tattoo shops that had girlie shows or better, in back, sported a pink and purple neon parrot in the window. And any girl over twelve who walked more than a block acquired a noisy escort of men in uniform. Just crossing the street involved staring down an angry driver and squirming through a line of honking cars jammed bumper to bumper. The heat, the noise, the crowds, and the traffic drove Combat Aircrewmen Carson Braddock and Max Bryson into the back alleys. All along the crooked roadside clumps of red hibiscus and purple Bougainvillea added the soft and heavy scent of hothouse blossoms to the warm afternoon sea air. Gritty but spotless in their tailor-made whites, the two beribboned aircrewmen admired the shoreline view as they entered the Canoe and Racquet Club.

"Notice how the shallows harbor orange and purple starfish nestled in the pink and yellow coral," Carson directed. "The ocean looks like a shifting carpet of bright tropical flowers."

"It's easy to see why the brass set up shop here," Max observed. "The war seems a million miles away."

The steady late summer sun reflecting off Diamond Head had a touch of afternoon orange that covered the cliff with its earliest hint of bronze. The bold rays slanting into the sea spread great swaths of daffodil yellow across the gathering surf just before it broke. The raw beauty held their eye until they were confronted by the two highly decorated U.S. Marines in parade dress uniform guarding the study. The tight collar on the dark blue blouse and the bright red stripe down the powder blue pants called attention to the rigid stance the men maintained as they blocked the thick mahogany door. The corporal checked the sailors' names against the list and the times he had on his clipboard. The gunnery sergeant took in the cut and the quality of the China-white bell bottom trousers and the zippered blouses the sailors wore.

"Those are tailor-made outfits," Gunnery Sergeant Martin Mann declared. "You men are out of uniform."

The accusation was fierce, grim, and technically correct even though hardly any sailor ever wore his regulation uniform on liberty. Nevertheless, the grizzled Marine glaring at them through mirrored sunglasses had to be faced. And he had to be dealt with decisively since he drew tremendous pleasure from the discomfort he inflicted.

"So are you, Gunny," Carson Braddock replied. "Unless cordovan Florsheim shoes are now Government Issue."

Gunnery Sergeant Martin Mann smiled and acknowledged the counter-thrust with a nod. Corporal Tony Regni took a step closer and checked the blue petty officer stripes, the aerial gunner's badges, and the radar operator's emblems the navy aviators wore on their sleeves. He completed his inspection with a look at the wings above their combat ribbons. Throughout he maintained the scowl and glower of a suspicious detective.

"Are you the two Airedales that attacked Hiroshima against orders?" Corporal Regni demanded. "And then fucked up the A-bomb?"

"That's right," Max replied. "With so many of you sea-going bell-hops getting knocked off on the island invasions it seemed a good idea to keep the war going a little longer."

The words tumbled out without thought or rancor. Bad mouthing Marines was a Navy reflex that bordered on instinct. And all Marines shared the same impulse.

"That's quite a mouth you've got, sailor," Gunny Mann observed.

"Do you know who's in there waiting for you?"

"Of course," Carson lied out of habit. "Doesn't everybody?"

The sailors uncovered and the Marines opened the doors to the richly furnished study. ARM2/C Carson Braddock and ARM2/C Max Bryson stepped inside without looking around and came to attention. Erect, charged, and set to defend themselves, they scanned the sumptuous early twenties tropical decor with expectations similar to those of freshly captured prisoners of war. The high ceiling and the rosewood walls of the club's intimate library absorbed the heat and the glare that entered through the picture windows framing the panoramic ocean view. Still, the airmen's eyes adjusted quickly as they picked out an attractive oriental woman seated on the settee near the fireplace getting ready to take notes. Yet before they could focus on the two senior officers and the civilian seated in high-backed leather chairs, a middle-aged chief petty officer blocked their path. He polished up the silver combat aircrewman's wings they wore above their campaign ribbons and picked the tarnish off their battle stars.

"Only speak when you're spoke to, sailors," Chief Gunner's Mate Lawrence Walsh insisted. "Don't argue, swear, use slang, or bad language of any kind. And for Christ's sake don't repeat anything that's said here outside this room. Irregardless."

The two cousins acknowledged the instructions with a nod. The chief's frown suppressed the smile of recognition that rose the moment the cousins identified "Knobby" Walsh as their recruiting officer in Seattle. *This is no place for a reunion*, Carson realized in an instant. *Besides, the old coot wouldn't remember us even if I had shot him in the foot.* The brief reflection sent a slight touch of distance across Carson's face and that was enough for the trim young secretary to single him out as the leader. Her black hair and the dark eyes took on added luster as she adjusted her cushions with barely a stir of the simple orange shift that she wore. Carson winked and Max gave her a broad smile but neither sailor could hide the surprise that flashed across his face. The young secretary's evenly balanced features and the glow of her high cheekbones announced her ethnic origin even before she spoke.

"This meeting is so top-secret," Miss Shirley Hashimoto declared, "it did not occur."

"Then what are you doing here?" Carson demanded. "You're a ...."

The remark was self censored without discomfort or embarrassment. A flier barely two days out of mortal combat had little time for rear echelon niceties.

"I am a translator," Miss Hashimoto declared, "with a major in physics."

The flush that rose through her slightly sunken cheeks emerged as a fire that made her dark eyes glow. Sensitive, volatile, and under tight control, the Japanese twenty year old exuded the special aura that a thin yet well-endowed young woman always provides. Across from her, the three high ranking officials were too deep in their discussion to notice the secretary or the enlisted men. Robust but well advanced in age, the trio sat in a tight circle closed by their indisputable authority. In dress, bearing, seriousness, and intensity it was obvious that they were men entirely accustomed to ignoring the presence of others.

"Formosa must be invaded and subdued before we invade Japan," General Douglas MacArthur insisted. "The Army cannot have such a powerful enemy bastion poised to strike from the rear."

"That will take six months and cost well over thirty thousand lives," Admiral Chester Nimitz said. "Worse yet, it would put the invasion off until next year."

The admiral was a short and stocky man with a wrinkled face crowned by a shock of crew-cut white hair. The thick gold braid, the chest full of ribbons, the gnarled hands, and the weather beaten face all added to the brightness of his starched and pressed white officer's uniform. Yet his authority was concentrated in tight lips that hardly moved when he spoke and piercing blue eyes that probed even as he listened.

"That can't be helped, Chester," General MacArthur asserted. "Formosa isn't some tiny Pacific outpost that can be by-passed and neutralized by a naval blockade."

"Ah, but that's where you're wrong, Doug," Admiral Chester Nimitz snapped. "The Navy is strong enough to seal off Formosa and mount an invasion of the home islands at the same time."

General Douglas MacArthur was just over six feet tall and somewhat thickened with age. The simple army shoes, the lightweight khaki pants, and the almost undecorated military shirt open at the neck gave the small ring of five stars attached to the collar points a magnetic attraction. And for all his years, the unblinking eyes and the firm jaw supported the vitality and the assurance that filled his voice. He spoke with the conviction of a disciplined leader.

"If you are wrong, admiral," General MacArthur proposed, "it will be the Army that pays."

"Right or wrong, the fighting men always pay," Admiral Nimitz countered. "But the cost is substantially higher when we operate under the curse of a divided command."

"Gentlemen. Gentlemen," President Harry Truman interposed. "You are jumping the gun. The atom bomb is at the heart of this dilemma and the Navy has arrived to help us resolve it."

The President of the United States of America wore a cream colored Panama suit and a pale green necktie that brought out the texture of his light-gray shirt and the darker streaks in his remaining hair. President Harry Truman was uncomfortable sitting down. He crossed and re-crossed his legs so often his beige pants were wrinkled above the knees. The wire-rimmed glasses and the yellowed teeth gave his round face a studious look that melted away when he flashed a smile. But the speed with which he changed from one thing to another marked him as a politician.

Quick to respond, the admiral looked at the sailors with seasoned eyes that carried out a lightning inspection. Even as he nodded his approval his squint warned of growing impatience. Since the radio-gunners' youth made their gold battle stars all the more impressive he softened his voice out of respect.

"At ease, men," the admiral ordered. "This won't take long."

Automatically, the two Canadians planted their feet eighteen inches apart. Swiftly, they folded their white caps and tucked them beneath the collars behind their necks. Then they thrust their hands behind their backs, and locked one hand around the other wrist.

Even "at ease", however, Carson Braddock and Max Bryson were rigid with the shock of recognition. The absence of any introduction and the speed with which they were shuffled about added to their insecurity. With all eyes on them they could only stare straight ahead and listen for clues from whoever spoke.

"Ready when you are, Chief," General MacArthur declared. "They are all yours."

Chief Petty Officer Lawrence Walsh paced back and forth in front of the two sailors until he felt their gaze shift from the book shelves that lined the far wall to himself. The brawny, bushy-browed chief gunner's mate was a veteran of naval aviation ordinance. His decorations included five campaign ribbons with bronze battle stars and the Navy Cross. Despite the summer heat, he wore the blue winter uniform that had all his rating stripes and service hash-marks in good conduct gold. Thick jowled, bare headed, and uncomfortable in snap-on cuffs, tight collar, and black tie, he checked the two men before him to see which one might be the easier mark. Finding no obvious weakness, he looked from one to the other as he spoke.

"We all know that radio gunners ain't taught nothin' about fuses and detonators," Chief Walsh declared. "So just tell me what happened in your own words."

Carson and Max ran through the trouble that Captain Pastor had wiring the bomb. The almost neckless chief listened so attentively that the sweat that his winter uniform generated in the tropic heat ran down his face in uninterrupted streams. His gray hair and slight paunch invited disclosure even though the strength in his hands as they grappled with each other warned against evasion. Whenever the sailors faltered, Chief Walsh took them through the next step with the patience of a crusty uncle. In a few minutes they reached the critical stage.

"I attached the blue and yellow wires to the left and right forward terminal, respectively," Carson explained. "And checked with Captain Pastor to make sure he meant my left and my right as well."

"Then we put the red plugs in place of the green," Max added. "And the job was done."

Chief Gunner's Mate Larry Walsh digested the testimony with

his entire body. He paced, shrugged, wrung his hands, and mopped his face with a fresh white handkerchief before all the bits fell into place.

"When ya connected them wires to the forward end of the detonator," Chief Walsh inquired, "is that exactly what the captain had told ya to do?"

"Absolutely," Max blurted. "I listened very carefully. Those were his instructions. No more. No less."

The disclosure was entirely truthful. Still, one word stood out like a stranger at a family reunion. Foolish though it seemed, Carson felt compelled to set the account straight right down to the last detail.

"Well, not exactly," Carson Braddock hedged. "He actually told me to connect the wires to the bottom terminals."

"Bottom. Forward. What's the difference?" Max demanded. "It's the same thing."

The forceful affirmation made the chief petty officer blink as if he had swallowed an olive whole. Unwilling to slow the pace of the proceedings, however, he set his reservations aside and plunged ahead.

"When you was finished," the chief pressed, "did Captain Pastor check it out hisself?"

"How could he?" Max demanded. "He was practically blind without his glasses."

"Did he feel the connections at all?" Chief Walsh asked. "Follow the wires down with his fingers and touch the terminals."

Each question cut off a fresh slice of turf like a penknife used to play mumbli-peg. Fascinated, the spectators watched in awe. The ground the sailors had to stand upon vanished before their eyes.

"No, he couldn't," Carson stated. "After an hour in that cold air without any gloves his fingers were useless."

"I felt each one for him," Max explained. "I took off my gloves and fingered the terminals. They were good, tight connections."

Finally, all the facts were in place and arranged in the right order. Confident, calm, and judicious, the Navy's top enlisted ordinance expert presented his verdict.

"I am sure they were," Chief Gunner's Mate Larry Walsh

concluded. "But they was in the wrong place."

The disclosure swept through the select audience like an Arctic breeze. The sailors braced themselves. The secretary wilted, slightly. The admiral ground his teeth. And the general looked away. Only the Chief Petty Officer stood firm as the President's intense gaze settled on him.

"How could that be?" President Harry Truman demanded. "The boys did exactly as they were told."

"Not quite, Mister President," Larry Walsh stated. "In the First War, when bombs were small, we stood the missiles on their tail-fins and screwed the fuse into the nose-cone where it served as an impact detonator. In that position, the bottom of the fuse was towards the tail. Most of the old timers still think of it that way. Irregardless."

"Do you mean that Captain Pastor wanted the connections made to the rear pair of terminals when he specified the bottom ones?" President Harry Truman asked. "Not to the forward pair!"

"Precisely, Mister President," Chief Walsh confirmed. "The forward or 'top' pair of terminals was dead posts."

Its simplicity drove the disclosure home with stunning force. But no one in high office wanted to believe it.

"Knobby," Admiral Chester Nimitz blurted. "That is such an elementary error only an ordinance striker would make it. Captain Pastor was one of our best men. I chose him for that assignment myself."

The admiral's use of the chief petty officer's nickname surprised everyone in the room except the gunner's mate, himself. As the admiral's former shipmate in the dirigible Navy, he took pride in being likened to the cagey bald-headed manager of the comic strip boxer, Joe Palooka. That pleasure showed as a rueful smile he could not suppress.

"The very best, admiral, I assure you," Chief Gunner's Mate Larry K. Walsh insisted. "If he had completed the assembly hisself the bomb would have exploded. Deke Pastor was much too good a man to make a technical error."

The implications took a while to settle in and register. The admiral was the first to move but he rose to his feet slowly. The general stood up quickly and walked to the fireplace. But it was the President who captured everyone's attention with swift and bouncy movements that made him look like a bantamweight boxer gearing up for a fight as he spoke to the chief petty officer.

"You're a Japanese ordinance expert, chief," President Harry Truman insisted. "You have never seen anything like it or even heard about it. Can you figure out why our atom bomb did not explode?"

The question was too simple to require any serious thought. Yet, out of respect for his Commander-in-Chief, the career petty officer pondered the matter for a long moment before delivering his reply.

"In about ten minutes, Mister President," Chief Larry Walsh declared. "Less, if I'm one of their best."

The verdict settled on the country's top decision-makers with the gravity of a death sentence. Accustomed to having the final word in his jurisdiction each one held his own council. The care they took to keep from looking one another in the face turned their silence into an exercise in preserving personal autonomy. Finally, the general, sometimes known as Old Acid Tongue, broke the impasse.

"Then it looks like the Air Force has delivered a perfectly usable atomic bomb into enemy hands," General Douglas MacArthur concluded, "with no little help from the Navy."

Everyone went rigid and swallowed the reprimand with shallow breaths. The general sucked on the stem of his pipe and sent moist gurgles around the room. Admiral Nimitz rubbed his brow and studied the distant waves breaking over the outer reef. The President interlocked the fingers of both hands and bent them back swiftly until the knuckles cracked. Head bowed and hands behind his back so that the sweat from his face did not fall on his uniform, the Chief Gunner's Mate intruded with a touch of hope.

"Unless the four-hundred plane back-up raid from Saipan destroyed it, general," Chief Walsh ventured. "We hit Hiroshima pretty hard. Between the five hundred pound high explosive bombs and the four pound incendiaries they lost most of the industrial core and some eighty thousand dead, overall."

"Did that raid produce a fire-storm, Chester?" President Harry Truman inquired. "Like the ones in Dresden, Hamburg, Cologne, and Tokyo?"

"No, Mister President," Admiral Nimitz replied. "There was only the normal blast and a horrid conventional burn."

The grave tone and the soft delivery was in respect for the thousands of lives so cruelly destroyed. Yet no one there had any qualms about the bombing itself.

"That's about forty percent of the city center destroyed," Larry Walsh explained, "and two thirds of the homes burned to ashes with their occupants inside."

It took a long and silent moment for the horror embedded in the facts to melt away. The terrible destruction and the tremendous loss of life loomed as a specter that gave the threat of a serviceable atom bomb in Japanese hands a ghastly presence. Everyone had to reflect on what it meant and somehow the formalities of rank and office vanished. The President and the flag officers showed their solemn concern in the way they stood. But the two sailors were too young and disturbed to recall the warning they had been given or to worry about their dignity. Charged up and burning with indignation, they simply blundered in with no thought to propriety at all.

"Why the Hell didn't you use the other atom bomb?" Aviation Radioman Second Class Carson Braddock demanded. "The one they call 'Fat Man.'"

"That son-of-a-bitch would have melted 'Little Boy' down," Aviation Radioman Max Bryson observed, "like butter in a furnace."

The profanity gave a hard edge to the raw common sense displayed. Annoyed, offended, and unaccustomed to such directness, the senior soldier was quick to probe the weak point in the sailors' argument.

"Unless it failed to explode, as well," General Douglas MacArthur growled. "And doubled the enemy's nuclear arsenal then and there."

"It hardly matters," President Harry Truman insisted. "They don't have any bombers big enough to lift it."

Suddenly, the President was out beyond his depth. When it came to the capabilities of enemy aircraft the combat seasoned Canadians were the experts.

"Don't under estimate them, sir," Carson Braddock cautioned. "They could stow it aboard one of their long range flying boats and make a kamikaze dive on Honolulu."

"IMPOSSIBLE!" Admiral Chester Nimitz declared. "It would be blasted out of the air before it flew five hundred miles."

"Hold it right there, Chester," General Douglas MacArthur scoffed. "Pearl Harbor was supposed to be impossible too. Or have you forgotten?"

Since the Navy had used just that possibility in war games the dig was doubly cruel. Anger made Admiral Nimitz's face flush. It took a moment for him to suppress an equally unkind retort about the general's failure to stay with his troops at Corregidore. The brittle silence created an opening that the female translator could not ignore.

"Ugh-humm," the handsome young woman mouthed. "Excuse me?"

Distressed by the discord, yet unable to contain herself, the fine boned Japanese-American girl was too shy and too polite to speak out uninvited. The long sigh that rose from Miss Shirley Hashimoto's throat settled on the heated discussion like a light but chilling spray. Nothing happened for a moment and then the color in her cheeks darkened to a salmon glow as each of the men looked at her in turn.

"Yes, Miss Hashimoto?" President Harry Truman inquired. "Do you have something for us?"

"If you will pardon the suggestion, gentlemen," a breathless Shirley Hashimoto pleaded, "you are not thinking like the—ahh—enemy."

"What are we overlooking, Shirley?" Admiral Nimitz asked. "Where would the Japanese focus their attention?"

Stepping forward and smoothing her tight fitting dress across the stomach and down the hips, she had the ravishing look of a shy temptress. Flushed, excited, and decidedly nervous, her bronze cheeks and slightly inflamed lips seemed to pulse beneath their glow.

"Before your backup raid arrived," Shirley explained, "the bomb was probably hauled out of the city. Even now, their experts are figuring out precisely how it works. Soon they will set up machine shops and start making parts for fifty or a hundred of them exactly like it."

The suggestion took everyone else by surprise. Disturbed, the senior members of the tiny group probed each other's faces and found an uncertain consensus. A curt nod from the president gave the admiral the floor.

"It can't be done that way," Admiral Nimitz explained. "Even in good times, it would take them months, maybe years, simply to refine that much uranium. As it is, our submarines are sinking just about every ore carrier that enters Japanese waters or tries to leave an Asian port."

The frank disclosures took some of the punch out of the young physics major's argument. Seeing her wilt before her boss's penetrating gaze, the President provided her with a bit of support.

"Intelligence is certain that the Japanese have an A-bomb project of their own," President Truman disclosed. "So they are bound to have a stockpile of the raw material on hand."

"And it is no small amount," Shirley Hashimoto assured them. "The radio intercepts I translate for Naval Intelligence are full of references to pitchblende, coffinite, bannerite, and other minerals with a high uranium content."

"The way our B-29s are bombing their industrial centers," General Douglas MacArthur observed, "it is hard to imagine where they would find the factory space to build such a war chest."

"Think a minute, general," Shirley pleaded. "You know the oriental mind."

The compliment drew a smile from the pencil browed general. But before he could step in with a rejoinder the sailors spoke up.

"She is right," Carson Braddock declared. "They will abandon the cities and build them in barns and underground work shops all over the countryside."

"This is what they have been waiting for," Max argued. "A super weapon powerful enough to turn the tide of the war in their favor at the very last hour. What could offer greater hope?"

"They will see it as the modern version of the Divine Wind that has saved the home islands from invasion over the centuries," Shirley Hashimoto announced. "It is the prophetic dream of national salvation fulfilled."

"If they've got the refined uranium," Carson speculated, "it will take them no more than a few months to make enough atomic weapons to annihilate any force that threatens their shores."

The urgency in the young aviator's voice and the power of the ancient myth took hold of the general like the bark of a menacing dog. Invigorated, focused, and inflamed he delivered his verdict in a voice that rumbled with conviction.

"Then they will not have that time," General Douglas MacArthur insisted. "We must by-pass Formosa and invade Japan as soon a possible."

President Harry Truman stopped his pacing and looked at his senior commanders over the top of his round steel-rimmed glasses. The admiral was a short but energetic man in a superbly turned out uniform. When the senior naval officer spoke, his words burst from his mouth like water from a fire hose.

"Now you're making sense, General," Admiral Chester Nimitz ventured. "That's what I have been pushing for all along."

"Good," the general replied. "Then you won't mind moving Operation Coronet up a bit. What do you say about invading Japan two weeks from now?"

The suggestion struck the admiral like a blow from a cop's Billy club. His body stiffened and his jaw locked shut and fixed his face almost as rigid as sculpture. With lips that hardly moved he delivered his rebuttal.

"An assault on the south island is at least as big an operation as the D-Day invasion of France," the admiral insisted. "It takes time to deploy the necessary air power, bring a twenty-carrier fleet into enemy waters, assemble thousands of landing craft, draw together an army of battle seasoned troops from all over the Pacific, soften the beaches, and bring on the eight hundred freighters needed to supply an extended campaign. The invasion of Kyushu can not possibly take place before early December."

The general was a tall and angular man with a theatrical bearing and a deeply lined face that did not smile quickly or often. Yet it was an effective mask that projected just the balanced mixture of confidence and authority needed to make a point without turning it into an order.

"That was before the Japs had the bomb, Chester," General Douglas MacArthur observed. "Now we must invade before they have a chance to bring their most battle hardened troops home from the Asian mainland."

"Even as we speak," Admiral Chester Nimitz declared, "we are mustering a naval task force capable of defending itself in the East China Sea. The goal is to straddle the Korea Strait with enough firepower to sink anything trying to cross from Pusan, Korea, to the home Islands of Japan."

The mental tug-of-war between the two senior officers had Harry Truman enthralled. The glint in the President's eyes and the taut muscles that stiffened his back like a bent leaf-spring told the senior Army officer to soften his stand.

"That's the spirit," General MacArthur insisted. "It is your brilliant advanced planning that gives me every confidence that the Navy can put us safely ashore on Kyushu before September. As to the exact date, I leave that to you and the tide-tables."

Since the general never flattered and seldom gave praise, his remarks carried extra weight. Clearly, the President liked the sailor and disliked the soldier for more reasons than he could name. Shifting his glance from one to the other, President Harry Truman looked like a well-turned-out handicapper sizing up two champion racehorses. Suddenly, his face brightened and he was ready to place his bet.

"With that decision, General," President Harry Truman announced, "you have become The Supreme Commander of the Allied Forces in the Pacific."

The strain that folded several dark lines down the President's cheeks prompted Admiral Nimitz to muster a wan smile and nod his acceptance of the decision. Relieved, President Harry Truman flashed a broad grin and stepped toward the general. General MacArthur's reticent bearing and serious frown left the President's outstretched hand with nothing to grasp.

"I do not wish to appear ungrateful, Mister President," General Douglas A. MacArthur stated, "but I think you mean Overall Supreme Commander."

The swift act of blatant self-promotion stunned the others. Nevertheless, their chorus of sudden gasps had hardly settled before the admiral spoke out.

"Of course," Admiral of the Fleet Chester W. Nimitz allowed. "After all, Doug will be moving much of Eisenhower's European troop strength out here for backup."

The consolidation of his two chief military antagonists caught the President by surprise. For years he had studied how President Roosevelt played one against the other in order to get his own way. Yet, with a street scrapper's instinct, he put all of that behind him and dealt with the fresh alliance that confronted him.

"You are right," the President agreed. "Congratulations, General. As of this moment you are in command of all the Allied Forces anywhere in the world."

The general took the President's handshake with a firm grip and a solemn nod. He cupped the admiral's outstretched hand in both of his own and thanked him with his eyes. Then he turned away from the group and stared out the window at the magnificent ocean view. Stretching away to a curved horizon, the sea caught just a hint of rolled gold from the late afternoon sky. Slowly, a broad and heartfelt smile of satisfaction invaded the general's craggy features as the silence deepened. No one spoke until a gentle cough broke the mood. As the senior enlisted man present the chief petty officer had certain mundane matters to settle.

"Aaah. Gentlemen," Chief Gunner's Mate Lawrence K. Walsh ventured, "I propose that all charges against these two enlisted men be dropped."

"Agreed," General Douglas MacArthur allowed. "Anything else?"

The invitation was addressed directly at Admiral Nimitz. The soft tone, the gentle nod, and the readiness to grant any reasonable request were all meant to put the Navy at ease. But it was too good an opening for the cousins to pass up.

"Against our pilots, too," Carson Braddock insisted. "It's only fair."

"After all," Max Bryson added, "they were in hot pursuit of a deadly enemy when we penetrated reserved air space."

The bold initiative on the part of the two enlisted men found the general in a rare mellow mood. Content, relaxed, and bent on lighting his pipe, he passed the decision on to his senior subordinate with a wry comment.

"It looks like the Navy could give lessons in pressing an advantage," General MacArthur observed. "What is your pleasure, Chet?"

Admiral Chester Nimitz looked away from the general and took in the anxious cousins with a mixture of compassion and pride. They had stood their ground and spoken their minds in a room dominated by the highest brass in the land. As he addressed them, the tang and thistle-like sting of cheap metal spread across his tongue. He did not know many senior officers who would have been so outspoken.

"Consider it done, sailors. I will have them re-assigned," Admiral Nimitz declared. "Maybe flying fighter planes will keep them out of trouble. Now get the Hell out of here."

Carson Braddock and Max Bryson fetched their caps from behind their necks. Swiftly, they unfolded them, squared them across their foreheads, saluted in unison, and left the darkening study. A quick escape was the only way to get out while they were still ahead. Suddenly the war was disturbingly close.

CHAPTER SEVEN

The liberal's dilemma
Is how to live better than the masses
And not be caught
Defending privilege.

Downtown Honolulu had a busy inner city that turned from a sober industrial center to a raucous entertainment capital soon after sunset. Not even the rumor that a Japanese submarine had sunk the cruiser, U.S.S. Indianapolis, with the loss of eight-hundred-eighty-three hands, could dampen the festivities. The fact that the cruiser had been carrying the only spare atom bomb back to Pearl Harbor for a thorough refit was not widely known.

In Chinatown, where the Nuuanu Stream emptied sewage into the inner harbor, the factory workers from the Dole cannery plant next door carried out a dramatic transformation every evening. The rickety wooden building with a high tin roof that was a noodle factory all day took on the color of hundreds of festive lanterns strung from the heavy timbers that framed the loft. Each of the ground level mixing vats was scrubbed and cleaned. Triple filtered water turned each one into a circular pond full of large black and gold carp. Early arrivals could fish for their dinner with dough balls on the end of barbless hooks.

By the time Combat Aircrewmen Carson Braddock and Max Bryson arrived at The Purple Parrot, however, the cooking fumes and tobacco smoke had all the lanterns wreathed in blue halos. The fish were gasping in the mixture of whiskey and beer-slop that turned their water brown. On the elevated dance floor made of packing crates, couples struggled to catch the beat of the eight-piece band pounding out an island version of a hillbilly classic.

Their athletic gyrations stirred up so much cigarette and cigar smoke that the slogan of the evening scrawled across the mirror behind the bar was hard to read:

A bordello is called a cat house
Because of the clitty-litter.

Dressed in freshly laundered tailor-made whites, the two aviation radiomen picked their way through the crowd of sodden revelers like fastidious preachers at a summer barbecue. Despite their care, however, the spillage from jostled drinks and the ashes brushed off cheap cigars gave their blouses a slept-in look before they reached their table on the edge of the dance floor.

"What is that song they're playing?" Carson Braddock demanded. "The combination of guitar, bongo-drums, and that whining mouth instrument makes it sound like Tarzan with his nuts caught in a vice."

"Hell, that's The Wabash Cannonball, Hawaiian style," Max Bryson revealed, "played on an electrically amplified Jew's harp."

The oriental twang in the music combined with the general clamor and din of rapping fists and stamping feet to drown out conversation behind a wall of almost impenetrable noise. Nevertheless, just about everyone was trying to talk at once. Indeed, the place was so crowded and the dancing was so vigorous that even the huge quantity of empty beer bottles on the rickety tables set up their own shrill timpani. Over it all, however, the new arrivals managed to express their disappointment.

"May the saints be praised," Carson groaned. "So much for the best night club in the Pacific east of Shanghai."

"I always suspected that those old China hands were Asiatic," Max observed. "But what they see in this place I will never know."

The serious drinkers were packed in so tight that the chairs to adjoining tables overlapped. A nearby neighbor had to shout to inject words directly into an ear that was only inches away.

"It will cost you a buck, sailor," the gruff voice trumpeted. "That is, if you really want to find out what made this joint so hot between the wars."

Max and Carson turned to see the older Marine from The Canoe and Racquet Club grinning at them. Casual, in his suntans,

Gunnery Sergeant Martin Henry Mann looked a lot older than a man just past his mid-twenties. The smile that cracked his face was lewd as he gave Max a silver dollar in exchange for his paper bill. The stack of round dollars on his table stood almost as high as the protective wall of empty beer bottles that surrounded it.

"Just hold the coin upright between your fingers," Gunny Mann directed. "Then stick your hand out with the palm up."

Within moments a young Chinese waitress carrying a tray of drinks eased her lithe torso through the crowd of seated patrons and set a chilled bottle of beer on the table. The daringly cut purple sarong hugged her hips and gave her unsupported breasts ample room to breathe. She worked the slit on the side of the sarong around to the front and gave the customers a close-up view of her neatly shaved Venus patch. Delicately, she eased her hips forward and enfolded the coin in its tender lips. She lingered just a moment to give the fingers that fed her vaginal-purse a chance to stroke the flesh and then she turned away.

"I'll be God damned," Max extolled. "Smoother than silk."

Quickly, Carson produced a five-dollar bill and obtained as many silver coins from the Marine gunnery sergeant. He bought himself and Gunny Mann two drinks, each from a different girl, and found himself stroking the original waitress as he purchased Max another round. Instinctively, the sailors and the Marine rubbed the ends of their fingers with their thumbs as a reminder of the satin soft and smooth pubic skin.

"What do you know," Carson said. "The ultimate slot machine."

Even though he was a Marine, the sailors' swift reappraisal of him enabled them to fall into easy conversation. After skirting the issue of the fliers' meeting with the top brass several times, Gunny Mann could not hold his tongue any longer.

"Well," the beribboned Marine inquired, "what did you think of the President?"

"All politicians put me on edge," Carson Braddock confessed. "I am always uncomfortable in the company of someone who lies better than I do."

The joke caught the Marine with a mouth full of beer that he sprayed all over the dance floor in a fit of uncontrolled mirth. The eruption, their chuckles, and the Marine's short coughing spell drew the attention of others around them. But any thought of broadening their circle of acquaintances was cut short by the high pitched yelp of pain that burst from the throat of a waitress some fifty feet away. Her distress raised a gale of laughter from a crowd of soldiers seated near her across the polished floor.

"Watch yourself," Gunny Martin Mann advised. "And stay out of this one."

The British commandos and the American paratroopers wore shoulder patches from outfits that had been prominent all through the war in Europe. Their mindless merriment was swiftly curtailed, however, by a beer bottle that knocked out their most raucous member with a fiercely delivered blow to the top of the head.

"Will wonders never cease," Carson remarked. "A waitress who takes her virtue seriously."

"Nothing as rare as that," Gunny Mann replied through a smirk. "But there is always some joker who puts his silver dollar on the corner of the table and heats it with a cigarette lighter."

The half-drunk commandos and paratroopers reached out for the retreating waitress and were showered with beer for their troubles. The unconscious Tommy was hustled from the room by a pair of bare-chested native bouncers in loincloths. In an effort to calm down the irate tangle of soldiers and civilians, the manager flicked the house lights on and off. The public address system urged the patrons to pay attention to the gray-haired master of ceremonies on stage. Having been a second-string vaudeville comedian most of his life, the out of shape, overweight, glassy-eyed impresario was accustomed to being ignored. Throughout the racket and the activity that filled the spacious room he waggled the handle of the push broom he used for support. Yet as soon as the noise abated he leaned into the microphone and delivered his lines in the deep and scratchy voice of a well-seasoned alcoholic.

"As a Jew, Sammy Yamamoto had to fight harder than any three swordsmen in ancient Japan just to stay alive," the bald headed announcer insisted. "As a result, the entire warrior class took its name from the cry that went up when a terrible saber slash blinded him on one side: 'SAM! YOUR EYE!'"

The jeers and hoots that drowned out the feeble laughter caught the attention of the servicemen and their dates sitting at the tables along the wall. Even though they had not heard the joke, they stamped on the floor, pounded on the tabletops, and bounced up and down on the planks suspended between the heavy studs supporting the rafters. The noise and the vibrations they sent through the tin roof forced the M.C. to turn up his microphone and direct his next offering at them.

"If Nickie Nacator and his bride had twins," the unshaven, flabby cheeked comic proposed, "what would the family be called?"

"THE FOUR NACATORS," Carson shouted.

A spirited clap and stamp that startled all the pigeons into renewed flight accompanied the howls and groans. Between the birds, the dust, and the feathers that swirled through the smoke filled haze the cavernous room resembled a grotto during an earthquake. Nevertheless, the master interlocutor, Tommy Heath Jr., detected a sense of readiness that had not been there before. As soon as the arm holding the push broom went up over his head he had the whole house in his hands.

"Why does a sailor's tailor-made trousers always remind us of Martin Block's famous Stateside record program?" the disheveled host inquired. "Why? Huh? Why?"

Suddenly, there was a hush throughout the vast barn-like structure. Only the pigeons flying around in the loft made any noise as the entire crowd of regulars drew in a deep breath and timed itself to reply in unison. The answer came back in a well-practiced chorus that shook the house.

"MAKE BELIEVE BALL ROOM."

The racket and rattle made the tremors pulsing through the ratty curtain that served as a backdrop go almost unnoticed. To call attention to it, the leering announcer ran his free hand from the breasts to the crotch of the girl poorly sheltered behind it.

"All right," the gravel-voiced master of ceremonies declared. "Now that I have everyone's attention I want you to give a Purple Parrot welcome to our new singing sensation: Pearl City's own passion flower—the regal—the radiant—the ravishing Queen of Chinatown—HONEY MOONS."

Shouts and applause rang out across the smoke-filled room as the patrons threw a cascade of silver dollars up against the curtain and cheered as the heavy coins clattered to the stage floor. Delighted, the smiling raconteur swept the loot into the wings with his wide push-broom before he opened the soiled yellow curtain.

There, in the haze softened spotlights stood a slender twenty-year-old woman wearing a deeply slit Chinese gown. The powder blue sheath hugged her narrow waist and gave equal exposure to her chest and her thigh. Her long black hair framed a heart shaped face that was both slender and seductive.

"Thank you, gentlemen," the lovely girl's soft lips mouthed, "from the bottom of my heart."

The audience screamed and howled as she stepped up to the microphone and bent low to allow the light to reach inside her gown and play across the curve and hang of her breasts. The ruddy glow of her smooth skin added warmth to her satin gown from the inside as she invited the band to play. As the musicians opening strains filled the room Carson Braddock took a closer look at Honey Moons.

"Either I've got dung-fever," Carson suggested, "or I have seen that luscious body before."

The opening bars dispensed with the hillbilly-Hawaiian twang and soothed the patrons with the smooth strains of a popular ballad. The soft lilt of the song cut the clamor down to an almost surmountable blare.

"That's Admiral Nimitz's secretary and translator," Max declared. "Shirley Hashimoto from The Canoe and Racquet Club."

"Not so loud," Gunny Mann cautioned. "Do you want to start a riot?"

The soft strains of "Sentimental Journey" quieted the crowd and the singer's voice could be heard searching out the key of E-flat that Doris Day used so effectively. As she worked her way into the song, Shirley Hashimoto waved her hands and her arms in the Hawaiian style. The weave and the hip-shrugs brought her lovely body forward in an unspoken appeal that emphasized the longing and the loneliness every serviceman felt. On the closing bridge, her voice opened up and filled the room with a rich and mellow sound that brought all eyes to her soft and beguiling face. Thrilled, she gave clear, sensitive, and careful expression to the slight alteration in the lyrics that tailored the song to her audience.

Who ever thought
Our hearts could feel such yearning
Since no one here would choose to roam,
Let's all take that soul-full voyage,
Sentimental journey home.

Those who listened let the mellow tones of her voice wash over them as they floated off into visions of that deeply treasured trip. The serious drinkers guzzled hard during the lull her song produced. Together, their applause and whistles of approval encouraged Miss Hashimoto and the band to consult on an encore. Before they could begin, however, the commandos and paratroopers who were being ignored by the waitresses took over.

"Tits or no tits," a drunken private shouted, "that broad ain't no Chink."

"From gash to gonads, I know a Nip when I see one," a battle-ribboned paratrooper insisted. "And that bitch is as Japanese as the pilots who bombed Pearl Harbor."

The loud declaration brought everything to a halt. A waitress snatching a coin from a merchant seaman's fingers let her skirt drop. George Brunus, the trombone player behind the singer, stopped blowing the spit from his horn. All eyes turned to study the seductive hang of Shirley Hashimoto's half exposed breasts as she bowed. Even the girl's lovely face lost its glow as the silence focused all ears on the swish and coo of the pigeons in the rafters.

"SHE'S PROBABLY GOT RELATIVES ON THE SUB THAT SANK THE INDIANAPOLIS," a chief petty officer shouted.

"THAT'S EIGHT HUNDRED GOOD MEN GONE TO A WATERY GRAVE, MATE," an Australian soldier declared. "AND YOU CAN BET SHE'S GONNA SING 'I'LL BE HOME FOR CHRISTMAS.'"

Suddenly, the room erupted with the savage fury of a madhouse. The air was filled with shot-glasses, beer bottles, pretzels, ashtrays, cutlery, dinner plates, live fish, and anything else close at hand.

The barrage aimed at the stage drove the girl back against the curtain. Frightened, splattered, and trapped, she stood there dodging like the victim in a knife-throwing act gone wrong.

"Honey Moons, indeed," a Highland Piper scoffed. "She is more like The Moon of the Misbegotten."

"Can't you SMELL the Jap in her?" a British Tommy wearing the Burma patch roared. "She reeks with the stink of rotten fish."

Braving the missile-storm, a young paratrooper and a wiry commando leaped up on stage and grabbed Miss Shirley Hashimoto by the arms. A robust merchant seaman raked the front of her gown with both hands and gaped at the full-blown breasts that shook and wobbled as she struggled to break free. The frenzy and the spectacle of the half-naked girl finally broke through the shock that immobilized those who knew her.

"I told her she couldn't get away with it," Gunny Mann insisted. "But she knew better."

The twisting girl's terror and partial nudity drove the half-drunken crowd wild. Women on the dance floor uprooted potted plants and swung the stalks around their heads before launching them across the room.

"Oh my God," Carson Braddock shouted. "They'll kill her."

All along the aisles, quick hands snatched up black and gold carp out of the deep vats and hurled the squirming fish at Shirley with all their might. The impact of a two-pound carp made her stagger as the sailor in civvies lunged for her with grasping hands and a face disfigured by lust.

"That merchant seaman is gonna rape her," Max Bryson allowed.

Alarmed, the three-man defense team rose to its feet and snaked through the crowd like a short Conga line. The Gunnery Sergeant stripped off his necktie and clamped a roll of dimes in his fist. The sailors slipped their wallets off the top of their pants and stuffed them inside their blouse pockets. Then they pushed their buttonless sleeves back above their elbows. As the merchant seaman took hold of Shirley's breasts the Marine vented his own desire.

"I could use a little of THAT myself," Gunny Mann confessed.

Propelled by loyalty, the three tablemates bounded up on to the stage and confronted Miss Hashimoto's assailants. More than half-drunk and filled with righteous anger, the two soldiers and the merchant seaman exchanged glances that forged a hasty alliance. As they turned to fight, Carson stepped up close to the paratrooper and grabbed the front of his shirt just below the neck.

"What the fuck do you think you're doing, Mac?" Carson demanded. "This China Doll is my comfort for the night."

"You lousy swabbies are all alike," the paratrooper protested, "a bunch of Jap lovers."

The young soldier's wild swing caught Carson Braddock on the shoulder but did not break his grip. Carson delivered a short but straight chop with his left fist that flattened the blond eighteen-year-old paratrooper's nose and bloodied his lip.

Fighting back-to-back, the two cousins made a good team. Max threw several punches at the British soldier struggling to get at the girl before he got his full attention.

"She ain't no Jap," Max Bryson insisted as he thumped the British commando on the chest. "She was born in Korea and THOSE Gooks are our allies."

Undaunted, the young commando brushed Max's hand aside and threw a chop at his neck. Blocking with a forearm that snaked around his unsteady assailant's biceps, the sailor threw him over his hip. A sharp kick to the ribs spun him around just as Gunny Mann backed out of his way. Nimble and alert, the Marine gunnery sergeant felt the heels of his shoes touch the box that half covered the footlights. With nowhere to go, he threw the roll of dimes at the commando's head and stripped for action. Short, light boned, yet thick in the upper body, the Marine gunnery sergeant took off his belt and wrapped it around his fist with the buckle hanging loose. He waved the carefully honed metal clasp in the merchant seaman's face and menaced him with a silent stare before he spoke.

"I would go now, if I was you," Gunny Mann advised. "The shore patrol will be here any minute and they take a dim view of a draft-dodger who has jumped ship."

Enraged, the merchant seaman grabbed for the dangling belt and missed. The reach earned him three swift raps with the razor sharp buckle that left him bleeding from his scalp and both cheeks.

The slightly balding British commando rose up slowly and

braced himself to take Max on from a solid footing. He advanced in a stalking crouch and made the young sailor dodge and parry a series of feints. The blond paratrooper from New Jersey tore free from Carson's grip with a kick and a roar that was immediately followed by a roundhouse right. Seeing it coming, Carson blocked it, countered with a jab to the jaw, then stepped inside as he delivered a hard left to the soldier's stomach. Hurt, yet angered more, the Army private vented his wrath.

"This ain't the Golden-fuckin'-Gloves, sailor," the angry paratrooper announced. "How are you as a street fighter?"

The soldier from Elizabeth-Port, New Jersey, advanced in a crouch with his head bobbing up and down. His powerful arms delivered a series of flailing blows that landed with sledgehammer force. Carson took a left to the cheek that made him dizzy and a right to the ribs that cut his breath short. Shaking his head, he calculated the moves that gave the soldier such power. With each step forward the paratrooper bowed and dipped his whole body in a weave that allowed him to punch from the ground up. Finally, as the soldier drew a deep breath and lifted his left foot, Carson Braddock brought his knee up. The blow caught the soldier under the jaw just as his head neared the bottom of a dip. The impact straightened the paratrooper up and bent him back like a sapling facing a sudden gust of wind. The rapid succession of body blows Carson landed on his stretched stomach and the jabs to the face that followed left the soldier gasping and feeling his puffed up cheeks. Even so, the punishment did not dull his brain or weaken his resolve.

"Here I am trying to keep it a nice, friendly fight," the private complained. "But the Navy's got to go for blood."

"Then let's give it to them," the British lance corporal insisted. "With no quarter."

The commando was a fit and seasoned veteran who waded in with short but rapid jabs that set Max's head bobbing like a woodpecker. The body blows he pumped into the sailor's chest and stomach drove the breath from his lungs in great bursts. The lance corporal was a methodical battler determined to overwhelm his opponent in an avalanche of blows. But Max drew him on by backing away. At the edge of the stage, the sailor bobbed around a succession of straight punches and fought back. Yet his opponent would not budge.

"You're as solid as a brick shit house," Max observed. "And twice as dirty."

A flurry of skillful counter-punches caught the commando off guard. In that moment of hesitation, Max let loose a right cross that carried shoulder, back, hip, and leg power. His strength rose straight up from a foot firmly anchored on the step leading upstairs. The blow to the commando's jaw buckled his knees. A one-two punch made him stagger. Moving forward, Max used his height to drive solid rights down on the Brit's chest and shoulders so that he had to catch his weight on trembling legs. Impressed, the foot soldier backed away until his shoulder brushed up against the merchant seaman.

"Not too shabby," the British lance corporal confessed, "for a deckie."

"Deck-hands or sea-going-bellhops," the burly furnace stoker roared, "they're all the same to me—gobs and slobs."

The heavy-set brawler from the merchant marine charged with the head-on deliberateness of a maddened ox. He lunged and swung at Gunny Mann with a lumbering abandon that earned him cuts, lumps, and welts with each pass. Gunny Mann sidestepped with the grace of a matador and brought his steel clasp down with the precision of butcher's cleaver. The cuts and scrapes on the merchant seaman's back streaked his midnight blue watch sweater in streams of darkened liquid. A vicious chop to the stoker's forehead opened up a gash that clouded his eyesight with blood.

"Gyrines and Gypsies," the wounded stoker complained. "Ain't neither one can stand still and fight like a man."

Well aware that the more a fighter talks the poorer his defense, the Marine came on strong. Suddenly the shrill whistle of the Navy Shore Patrol broke through the din of the riot and put the merchant seaman on the run. Without him, the two soldiers quit the stage and pushed through the crowd toward an exit. Surrounded by protectors, Miss Shirley Hashimoto struggled to cover her bare breasts with strips of the torn satin gown as she sobbed and trembled from shock. The tears, sweat, spilled drinks, and blood stains that soiled her body-hugging blue dress made her look like a refugee from a ruined bordello.

"Let's get you home, Missey," Carson suggested. "One Sentimental Journey is enough for tonight."

"Your song was terrific," Max offered. "You have a real American sound."

Aviation Radioman Second Class Max Bryson removed the black silk neckerchief that was the only regulation part of his tailor made uniform and draped it over Shirley's bosom so it covered her breasts. Combat Aircrewman Carson Braddock put his arm around the trembling girl's bare shoulders and guided her off the stage and down the steps to the dance floor. In the din raised by the struggle with the shore patrol, Shirley's gasps and slight convulsions went unnoticed. With almost each step across the raised dance floor she either dodged or balked to avoid being struck. Their squirms through the crowd milling around the tables were continuously accompanied by a cup, a glass, a shoe, or a purse that came close enough to give her a fright. Suddenly, Carson Braddock staggered, dropped to one knee, and struggled up again. The blow to his head had seemed to turn his brains to soup and left him as weak in the knees as a newborn lamb.

"What the fuck," Carson swore. "Who hit me?"

"It was an unopened beer bottle," Max disclosed. "It came sailing in over the crowd from somewhere behind the bar."

"You can bet it had my name on it," Shirley sniffed. "Are you OK?"

Unsure of his legs, Carson Braddock found a chair and sat down at an empty table. Swiftly, Max Bryson pulled out a clean handkerchief and pressed the folded cloth against the wound. He pressed hard to stem the flow of blood but the facial wound was too long and jagged to be covered all at once.

The gash started at the temple and tore loose the top of his ear. The nasty opening ran down behind the loose flesh to follow his jawbone all the way to his chin. The bruise that the bottle made before it broke, darkened the flesh around his right eye. And sharp slivers of shattered glass lined the deep gash that the broken body of the bottle had carved down his head and face. An inch lower and the broken glass would have sliced the jugular.

Max was quick to press a second clean handkerchief over the severed veins. But the needle sharp jabs of the slivers embedded in his flesh made Carson draw away. Gunny Mann retrieved a dinner napkin and wiped at the fast flowing blood that streaked Carson's neck and blouse. Taking greater care, he tried to brush aside the slivers of shattered glass that showed up like pink ice in the wound. He saw, quickly, that the cut was too deep to clot even under pressure.

The dark seepage that ran down Carson's neck and spilled across his shoulder spread out in a bright red stain that soaked his white jumper. Alarmed, he grabbed Max's handkerchief and clamped it down over the top of the wound with both hands. No matter how much pain Carson swallowed or how hard he pressed, however, the red stain that spread on his sleeves and his blouse continued to grow.

"We have to get you to a doctor," Shirley Hashimoto insisted. "You're gonna pass out from loss of blood."

"NO DOCTORS!" Carson declared. "No matter what."

The protest was so loud and vigorous that the blood starved veins in his pale cheeks stood out as if they were drawn on the skin with blue ink. As he shook his head to clear his eyes and his brain, Max gave the reason for his cousin's concern.

"We fly out in the morning," Max said. "If the croakers get him it means a week in sick-bay, at least."

"I could miss my ship," Carson lamented. "Maybe lose our squadron."

The problem made the table of four a momentary and troubled haven of reflection in a sea of turmoil. All around them, shouting young men and screaming girls jostled and shoved their way past in their rush to get to the unguarded kitchen exit. The shore patrol followed at a discrete distance just to keep the crowd moving at a good pace. A glance assured the SPs that the quiet quartet would not stir up any trouble so they left them alone.

"God damn," Gunny Mann said. "You're road kill at a vulture's picnic."

Concerned for his newfound friend, Gunnery Sergeant Martin Mann climbed up on a chair and searched the room until he spotted a short, sandy-haired Marine wielding a broken whiskey bottle. Deftly, the sergeant scaled a metal ashtray across the room so it caught the young Marine's attention.

"CORPSMAN," Gunny Mann bellowed. "On the double."

The words were lost in the first few feet of travel but the summons was unmistakable. As Gunny Mann stepped down from the chair, the compact medical corpsman went into high gear. He threw his jagged weapon at a menacing bouncer and grabbed an open bottle of vodka from behind the bar. Wherever the going was slow he took a large swig from the bottle and sprayed the whole mouthful into the faces of those who blocked his way. The stream he spit into the eyes of a piano player passing behind the gunnery sergeant was just to keep in practice.

"Casey?" Martin Mann inquired. "Have you got your emergency first-aid kit with you?"

The Marine corpsman glanced at the gunnery sergeant with the hurt look of an offended professional. The slack jaw, the soft lipped scowl, and the baleful expression in his wide eyes all signaled disbelief.

"Aw, come on, Gunny," Corpsman Casey Dworkin protested. "You know I would sooner part with my balls than leave that behind."

"That won't be necessary," the gunnery sergeant concluded. "Just give this sailor a shot of morphine and sew his ear back on as best you can."

The mention of sedation brought the sailor's head around with a belligerent snap. A wheel of blood droplets spewed from his wound like sweat from a whip-lash injury.

"No pain killers," Carson declared. "If I can't walk out of here on my own those shore patrol bastards will haul me away and ask questions later."

The corpsman laid out his field kit and sterilized the stitching needle in a tiny trough that burned pure alcohol. While it flamed and boiled, he found the pressure point that controlled the blood flowing from the gash and had Max press hard to bring it under control. Gunny Mann fished a hand full of ice-cubes from the only upright whiskey glass he could find and used them to counteract the swelling that was raising the bruise around the cut into a thick-lipped bulge. Deftly, the young medical corpsman picked out the glass slivers with a tweezer and wiped the wound clear with cotton swabs. To make sure all the glass was gone he flushed the wound with a steady flow of vodka. Carson jerked his head away as the sharp sting of the whiskey slashed at his brain. Corporal Casey Dworkin grabbed the sailor's jaw in an iron grip and cauterized the exposed veins with a blunt septic pencil as he spoke.

"Now, that is just what you can not do," the corpsman insisted. "Unless you hold your head rigid and eat the pain through all sixteen stitches you're gonna end up looking like the bride of Frankenstein."

The warning made the others gathered around the patient reappraise their roles. Max gave his cousin a comforting pat on the shoulder that delivered some assurance but only the girl offered her services.

"Let me help," Shirley Hashimoto pleaded. "After all, I'm the one who is responsible for this mess."

"You're not strong enough to hold his head still against such an involuntary reflex," Gunnery Sergeant Marty Mann declared. "For that matter, neither am I."

"No one is," Corporal Casey Dworkin ventured. "I've been through this with a poor wounded bastard a hundred times. In the end, it's always a matter of rigid self-control."

The sober professional advice took a moment to sink in. Impressed but undeterred, the girl came back with a reply that surprised the men.

"Don't write me off so fast," Shirley urged. "I may have a different kind of strength to offer than you find on the battle field."

The dark haired young woman in the ruined blue gown took the black kerchief from around the neck of Carson's middie-blouse and dipped it into the liquid in the nearest vat. Then she used the wrung out cloth to wipe the blood from his hands and wrists. Satisfied, she did a half-twist as she sat down on her legs and settled at his feet with her back against his knees. Carefully, she covered her exposed breast again.

"There is power," Shirley said, "even in the softest touch."

Gently, she took Carson's hand in hers and held it until the fist uncurled. Moving easily with a slight flush that gave a bronze glow to her golden skin, she slipped the relaxed hand beneath the black silk neckerchief that hid her breasts from view. Shy and driven by instinct, Carson Braddock pulled his hand back.

"It's all right," Shirley Hashimoto assured him. "I want you to hold me there."

She drew his hand down again and squeezed it in hers until his palm cupped her bare breast. Her nipples swelled in excitation and her flesh quivered beneath his uncertain touch. The feel of the naked flesh and the softening of the strain on Carson's face reached his cousin as well.

"Oh, God, hit me with a beer bottle, quick," Max demanded. "Before the other one is taken."

The witty outburst made the other men chuckle. But Shirley was too deeply involved to find it funny.

"Remember," the Japanese-American girl warned. "If you squeeze too hard you'll make me cry-out in pain."

As his fingers kneaded the pliant flesh, Shirley Hashimoto closed her eyes and gave herself to the mixture of arousal and compassion that made her body tremble. With each stroke and clasp her breath surged in semi-controlled gasps that drove the young man to state his regrets.

"I don't want to hurt you," Carson explained. "Or shame you, either."

"That's what makes it all right," Shirley insisted without opening her eyes.

Intrigued, Corporal Casey Dworkin waited as the girl's surrender aroused the sailor's desire. The corpsman rinsed his hands in alcohol again before he threaded the catgut through his stitching needle. All the while, he noted the swelling around the edges of the sailor's head wound. There was no time to waste if he hoped to avoid leaving a disfiguring scar.

"Ready or not," Casey Dworkin said. "This is it."

Eyes bright, wide, and unfocused, Aircrewman Carson Braddock fixed his mind on the throb and texture of the flesh that surged against his greedy grasp with such tender pressure. His fingertips searched the curve and thrust of her bosom and the touch traced a full-bodied line-drawing in his brain. The sensation and the image mixed with such satisfaction that he hardly felt the sting of the stitching needle at first. But the whistles and baton-bashing of the newly arrived squad of Army MPs hampered his concentration and forced the corpsman to address the stitching with fresh urgency. Each puncture hung in Carson's flesh like the claw of some tiny beast that was crawling along his jaw and up his neck. Despite the renewed pain, however, the soothing effect of Shirley's seductively curved breast and firm nipple kept Carson's head as still as the knob on a knurlpost. Somehow the tide of the girl's inner being flowed in through the young radio-gunner's palm and it put him in a state of punishing grace that only the corpsman's voice had the power to penetrate.

"You can come back now," Corpsman Casey Dworkin declared as he snipped the catgut close to the knot. "It's done."

"He did a good job," Gunny Mann volunteered. "The scar will be no more than a crease that runs along your jawbone and disappears into your hairline."

The assurance and the release spread a dry heat that filled Carson's face and brain. Yet his head and neck was cold and wet from the vodka that the corpsman was using to wash the blood off his scalp and out of his hair. As he removed his hand from Shirley's breast the rest of him vibrated with the tension of a bell that has been struck a solid blow.

"EEEEEYYOW!" ARM2/C Carson Braddock yelled. "HOT DAMN!"

For a moment the girl and the sailor locked eyes. Innocent as they were neither knew how much the one wanted the other. They were too young to know that once the feeling goes deep enough it never dies.

CHAPTER EIGHT

No skeptic
Ever toiled long
As a fisherman
Since casting
For what might not be there
Runs counter to his nature.

As soon as they returned to the fleet some three-hundred miles off the coast of Japan the Canadian cousins were embroiled in the Brandywine's crash program to outfit two Helldivers with enough extra fuel tanks to double their range. Each refurbished SB2C-4E was stripped of its radar pod, two twenty-millimeter wing cannons, eight zero-length rocket launchers, and the pilot's seatback armor plate. In place of a bomb load she took on four one-hundred-fifty-gallon wing tanks and a large self-sealing gas tank fastened into the empty bomb bay. Armed only with their twin thirty-caliber machine-guns Carson and Max's Helldivers flew through the Bungo Channel and across Japan's Inland Sea to reach Korea Strait before dawn. Their mission was to patrol the waters off Korea ahead of the three U.S. light cruisers and the battlewagon moving up from the China Sea at flank speed. The Navy knew that the Army Airforce B-29's bombing the Pusan docks and troop martialing yards would force a hasty evacuation. With just over a hundred miles of open water between Korea's Pusan Harbor and the coast of the Japanese main island everything hinged on precise timing. Even so it was worth risking three top-of-the-line fast cruisers and the forty-five thousand ton battleship Missouri in an effort to prevent Japan's crack Asian army of almost half a million men from reaching the homeland.

At dawn on the third day the Brandywine's two long-range Helldivers took reconnaissance photos of the troops embarking for the impending evacuation. Orbiting over the bay, rear-seat radio-gunners Carson Braddock and Max Bryson witnessed the destruction rained down on Pusan Harbor by Superforts flying above thirty-thousand feet. Long sticks of five-hundred-pound bombs turned the docks and ten square miles of crowded assembly yards into cratered Hell. The dead and the dying were tossed around like dismembered bodies in a squalid slaughter house. The strings of monstrous "daisy cutters" were even worse. Each one floated down on a small parachute and went off three-hundred feet above the ground. Japanese soldiers were felled by concussion and killed by a circular shower of steel pellets and razor sharp fragments that punctured, chopped, and sliced flesh for a radius of two hundred yards. Briefed for land targets and loaded with anti-personnel bombs the bombardiers in the nose of the Superforts left the ragtag enemy fleet boarding troops and deck cargo out in the harbor alone. Besides, the batteries of Japanese dockside anti-aircraft guns protecting the fleet at anchor sent up a steady barrage of shells that exploded just under 31,000 feet and provided a clear warning.

"Oh shit," Max lamented. "They got lucky."

The 35 pound shell from a Japanese 106 millimeter Model 14 anti-aircraft cannon went off beneath a B-29 that dropped out of formation. The blast crumpled the right wing and set the fuselage on fire as the Superfort tumbled out of the sky. Three chutes cleared the wreckage before the plane exploded.

"I'm contacting the nearest cruiser," Carson declared over the VHF channel. "They've got to catapult a float-plane and start it on its way just in case there is a chance for an air-sea rescue."

As Carson radioed the U.S.S. Cleveland and gave her combat control center Pusan Harbor's coordinates Max kept his eyes on the descending parachutes. The one caught in a stiff breeze that was driving it out to sea had a chance. The two angling toward the docks were out of luck.

"Those army fliers are still three thousand feet above the shore line," Max stated over the VHF. "And there must be seventy thousand enemy rifles zeroing in on their limp bodies."

Even in bright sunlight the deep waters of Pusan's well sheltered harbor took on a gray sheen darkened still more by the reflection of the trees that covered the steep hills almost to the shore line. The murky surface collected a residue of industrial waste, wood chips, and wreckage that filled the sea-lanes with flotsam nearly thick enough to walk upon. For miles the eighty-three-foot-long whaler setting out to pick up the downed flier had to nudge through that wall of debris.

"Watch out for the fanatic Yankees in those dive-bombers," the helmsman aboard the whaler shouted to his shipmate. "They'd rather kill a downed flier than let him be captured."

The circular steel cabin sat well forward on the pirogue's dory-like hull. The squat steel shelter gave the sailor manning the heavy machine-gun atop the wheelhouse a panoramic view of the bay. On the bow the short barrel of the four-inch harpoon cannon stuck up like the broken horn of a narwhale. Wearing navy work-whites, the gunner's mate aloft and the bosun at the wheel of Delightful Dancer tracked the flier floating in a yellow Mae West and the two planes overhead.

"Here they come," nineteen year old Gunner's Mate Takijiru Sugihara warned as the Curtiss Helldivers did wingovers and started down. "Praise to Buddha, they don't have any rockets."

At wave-top level the leading Helldiver banked steeply as the rear-seat gunner dropped an inflatable life raft to the downed aviator. His wingman circled to attack the pirogue from the rear.

"These Yankee-dogs have been here quite a while," twenty-one year old Bosun Chiconori Kaijitsu observed. "They must be low on fuel."

The dark blue U.S. Navy Helldivers leveled off twenty feet above the waves and rushed in at the Korean whaler from opposite directions. Turning the spry open hulled pirogue swiftly, Bosun Chico Kaijitsu swung Delightful Dancer out of the crossfire. That spoiled Gunner's Mate Taki Sugihara's aiming angle as the Helldivers' rear-seat gunners prepared to open fire. Mindful of the approaching plane's flight path, Max held off for a moment. Then he clobbered the pirogue with bursts of machine-gun fire that broke all the glass in the bulletproof wheelhouse. Carson's three second bursts shattered the dinghy behind the cabin, ripped up the latticework that covered the bilge, and shredded the Japanese ensign that flew from the stern.

"Clever bastards," Carson observed, "the helmsman swung his gunner out of our sights."

"That hairpin turn was perfectly timed," Max allowed. "If I hadn't hesitated, my opening rounds would have ricocheted into your fuselage as you flew by."

For the better part of an hour the Korean pirogue and the U.S. Navy Helldivers played chess on the surface of the sea. Each time the whaler headed for the downed flier rowing out to sea the gunners in the dive-bombers drove the Japanese vessel to seek shelter in the trough of a wave that took her off course. When one Helldiver circled back to mark the flier's location with a yellow dye marker and a smoke bomb the pirogue struggled to get up wind of the orange raft. Stalemated, both parties redoubled their efforts when the rescue plane off the Cleveland flew in from the open sea.

The Navy's OS2U Kingfisher was a single engine, midwing, float plane. Her eight hundred horsepower radial engine gave her a top speed of 122 knots. The pilot's cockpit and the rear seat gunner's sliding canopy were at opposite ends of a long greenhouse. The small wingtip balance-floats seemed out of proportion to the fat radar pod on her port wing. And the large main pontoon directly below the untapered white fuselage made her look like of hot water boiler strapped atop an Eskimo kayak. Awkward and obsolete, the Kingfisher taxed the skill and the nerve of the navy's best pilot and most seasoned radio-gunner whenever it set out to rescue a flier in enemy waters.

"Lighten the load, Knobby," Enlisted Pilot Pete Cramer ordered.

Working quickly, Chef Petty Officer Larry K. Walsh heaved his belted ammunition overboard and muscled the one hundred seventy-five-pound matched pair of Browning thirty caliber machine-guns off the modified Scarff-ring. As the plane banked he dropped the weapon over the side clear of the main pontoon. CPO Pete Cramer used the added lift to ease the Kingfisher down on the surface of a shallow trough without a splash. Afloat, the under-powered rescue plane bobbed and dipped in the whitecaps and swift running swells like an empty beer can in a riptide. With each wave that washed over the main float, another gallon of seawater poured in through the poorly fastened servicing plate overlooked in the haste of the emergency catapult launch. In minutes the plane's buoyancy began to fade. Sensing danger, the pilot gunned the motor to keep the plane afloat. Using the ailerons, he dipped the small wingtip floats to steer the plane over the waves as they taxied to within a wingspan of the downed flier's life-raft.

"Get him aboard and secured pronto," Chief Cramer urged. "That Jap patrol boat is closing on us from windward."

"It's gonna take at least five minutes," Knobby insisted. "Even in a raft, an hour in these frigid waters makes the young ones stiffer than a fence post."

Chief Gunner's Mate Larry Walsh got out of the rear-cockpit and climbed down to the main pontoon without taking his eyes off the Japanese vessel charging toward them. Shedding his Mae West, he leaped into the water and swam to the dazed flier. The chill in the blue-green sea strapped the fifty-year-old chief's chest and stomach in tight bands of pain as he dragged the life-raft back to the main pontoon. Once both men stood upright on the pontoon their added weight depressed the loose servicing plate below the water. The climb up into the rear-cockpit was an agony of ache and strain for them both and a challenge for the pilot. As soon as they were aboard Pete Cramer turned the Kingfisher around and picked up speed. He needed more distance to take off into the wind. Meanwhile Knobby Walsh put him in radio contact with the two Helldivers orbiting overhead.

"What the fuck are you guys doing up there?" Chief Petty Officer Pete Cramer demanded. "Get that Goddamned whaler off our backs before she guns us down."

Enlisted pilot Peter Cramer had taught fledgling fighter pilots to fly pint-sized Curtiss bi-planes off the airships that the U.S. Navy built after the First World War. The drop from the crane in the dirigible's cavernous bay gave them a launch like a clipped-wing falcon plunging from the nest. But the trick was to bring the tiny F9C-2 Sparrowhawk in for a landing down along the curved underbelly of the airship. His students soon mastered the art of skimming the dirigible's underside so smoothly that the rack mounted just above the Sparrowhawk's top-wing would click into the dirigible's extended skyhook without a jolt. And his voice made it clear that he accepted no less from others. As a result Carson Braddock's reply sounded like an apology.

"These aren't bombs on our wings," Carson insisted. "They're empty gas tanks."

"Then what the fuck are you saving them for?" Knobby Walsh inquired. "One plane drops them in the enemy's path and the other shoots them up until they explode. It's better than nothin'."

Larry Walsh had learned to improvise as the helmsman aboard the navy dirigible U.S.S. Macon. When a sharp gust of wind tore off her top fin and ruptured three of the gasbags in her stern his skill at the wheel softened the drawn-out crash into the raging sea. His courage in the ever-insatiable Atlantic kept the death toll to a minimum. Only the Macon's radio operator and a Filipino mess cook drowned. And that earned Larry his chief's stripes along with the Navy Cross.

Acting on impulse Carson's pilot dove their Helldiver down to the deck and whipped in toward the whaler. When the almost empty wing-tanks hit the water they skipped across the waves helter-skelter. Firing in short bursts Max blew up two of the tanks in the pirogue's path and forced her to swerve away from the short-lived screen of orange and yellow flames. Unimpressed, Max's pilot overtook the pirogue on the verge of a stall and dropped his four canisters as they approached her fantail. The two that hit her deck showered the steel cabin with several gallons of unused gasoline that Carson ignited with tracer bullets. The heat drove Bosun Chico Kaijitsu out of the wheelhouse and cooked off all the ammunition for the Mate's eleven millimeter machine-gun. And even though the Japanese sailors were vulnerable out on deck smothering flames both Canadians were out of ammunition. Singed and doused by the heavy seas the purple-hulled pirogue rode high on the waves and surfed like a sleek harbor seal as the Japanese sailors regained control. Down wind, the rescue plane wallowed with the bulk of an elephant seal pushing through a mountain of water.

Without slowing down, Pete Cramer slid the Kingfisher through a swift turn that drove her main float beneath the waves and almost ripped her wingtip floats off. Feeling her shudder subside, he opened the throttle and cut-in the specially installed water-injection power booster as she came around into the stiffening breeze. The engine roared and rattled with piston slap as it picked up an extra hundred horsepower from the steam in the cylinder heads. Even on combat emergency power, however, the overloaded seaplane strained hard to gather speed as the float rose to the surface of the water. The struggle to rise up on the step of the waterlogged pontoon made the pistons clatter and the propeller scream. Cutting through frothy waves that grabbed at her main float while the whirling propeller churned and chewed the crest off the higher breakers, the thin skinned Vought OS2U Kingfisher sped through short leaps and settled again on the long and turbulent swells. The thud of the pontoon's curved metal plates pounding against oncoming waves swept across the intervening sea with the soggy beat of a waterlogged kettledrum.

"Here she comes," Taki warned from atop the wheelhouse. "Thrashing the waves like a pregnant trumpeter swan."

Gunner's Mate Taki Sugihara was short and wiry with a full face that blushed like a ripe peach with exertion. He had passed his university entrance exams before he enlisted. Even so, the Navy put him in submarines and trained him as an anti-aircraft gunner because of his good eyes and quick reflexes. When an American destroyer rammed his I-boat off Bungo Strait he was the only man to make it up and out of the open conning tower as she went into her final dive.

"Make it good, Taki-san," Chico urged. "You're only gonna get one shot."

The Bosun's long jaw and the mahogany glow in his cheeks masked eyes that were extra dark and sensitive to detail. Although he was not yet twenty-one he had fought in three naval engagements and survived the sinking of his destroyer in Leyte Gulf.

Gunner's Mate Takijiru Sugihara scampered down the ladder

welded to the side of the wheelhouse and sprinted forward to the harpoon gun. With well-practiced skills he readied the weapon for use. After setting the winch for rapid retrieval and barely dogging down the drag on the reel he cleared the coiled rope so it would play out and not foul. Sweating and drenched in spray, he wet down the line, unplugged the barrel, and loaded the harpoon into the muzzle. Panting like a wrestler, the young sailor put a heavy powder charge in the breech and readied the trigger for electrical and manual firing. Yet, only as he hunched down, took hold of the handles, and sighted along the barrel did he notice that the Kingfisher was firing the machine-gun she had poking out through her cowl. The bullets from the buffeted rescue plane skimmed across the deck and hit the wheelhouse where they rang through the rippled thunder of the surf with a high pitched hum.

"She's about to go airborne," Chico announced. "When she does, we should be closing head-on at over eighty-five knots."

"She better climb fast," Taki observed, "or she'll ram her main pontoon into the wheelhouse."

The salt-crusted seaplane bounced off the crests of two waves and took to the air. Barely able to climb, she hung on the wind with her nose up as torrents of seawater spilled from her main pontoon. Slowly, the screeching engine lifted her above boat level as she raced toward the whaler.

"Take a firm grip on the wheel," Taki shouted. "She's a monster."

"Go easy on the drag," Chico insisted. "A sharp tug could swamp us."

Sighting well ahead of the speeding aircraft, Gunner's Mate Taki Sugihara fired the harpoon gun straight up into the air. The kick of the powerful cannon buckled his knees.

"Harpoon away," Taki yelled. "It's climbing like an Indian Fakir doing the rope trick."

The stubby steel spear carried the heavy whaling line up in front of the American rescue plane in loops and curls. At three hundred feet the barbed harpoon arched high over the wing and the long greenhouse that sheltered the pilot, the rear-seat gunner, and the recovered flier. Making seventy-five knots, the laboring Kingfisher snagged the wet hemp with its starboard wing just outside the arc of the propeller. The impact whipped the harpoon down across the tail surface where the spread-barbs swung up and grabbed the underside of the elevator. For a long moment the rescue plane drove forward as the drag drew the line tight. The ripple and sheer of the heavy harpoon tearing through light aluminum sounded like the grind and crunch of a deadly claw.

"What the fuck is that?" Chief Knobby Walsh demanded. "Where did it come from?"

"An overdue hand from the sea," Chief Pete Cramer noted. "With a grip of steel."

A moment later the whaling line stiffened and the drag cinched the wet hemp as tight as piano wire. The cable-hard rope cut through the leading edge of the wing and the tension yanked the embedded hook so hard it dragged the plane's tail high above its nose. In mid-air, the fuselage began to fold just behind the wing. Quickly, the unaccustomed drag tugged the port wing down toward the water. Spewing rivets, scattering wing panels, and twisting pontoon struts, the ancient Kingfisher went down. The heavy line swung the floatplane out of the sky like a vulture on a leash.

"Brace yourself," Taki Sugihara shouted. "We've hooked a flying sea serpent."

The Navy Kingfisher slammed into the sea nose down. The gray-green wall of solid surface water crushed the forward section of the main pontoon and drove the overheated engine back into the pilot's cockpit. Death was as brutal as it was swift. No one had a moment to fend it off.

The rescue plane's steam-drenched engine splintered Peter Cramer's legs and the shock of the impact broke the catch on his shoulder harness. His head snapped forward and struck the windscreen. The blow to his forehead broke his neck and split his skull. He was dead even before the long, thin tube of the gunsight penetrated his eye socket and pierced his brain.

Unbelted to make room for his passenger, Knobby Walsh was reaching for the red button that would melt down the airborne radar when the plane hit. His body was driven up against the steel chassis of the radio transmitter where it folded into itself. The crunch of broken bones that accompanied his fatal wheeze sounded like the final collapse of a brittle accordion.

The recovered flier was thrown out through the long greenhouse that covered the rear-cockpit. Stiff wedges of broken glass and long slivers of torn up steel sliced both legs to the bone. Numb and ringed in a dark cloud of blood, Ensign Rusty Trimble bled to death in a frigid sea as the plane settled on the waves. Alert to the danger of an explosion the Japanese bosun brought the whale boat in toward the aircraft's damaged pontoon with care.

"Not all the big ones get away," Gunner's Mate Taki Sugihara shouted.

The words were as painful to utter as they were impossible to suppress. The rope that the harpooned aircraft had whipped across the staggering Japanese gunner's chest left a friction burn as wide as his hand. Nor had the bosun escaped injury. The sudden yank of a four-ton aircraft hitting the end of its tether at ninety miles an hour turned the twenty ton boat around and spun the wheel so fast that the spokes extending from the helm slipped from Chiconori's grasp and hammered against his ribs. Even so, the excitement of the catch took the sting out of their injuries for the moment.

"Let's winch up that wreckage," Bosun Chico Kaijitsu said. "We've got salvage rights."

Despite the mangled front end and the water between the gas tanks inside the main pontoon, the Kingfisher had enough buoyancy to keep her afloat. As the winch went to work, the crumpled wing rose above the waves and the aircraft came to rest on her right side. The tethered wreckage was massive and ugly on the surface but it served as a kind of sea anchor that allowed the eighty-three foot long pirogue to slide in close. Both men worked hard coupling the ruined rescue plane and the whaleboat together. Hardly anything disturbed their concentration. All through the grisly task of weighting the American bodies for ocean burial and searching the blood stained waters for the lost flier, however, there was a distant rumble that rose over the surf and drifted out from shore. Whenever the Japanese sailors lifted their heads and searched for the source a blend of wild shouts, rifle shots, and fanatic cheers went up from the troops standing on the cliffs all around the bay. Finally, Colonel Matome Tadashi's Rats of Pusan had a pair of heroes worthy of their praise.

A thousand feet above and powerless to interfere, the two Navy Helldivers made a final flypast over Delightful Dancer. Carson Braddock contacted the USS Cleveland and radioed the loss of the Kingfisher and crew. Max Bryson took pictures of the wrecked Kingfisher with his reconnaissance camera to prove that the Navy's top secret aerial radar pod was intact and in the hands of the Japanese Imperial Navy. Then both dark blue dive-bombers climbed away and headed back to the USS Brandywine.

On the nine-hundred mile flight back to the aircraft carrier the cousins considered what the enemy might do with the newly acquired AN/APS-4 airborne radar if the crashed Kingfisher's transmitter, receiver, and four inch viewing scope were all in tact. Speaking to each other over VHF radio they exchanged thoughts in plain language once they were out of enemy air space.

"They couldn't install it in a plane fast enough to help the fleet cross the strait," Max ventured. "We haven't even seen a Jap Zero all week."

"The pod weighs about a hundred fifty pounds," Carson ventured. "Suppose those sailors built a man-sized box kite and used the pirogue to tow it up to twelve hundred feet on telephone wire. They could search the sea and the lower altitudes a hundred miles further than the Cleveland's masthead Radar."

"Could they be that smart?" Max wondered. "They looked pretty young."

"They made good use of that harpoon gun on the whaler," Carson observed. "Didn't they?"

Both men knew that it was foolish to underestimate the enemy. And they doubted that the Navy's top brass would buy a theory from two discredited enlisted men. Much less a pair of Canadians. So they planned accordingly until their Helldivers were challenged by the IFF of the combat air patrol guarding the U.S.S. Brandywine.

CHAPTER NINE

War and capital punishment
Are state sanctioned slaughter
Taken by almost all patriots
To be within the moral code.

Back aboard the U.S.S. Brandywine Carson Braddock and Max Bryson accompanied their pilots to the aircraft carrier's combat control center and explained how the enemy might use airborne radar to help their troop transports avoid interception. Thanked and dismissed by the commander in charge they sought their pilots' permission to have their Helldivers modified.

"If the Japanese high command is as close minded as ours," Carson said, "all the captured airborne radar equipment is probably still on that whaler."

"So if we're gonna sink it and avoid the fate of the Cleveland's Kingfisher," Max declared, "we're gonna need a couple of combat worthy dive-bombers."

"Hell," Carson insisted, "the battleship and the three cruisers making the intercept will have enough to do without looking for a little wooden pirogue that will hardly show up on their radar."

By the pre-dawn takeoff, Carson's SB2C was re-equipped with a twenty millimeter cannon in each wing and Max's dive-bomber had its radar pod back. Each plane gave up both outboard wing-tanks so that one could carry four three-inch rockets on zero-length launchers and the other had a pair of two-hundred-fifty-pound bombs. Reconfigured for combat, each Helldiver took to the air with barely enough fuel reserves to spend half an hour over target. Radar and routine radio contact with the battleship U.S.S. Missouri enabled them to zero in on the enemy squadron of six twin engine bombers before they started their run on the American battle fleet.

"Those Bettys are here without fighter escort." Max noted. "Flying in tight formation."

"That's a seasoned Army squadron," Carson said. "Not a gang of kamikaze amateurs."

The dive down from ten thousand feet allowed the pilots and the rear seat gunners to arm and test fire their guns as they surveyed the battle scene developing below. Moving slowly on a silver sea the Japanese destroyer protecting the rag-tag armada of troop transports, cargo ships, and ferry boats was accompanied by a minesweeper, an armed net tender, and a river gunboat. Each was just out of range of the U.S. battle fleet. Sensing their pilots' single-minded concentration on the medium bombers below, Carson interjected a thought.

"I know the first order of aerial combat is to drop all bombs and external gas tanks before engaging the enemy," he said. "But if we keep the bombs we can paste at least the Jap destroyer. And the extra gas will help us search out the Korean whaler."

"Make a quick pass at the lead planes with your cannons," Max suggested. "And we'll pepper the fuckers with our pea-shooters."

The two battle blue Helldivers swooped in on the cigar shaped Japanese bombers like falcons after pigeons. Since the brown Mitsubishi G4Ms were flying without bomb-bay doors Carson's pilot dropped his estimate of their speed by thirty knots before firing off his rockets. Arcing in slow motion, the four smoking missiles bracketed the leader. The one that hit the fuselage set off a tremendous explosion. The blast blew the plane apart before any of the seven-man crew could leave his post. Banking away from the yellow eruption, Max's pilot trained his twenty-millimeter cannons just ahead of the next plane's glassed in nose. The chug of the twenty-millimeter cannons blurred Max's vision as a string of tracers perforated the gas tanks built into her eighty-one-foot wingspan. Three men dropped through the open bomb bay just before the wingtank exploded. As their parachutes opened, the top turret guns on the remaining four Bettys began to find the range of the two American Helldivers. Rocked by hits but feeling no serious damage the pilots banked their planes and reefed their turns in tight to give their rear-seat gunners a crack at the nearest Betty.

"Who nicknamed her the one shot lighter?" Max inquired. "Them or us."

"The joker who first took those bomb bay doors off," Carson ventured. "What other plane needs a permanently open escape hatch."

Chinning his weapon hard, Carson pumped two three second bursts into the Betty's port radial engine. As the one-thousand-eight-hundred-fifty-horsepower Kasei engine began to smoke two crewmen exited through the bomb bay. Max's extended burst into the pilot's cabin sent her spiraling nose-down toward the sea. Before she hit, the remaining Bettys dove out of gunnery range and made staggered runs on the American warships. Two were splashed by the combined gunfire of the cruisers Cleveland, Philadelphia, and Santa Fe. The one that reached the Missouri lost a wing to the battleship's massive anti-aircraft barrage and plummeted into the sea just a hundred yards short of her target. Free of distractions, the American cruisers directed their six inch guns at the enemy ships within range.

The armor piercing shells that fell out of a cloudless sky plunged sixty feet beneath the surface and exploded like depth charges. Hits on the leading Japanese freighter blew the deck cargo overboard, tore open the crews' quarters, started a gasoline fire amidships, and opened the forward hold to the sea. Troops struggling to escape crawled all over the weather deck like ants on a burning leaf.

The next salvo arrived in the convoy half a minute after the flash of the cruiser's guns glittered on the horizon some fifteen miles away. The bridge of the leading American cruiser was just high enough to give her officers a glimpse of the action. Pumped up and exhilarated by battle, the commander held his binoculars steady and offered his companions a running account of the enemy's disposition.

"The Japanese freighters and cargo vessels are running to the south," the executive officer of the U.S.S. Cleveland reported. "But there is a tiger out there that is out-distancing her escorts and charging straight in on us at a speed of more than thirty knots."

"That must be one of their destroyers," Captain Willard Suffolk concluded. "She will be pushing in to point-blank torpedo range so she can send a full salvo of fish in at top speed."

The captain's crisp account of the enemy tincan's tactics produced an immediate reaction. Without a moment's hesitation the lieutenant commander on the phone to the cruiser's command control center issued fresh orders.

"Switch from armor piercing shells to contact-fuses," the fire-control officer directed. "We can't have our hits passing right through her thin hull-plates and exploding out in the water."

Instantly, the order to open fire on all viable targets went out to the other ships in the squadron. Inside a minute, all three U.S. cruisers divided their fire between the approaching Japanese gunboat and her armed escorts. The American battlewagon that had caught up with the cruisers following the aerial attack fixed its sights on the troopships and escaping cargo vessels.

A dozen salvos tore the fabric of a clear sky before any more shells found their mark. A one-ton missile from the Missouri struck the stern of a heavily loaded Maru and tore the entire aft-end off from the main deck to the water-line. The "black gang" in the engine room were blown to bits along with the boilers. Deck hands and wipers near the exposed cargo hold suffered terrible burns. Bones broken by shock poked through their skin like shattered hockey sticks. Thrown into panic, the mixture of Korean, Burmese, and Thai natives manning the freighter and the Japanese soldiers crammed on board began to leap overboard before their officers could intervene.

A mile astern, a troop ship took a hit amidships that wiped out the bridge, demolished her superstructure, blew her smoke stack overboard, and started fires in her engine room. The third mate was struck by a shattered cargo boom that came down so hard it broke his back at almost every vertebrae. The first mate was hosing the deck cargo with seawater when the fuel that a Korean saboteur had deliberately left in a truck's gasoline tank exploded and blew him overboard. The incident created a panic that drove hundreds of Japanese soldiers into the sea.

A rusty freighter, deep in the water with a deck cargo of trucks and artillery, lost all headway when a shell tore her boilers apart and opened up her fuel bunkers and her bottom to the sea. The mates managed to get the crew and a few soldiers off in three lifeboats but near misses capsized each one before it could get outside the ring of burning crude oil. The agony of hundred of enemy soldiers leaping into the flaming sea came into view as the captain of the Cleveland scanned the sea with his binoculars. Regardless of the suffering, however, others were pleased.

"Thank God for radar directed gunfire," the fire control officer declared. "Without it, each of those ships would have been in among the islands before we ever got off a shot."

The gunfire from the three American cruisers was effective against the convoy's trailing vessels because they traveled as slow as the ferryboats. But the enemy warship charging directly into the Americans' forward guns was much harder to hit. Even so, the advancing Japanese destroyer took heavy shells in the superstructure that wiped out fire control. The two-hundred-fifty-pound bombs dropped by Max's Navy Helldiver, decimated the officer's quarters and made sieves out of both her funnels. The junior officers and ratings posted on the wings of the Nenohi's bridge to direct the gunfire of her forward five-inch rifle were repeatedly picked off by shrapnel bursts from nearby hits. But the ship's prow and her mighty diesel engines continued to raise a bright bow wave and churn out forty-five-thousand horsepower as she rushed along at just over thirty-four knots. Far astern, the surviving escorts put on short but feeble bursts of speed and steered into violent turns to swerve out from under descending salvos. Unhit, the minesweeper, the armed net tender, and the river gunboat set about rescuing some of the soldiers swimming toward the shores of the Tsushima Islands. And that troubled the Americans studying them with their binoculars.

"Son of a bitch," the captain of the U.S.S Cleveland complained. "Driving those little bastards out of those shallow coves will be worse than diggin' the meat out of a lobster claw."

Even though it took time, however, the cruiser's persistence and the skill of her crew paid off. Directing its gunfire in among the larger outcroppings, the USS Cleveland sent salvos of six-inch shells after anything that moved between the heavily treed islands. The shells that bracketed the Japanese minesweeper split timbers all through her wooden hull and left her struggling against the pressures of the sea like a swimmer with broken ribs. The explosion that went off under the river gunboat tossed the ninety-foot vessel clear of the waves and dropped her back down on a cracked keel that cut her speed to a few knots. The pressure waves from a pair of near misses that straddled the net tender stove in hull plates on both sides and left her wallowing in the shallows. Even with all the cruisers' guns free to concentrate on the Japanese destroyer, however, the charging Nenohi was almost too tough to sink.

A six-inch shell from the Cleveland tore into the enemy destroyer's fantail and scattered her depth charges into the ocean throughout a whipsaw turn. The sailor who struggled to stop the run-away ash cans lost an arm above the elbow. A hit by the Santa Fe demolished the Japanese destroyer's after deck gun, split one of her three Kampon boilers, and damaged her port turbine. The chief boiler tender and three of his strikers were riddled with shrapnel. Half the ratings on the overhead lattice work were broiled to death by escaping steam. The salvo from the Philadelphia that straddled her bow opened up seams in her double-welded hull. Injured work crews in the inundated compartments dove through the hatches in the watertight doors and dogged them shut with the cries of the severely wounded embedded in their ears. Even so, the unwanted weight in her flooded forward compartments forced the destroyer's bow to dip beneath every other advancing wave. The force of six feet high waves rushing down the narrow weather deck swamped gunners at their forty-millimeter cannons and swept men in transit overboard. Nevertheless, the Nenohi drove in through the bombardment with a black plume of boiler smoke pouring from both funnels.

Swiftly, the three cruisers closed to within ten miles and turned to bring their fore and aft guns to bear. A string of hits shattered the Nenohi's bow. The rescue team making dressings in the chain locker perished from the lacquer fumes let loose when the paint compartment exploded. Two shells in quick succession demolished her remaining gun turrets. The loader on the decimated forward five-inch gun continued to try to ram empty casings into the breech even though his stomach was gone and most of his insides were charred black from powder burns. A whistling six-inch shell blew open the ship's main fuel tank and spread flaming crude oil through the bilge and the corridors of the lower machinery deck. Sailors struggling to climb up slippery ladders fell down into pools of burning bunker crude that cooked them as they screamed. And still the Nenohi continued to forge ahead. But the devastation had already taken a heavy toll.

Out of a crew of two hundred seventy men a third were dead, a third were disabled, and the rest of the injured and the able did double duty to keep the ship afloat. Machinists and carpenters shored up threatened bulkhead while electricians and wipers lowered mattresses and heavy canvas over the damaged plates that were open to the sea. The surviving gunners lugged fire hoses into the main magazine and doused the glowing brass shells. Across from the crates full of primers, an explosion ripped open the far bulkhead and sent the soaked cotton bags of gunpowder sizzling around the compartment in a cloud of dense smoke. Listing and belching flames like a stricken dragon, the Japanese destroyer swung through a wide turn and launched a full salvo of torpedoes at the passing squadron of American ships. The Helldivers racing away from the hail of descending shells reported the danger to the bridge of the leading cruiser the moment the enemy salvo left the torpedo tubes. Grateful, the battle commander acted on it at once.

"All fighting ships make a ninety degree turn toward the target," Captain Willard Suffolk ordered. "Let's point our narrow bows at those incoming fish and close on that Jap tincan before she can reload."

"All ships," the executive officer broadcast in plain language. "Ready? Execute!"

The Cleveland, the Philadelphia, and the Santa Fe swung their six-hundred-foot-long hulls around in unison. Each churned up a lime green slick in the blue-gray noon hour sea. The flat water mirrored the flash of the salvos fired off by the battleship swinging in behind them.

Swiftly, the three U.S. cruisers headed for the crippled Japanese destroyer like predators suddenly unleashed. Intent on total destruction, they bore down on the Nenohi without firing a shot. After the endless bombardment of heavy guns the comparative silence of powerful engines pumping full-bore and the swish of narrow prows churning and slicing up the sea was a grim relief.

In just under five minutes the Cleveland's lookouts caught sight of the faint traces of the enemy's liquid oxygen driven torpedoes. Before they could shout a warning the deckhands were staring down at the gray-green wakes of the speeding missiles traveling the length of their ship. At a combined closing speed of just over a hundred miles an hour, the hulls and the missiles passed each other inside the space of a tightly held breath.

"Give me a torpedo count," Captain Suffolk demanded. "Port and starboard right down the line. All told, how many?"

"Six enemy long-lance torpedoes fading astern," the fire-control officer reported from the communication center. "One of the spotters claimed that they rushed by like bottle-nosed dolphins in a race."

"For a Hatsuharu Class tincan," the executive officer added, "that's a full spread. Those flyboys had it right."

The collective sigh that spread around the bridge was as soft as the first traces of steam from a tea kettle. The relief was palpable. Even so, officers and enlisted men swiftly focused on a possible danger to follow.

"Given the benefit of every doubt," Captain Willard Suffolk insisted, "how long will it take the Jap to reload and be ready to launch again?"

"With this six-foot chop it would take a good crew at least twelve minutes," the fire-control officer estimated. "A fleet championship team might cut two minutes off that time. But they wouldn't be working on a sinking ship."

Delivered in clear and confident tones, the information settled in no faster than cold butter on warm toast. Each officer studying the Japanese destroyer's burning superstructure took the time to appraise the enemy's potential to inflict further harm. Yet it was the second in command who answered the question on everyone's mind.

"If they had armed torpedoes standing by on deck despite the risk of incoming shells exploding the warheads," the executive officer proposed, "they could be ready in eight minutes. Perhaps."

The assessment was fair, professional, and conservative. No U.S. destroyer torpedo crew had ever earned the Navy E for excellence with a time that good. And the one that had come the closest earned it in peacetime under Lieutenant Commander Willard Suffolk's direction.

"Send a blinker message," Captain Suffolk declared. "Each ship turn broadside to the target to bring all heavy guns to bear. Hold that course for four minutes from now. Mark. No more. I repeat, not one second over four minutes."

On signal, the USS Cleveland, Santa Fe, and Philadelphia turned and ran parallel to the limping Japanese destroyer at five-thousand yards. Separated by a half mile, each of the three formidable cruisers opened up with a combined thirty-nine gun broadside that thundered across the sea. Fired at point-blank range for capital ships, the streams of ninety-pound shells hit the Nenohi like an avalanche of high explosives. Round after round blew her bridge apart, tore gun turrets from their mounts, toppled both smoke stacks, demolished her steering, ruined her boilers, and turned her topside into scrap. The blast that dismembered the captain and the executive officer blew the helmsman over the side with his hands clutching the wheel. Rounds that fell short skimmed through the water like high-speed torpedoes and opened up holes below the waterline that threatened to capsize the smoldering hulk. The smaller American anti-aircraft guns peppered the Japanese wreck so hard metal peeled off her burning superstructure like cardboard being shredded by firecrackers.

Caught in the murderous fusillade, the Nenohi's torpedo master and his crew crumpled to the deck and slid astern on slicks of their own blood. The thunderous explosions, the rumbling destruction below decks, and the roar of ascending flames rolled across the water as a chorus of doom. Even as the noise swept over the leading American cruiser the Cleveland's guns fired their closing salvo.

"Cease fire," the fire-control officer ordered. "Give the poor bastard time to sink."

As the American guns fell silent a great geyser shot up alongside the Santa Fe and drenched the bridge with its crown. The Japanese torpedo penetrated the hull eight feet below the water line. The explosion killed half a dozen men in the forward fuel pumping station and a rush of water drowned the emergency repair team posted in the lower-deck companionway. Collapsing bulkheads filled the bilge with seawater and drowned the seamen manning the pumps. Even so, counter flooding kept the Santa Fe on an even keel but the damage slowed her down by ten knots. Being thinly armored, the light cruiser suffered severely from the gaping hole that let in so much water it poured through the crew's quarters like a river.

The blasts of the two torpedoes that struck the Cleveland drove her over on her side. The waves rushing down the main deck washed several anti-aircraft gunners overboard before the vessel righted herself. Flooding on the machinery deck cut off power to the pumps needed to fight the fires in the galley. Seamen coupled up long length of hoses and ran the hastily built line back to a working connection in the laundry. As the water came through, however, the eruption of the after-magazine blew out two boilers that scalded the black gang with live steam. Reduced to twelve knots and forced to fight her fires, the Cleveland swung away from the battle line in the company of the Santa Fe and signaled the Philadelphia and the Missouri to cover their withdrawal.

"All fires are confined except for the blaze in the crews' quarters," the damage control officer reported. "As we have hoses working on that it should be under control in short order."

"Water tight integrity has been restored below deck. Work details are sealing off the twelve compartments open to the sea," Engineering Officer Barry Langdon disclosed. "Repair parties are hard at work on the damaged boilers, the aft magazine, and the power-turret drive train."

The cruiser's structural damage was serious but not bad enough to cripple her for long. Yet coming as a blow that seemed to be impossible, concern for any life lost settled on the high command with the crushing weight of an unforgivable error.

"How about the men?" Captain Suffolk demanded. "Have we taken many casualties?"

"We have thirty-seven dead," the senior medical officer declared. "Eight of the fifty three critically wounded won't survive. Five missing. Forty-one confined to sickbay. But the working wounded are too many for my pharmacist mates to tally. Plus twenty-three dead and sixty-one seriously wounded on the Santa Fe."

Torn away from his own vessel's agony by the news, Captain Suffolk glanced across the water to where his sister ship burned like an Oklahoma oil well. The fire that leaped up from the bunker tanks at the waterline enveloped the superstructure in yellow flames so blackened with crude oil that they sent a great spire of smoke churning up into the soiled sky. But nothing troubled him so much as the terrible loss of life his small squadron had suffered.

"Son of a bitch," the captain muttered. "Nobody can re-load torpedoes that fast."

Stunned, Captain Suffolk sank down into the elevated bridge chair and tugged at the peak of his baseball cap as the Nenohi's burned and shattered hull slipped beneath the waves. On the cruiser's listing bridge, senior ratings monitored their instruments and used runners to coordinate the efforts of the fire brigades and the rescue teams. The junior officers kept in touch with the damage control units and the repair parties over the ship's hastily patched telephone lines.

"There are too many targets heading south for the Missouri to handle all by herself," the chief radar operator announced. "She's calling two fast fleet destroyers in off coastal patrol."

The captain of the Cleveland bit his lip, clenched his fists, and ruefully accepted the news. The thought of having a couple of upstart tincans finish the job was too much for his pride.

"By God, we can still take on a couple dozen unarmed freighters and half a dozen troop transports," Captain Willard Suffolk insisted. "Off-load three Carley rafts for the missing and square the decks for action."

Despite her fierce fires, extensive damage, flooded compartments, and reduced speed, the Cleveland led the Santa Fe and the Philadelphia into the firing zone controlled by the battleship Missouri. For almost half an hour the sound of heavy guns echoed off the cliffs of the Tsushima Islands as the two U.S. Navy Helldivers searched the shallows and the bays for Delightful Dancer. Finally they found her alone in a teal-blue cove fingered with Nile-green streaks of kelp strung along the shallow bottom. A pass over the crowded whaler raised a dilemma.

"She must be carrying sixty or eighty unarmed soldiers she's picked up out of the sea," Max noted. "Mowing them down would be like shooting enemy fliers hanging from their parachutes."

"Your call," Max's pilot allowed. "But this ain't no Sunday school picnic."

"The sailor tracking us with that eleven millimeter machine-gun atop the wheelhouse is holding his fire," Carson noted. "He seems to be waiting for us to make the first move."

"Do it fast," Carson's pilot insisted. "If we're gonna make it back to the Brandywine."

On instructions the two pilots flew their Helldivers over the pirogue in wingtip formation. Pointing toward shore, Carson and Max each dropped ten smoke bombs at even intervals so they made a narrow path all the way to the deserted beach. In moments, the Japanese sailors got the message and started the soldiers swimming and then wading ashore. Last to leave, Bosun Chico Kaijitsu and Gunner Taki Sugihara each supported a disabled soldier in the long swim to the beach.

Assured of an empty vessel, the pilots dropped their almost empty wing tanks on Delightful Dancer in low passes. Two missed, one split open inside the canoe-like hull, and the other smashed against the steel wheelhouse. Firing short bursts, Carson and Max ignited the spilled gasoline. Flames spread rapidly all around the teakwood pirogue. Rather than wait for her to sink, the pilots riddled the burning hull with twenty-millimeter cannon fire and waggled the Helldivers' wings as they climbed away and headed back to the carrier. The two enemy sailors replied with a wave.

CHAPTER TEN

The illusion that problems vanish
When ignored
Is fostered by the speed
At which they are swallowed up
By larger ones.

When Max and Carson's dive-bombers reached the Brandywine their radio warning had the aircraft carrier streaming into the wind. The red flare Carson fired on approach told the deckhands that their Helldivers were almost out of fuel. Recovered quickly, the planes were loaded on to the after elevator and taken to the hanger deck to be re-equipped for full combat readiness. Hard at work installing extra cans of belted ammunition the cousins learned of their promotions to petty officer first class. But there was no time to celebrate. The entire armada was on yellow alert.

Each of the eighteen large aircraft carriers had half a dozen light cruisers guarding her for and aft as well as an entire squadron of destroyers circling the perimeter on the lookout for enemy submarines. The battleships, heavy cruisers, and destroyer escorts kept close watch on the scores of troopships in their midst. The subchasers and minesweepers accompanying the fleet of carrier escorts looked after the convoy of hundreds of freighters and cargo ships steaming in toward the coast of Japan. And fifty miles out ahead of them all, a combat air patrol of sleek navy Grumman F8F Bearcats and F7F twin engine Tigercats shielded the armada from enemy aerial attack. High above them, the vapor trails left by Superforts from Tinian, Saipan, and Iwo Jima, showed that the softening up of the Kirishima Peninsula at the south end of Kyushu was well under way.

For five days massive flights of silver B-29s unloaded strings of high-explosive bombs that dug deep craters in the soft earth of the peninsula. Carpet-bombing blew the limbs off trees, shattered trunks, and raised moist clouds of red sand that made the ground itself seem to bleed. The sticks of heavy bombs dropped five hundred yards behind the beach of Shibushi Bay sent out underground shock waves that made the bay's blue-green water boil. Yet few enemy troops were caught in the softening up process. Since no one was safe within five miles of the water Colonel Matome Tadashi pulled the shock troops that had survived the crossing from Korea behind the junction that handled the traffic coming in from both ends of the bay. He knew an invader had to take that strong point before making an amphibious landing. And his confidence was contagious.

"One of ours is worth ten of theirs," the sergeant major insisted. "Now we will prove it."

As battle seasoned veterans, the surviving Rats of Pusan believed that morale made all the difference against a vastly superior enemy force. Wherever they looked they saw a horizon full of American ships poised to move in from the open Pacific Ocean on a wide front. The troop transports alone carried fifty thousand U.S. Marines and twice as many battle seasoned soldiers.

In the purple light of a clear dawn the first wave of the American armada converged on the wide mouth of Shibushi Bay. From twenty miles off shore, a flotilla of capital ships shelled the ring of beaches. Three-gun salvos from a dozen battleships split the air so often that the rumbles rushing ashore swept across the deserted sand dunes like relentless aerial surf. The eight-inch guns of the American heavy cruisers sent shells pounding into the shattered tree line. As the dawn patrol flew in toward the beach the naval bombardment crept a mile ahead of the aerial attack force.

"I haven't seen this many planes—ever," ARM1/C Max Bryson broadcast. "We are all winging in like geese at a mountain flythrough."

"And you will never see such a gaggle again," ARM1/C Carson Braddock replied. "This is probably the world's last single engine aerial armada."

Unable to wait, whole squadrons of carrier planes darted in beneath the overarching steel umbrella of shellfire. Later waves of fighter planes peppered the empty Japanese trenches, the poorly camouflaged bunkers, the parked tanks, and the abandoned troop trains with machine-gun fire. Each Grumman Hellcat and Curtiss Helldiver launched full salvos of wing rockets at the unmanned gun emplacements. The battle blue torpedo bombers swung in off the water and dropped thousand pound bombs that ripped up road beds with earthquake force. Coming in wave after wave, the Helldivers dropped five hundred pound bombs that raised a racket so ragged and thunderous it invaded their cockpits. Often it blotted out all but the whine of the engines as they swept through their shallow glides. Such blockages forced the rear-seat gunners to cinch up the straps on their goggle helmets and draw the earphones mounted inside tight up against their heads.

"If there is anything alive behind the beaches," Aircrewman Max Bryson stated from the rear-seat of his Curtiss dive-bomber, "it is either twenty feet under ground or encased in concrete."

"Those battleship broadsides are effective," Carson Braddock confirmed from the adjoining SB2C Helldiver, "but it seems odd that the Japs haven't sent up a single kamikaze plane?"

The ache from the half-healed wound across his jaw forced Carson Braddock to undo his goggle helmet's leather strap. Relieved, the radio-gunner helped his scout-bomber pilot scan the devastated landscape for signs of any anti-aircraft guns or coastal defense artillery still able to shoot. Working in four-plane units, the spotter and marker teams raced along just above the battle-haze that covered all but the tops of the remaining trees. Ignoring the threat of friendly shells falling short, Max's pilot led them along the line of destruction at five hundred feet.

"What could they be saving their best weapon for?" Max inquired. "The troop transports?"

"If so," Carson mused, "where the Hell are they hiding them?"

"That's a point," Max allowed. "In two days of tree-top bombing and ground strafing all over this-here-now-island nobody has reported any planes aloft or on the ground."

The air assault on the five-mile belt behind the main invasion beaches doubled as the light from a brightening sky revealed untouched enemy positions. Additional dive-bombers and torpedo planes from the fast fleet carriers far offshore joined the swarms of fighter planes burning up the tree line with napalm. Although their planes had a full load of bombs, rockets, and napalm, they were flying too low and fast to use them. Instead, Carson and Max marked targets with small hand-held smoke bombs. But the smoke and debris kicked up by fire and massive explosions coated the low flying Helldivers and the gunners' goggles with a gummy residue of battle grease. Taking time out to clean their goggle-lenses the cousins took a look around. Above them, the bellies of the twin engine Curtiss C-46 Commandos flying paratroopers in from Okinawa flashed red with the glare of thousands of rockets launched from barges just off shore. Riding in the leading C-46 Commando, the jumpmaster gave advice to his battle seasoned Marines.

"Jap infantry units have very few marksmen," Gunnery Sergeant Marty Mann said. "So they lay down a field of fire about knee high and back it up with an all out Banzai charge. Just lay low and save your ammo until they're on their feet. The faster they run the worse their aim."

As he opened the exit door Gunny Mann was startled by the sea of red flashes zipping across their jump point. A brisk order had his radioman using the emergency broadcast band to issue a cease-fire order to the seaborne rocket launchers in plain language. Monitoring the radio traffic, Carson was certain it would not get through in the heat of battle. A hand signal brought it to Max's attention, and they each relayed the message to Fleet Central Combat Control as a top priority signal. And they picked up a coded message from Fleet Central in return.

"We are ordered to check out a blip that seems to be shadowing the invasion fleet," Aviation Radioman's Mate First Class Carson Braddock declared. "It is a top priority command."

"Fleet-radar off Toi Point at the north end of the bay has been trying to get a fix on it." ARM1/C Max Bryson explained. "It comes and goes on their screen like a persistent ghost."

The two Curtiss Helldivers banked away from the blazing

shoreline and skimmed out to sea. The full expanse of Shibushi Bay spread out beneath them like a vast aquamarine bowl edged by the scorched crescent that marked the beach. Climbing away, the two SB2Cs dipped their wings to the frogmen and sailors on the minesweepers clearing the twenty-mile wide bay. Withdrawal from combat gave the cousins a chance to share information.

"Combat Control reports it as too high to be a boat and too slow to be a plane of any sort," Carson insisted. "And since it keeps pace with the fleet it can't be a tethered barrage balloon."

"It behaves a lot like a low flying blimp," Max said. "But the Japs don't have any left."

Out where the deep water turned dark and rough, the huge invasion fleet was converging on the entrance in full force. The half dozen cruisers and destroyers protecting the troopships circled them like guard dogs. Overloaded, the seventeen troop ships held fixed stations in the middle of the inner bay. Hundreds of landing craft nearby bobbed about like ducklings on an agitated pond.

"The troop transports have finished off-loading the first wave into the LCIs," Carson observed over the inter-aircraft frequency. "And nobody has come under fire. It's uncanny."

From overhead, the bright sky that played across the one hundred square miles of Shibushi Bay gave the dark surface the gray highlights of pebbled glass. The loaded landing craft lining up on that fragile surface looked like nervous steeds impatient to start the long dash into the beach.

"All the enemy guns are silent," Max said. "This is the largest unopposed landing ever."

The dozens of ship length LCIs threw out wide bow waves. The white water extended beyond their raised disembarkation ramps in froth and foam that surrounded them with watery carpets. Burdened by tanks, the LCTs plodded along in straight lines and hung in the shelter of destroyers as they edged in toward the shallows. The hundreds of thirty-six foot long LCPs bounced like overloaded speedboats leaving pale green feathered wakes behind. The numerous wheeled-personnel-carriers and tracked floating vehicles milled about in ragged lines that bent and twisted as they fought to stay out of the rip tides and currents. Massed together, the great armada of landing crafts seemed to fill the bowl shaped bay with long shadows stretching toward the shore.

"It's all very impressive but it worries me," Max said. "Everyone knows that the Japs fight like cornered rats when their real-estate is invaded."

Out beyond the landing force, the Brandywine's pair of stubby Helldivers flew over a battle fleet yellowed by the early rays of dawn. The sleek destroyers and the heavy cruisers traveled at high speed and left lime-green wakes that stretched out behind them for miles. The battleships churned up dark water disturbed by their deep and powerful screws. But the almost motionless convoy of light gray tenders, wide-hulled tankers, battered supply ships, and rusty tramp steamers stood out in the early rays of direct sunlight as vessels without any wake at all. Further out to sea, the separate task group built around each of the fast-fleet aircraft carriers completed the ring of offshore naval support. It was a mighty armada. Neither Carson nor Max believed that it could be menaced by the faint and recurring image that sporadically appeared on the tiny orange radar screens in the rear cockpit of their Helldivers. Nevertheless, the two cousins directed their pilots toward the source less than a thousand feet above the water.

"I've got a blip just under ten miles ahead. Three hundred twenty degrees, magnetic," Max Bryson reported. "But the lousy thing is so weak it makes a real ghost look like the Iron Maiden."

"I have visual contact," Carson Braddock declared. "It's a God-damned glider being towed by that Korean whaler we burned out off the coast of Tsushima Island."

Straining to get his head a few inches out into the slipstream without loosing his goggles, Max got a better look at the target. It seemed to be some kind of seaside-park pleasure-ride except for the teardrop metal pod that extended the sailplane's stubby nose.

"Oh oh," Carson said. "The fleet's been under radar surveillance for more than an hour."

"The blasted sailplane is made of wood and canvas and goes up and down like a yo-yo," Max insisted. "No wonder fleet radar called it the specter of a ghost."

The two Curtiss Helldivers dropped down and rushed in at the small high-wing glider and the Korean whaling boat that had it in tow. To slow down and give their gunnery a chance, both pilots opened their dive brakes and lowered their landing flaps as they approached. A glider and a wooden whaler were minor targets unworthy of rockets or bombs. Consequently, Carson's grease and ash-coated dive-bomber strafed the single-seat glider with twenty-millimeter cannon fire that shattered wing ribs and punched holes in the embedded radar pod. Moments later, the other Helldiver came in on the whaler's beam and peppered the metal wheelhouse with cannon-fire that churned the sea around it into a froth of white foam.

"We have an enemy glider equipped with airborne radar under fire," Max radioed to Fleet Control Center. "They know every detail of our approach to Shibushi Bay."

"They may be planning something big," Carson warned. "Tell the Marines to watch out."

In the rear-cockpits, the radio-gunners had to undo their seat belts and stand up to bring their weapons to bear on each of the fragile craft. Circling around to rake the whaler and the glider with their wing cannons again, the pilots dropped the SB2Cs below a mountain ridge that hid the invasion fleet from view. Sighting and finding their aiming point far behind the slower aircraft as they overtook her was a novelty. Max and Carson marveled at how such a slow vessel managed to raise a land based training glider off the short stretches of beach that lined the bottoms of the cliffs.

"Christ," Max sneered, "that whaler couldn't do more than ten knots going down hill."

"And the glider is a modified German Rhon Bussard," Carson noted. "She won't lift off with less than twenty knots of wind moving over her wings."

Zooming in, their eight-ton dive-bombers overtook the five-hundred-fifty-pound glider from the rear. Seated just behind the damaged radar pod embedded in the nose, the Japanese pilot bent forward to grab the tow-line release-handle and note his altitude and airspeed. In a quick glance, he took in the two radio-gunners training their machine-guns just behind his tail. As they broke eye contact, the cousins locked on to the proper sight picture and opened fire. Short bursts from their thirty-caliber machine-guns sent slugs through the fabric and the wing struts with little more effect than bullets puncturing a target sleeve. Then suddenly the towline separated and dropped into the sea. Free of its tether and over loaded with lift, the damaged glider leaped up three hundred feet, turned inland, and dove for shore. Slow and heavy as they banked to follow, the Helldivers circled and descended on the whaler as the helmsman searched for a break in the heavy surf.

"Here come the pelicans," Bosun Chiconori Kaijitsu mused, "diving on a herring."

Hunched against the twenty-millimeter cannon fire pounding against the whaler's round metal cabin, the Japanese bosun was shaken like a cockroach inside a steel drum. Despite the din, however, he managed to receive the bulk of the radio message coming in from his friend aloft.

"Radar contact with the enemy fleet is lost." Gunner's Mate Taki Sugihara said from the glider's cockpit. "Make a final report on the last sighting. Out."

Even though the small orange radarscope inside the wheelhouse was blank, the bosun consulted it out of habit. He imposed the recent pattern of blips upon it from memory and studied his compass before making another mark on the map laid out in numbered squares. Confident, at last, the young Japanese sailor activated his ship-to-shore frequency.

"Blind Pirate this is Shy Snooper," Bosun Chico Kaijitsu broadcast. "The main invasion force is spread out across hyacinth grids seven through twenty three. The troop ships are clustered among the landing craft that are milling about in delphinium square seventeen. Over."

On receiving confirmation the bosun gave the rest of his message as the pirogue skimmed into shore on the crest of a wave. Exhilaration drove him to add a naughty flourish to the text that embarrassed him so much he tried to cover it with an exceptional honorific.

"Enemy in position for a fatal blow," he said. "Locked in tighter than a sumo wrestler's finger in a geisha's purse. May white cherry blossoms grace your memory forever. Out."

Bosun Chico Kaijitsu's radio signal was received in the basement of a ruined lighthouse and automatically forwarded by telephone. The phone's shielded cable carried the message beneath the beach and ten miles out into the middle of Shibushi Bay. There, the wire made contact with a half-buried submarine that hugged the ocean floor like a giant sturgeon. The circuit was crisp and clear.

The fifty-year-old captain of the Japanese submarine smiled to himself as he took the message and pressed the plunger that severed the connection. Resigned and yet relieved, he looked around at the men who monitored the instruments and handled the controls. Despite five full days and nights on the bottom, they kept the vessel ready to move out at a moment's notice. Even at three-hundred-fifty feet below the surface, however, the sound of the enemy invasion fleet penetrated the "S" boat's welded hull. Since no one spoke, the hum from the engines and the churn of hundreds of screws overhead made the submarine sound like a hive full of busy hornets.

"Our moment of destiny is here." Captain Tomoyuki Nakao announced over the intercom. "Soon the Emperor will know the kind of sailors that await him in Eternity"

The sweating faces and the unshaven cheeks of the Japanese sailors were as grim and unkempt as the wrinkled pants and the soiled jumpers they wore. The stench of unwashed bodies, the odor of stale breath, and the stink of feces made the control cabin smell like an oriental chicken market during a heat wave.

"Empty all ballast tanks," Captain Tomoyuki Nakao ordered. "Stand by to surface."

"Rig for silent running," Executive Officer Chikako Yagisawa directed. "Bring her up in the center of delphinium square seventeen. Execute."

Reduced to a skeleton crew, practiced hands moved to wheels and valves as the S-67's electric engines began to hum. The creaks and cracks of tortured plates yielding to intense pressure brought the vessel to life as compressed air hissed into the giant flotation tanks. Buoyant but restrained, the carefully buried submarine shifted from side to side as she struggled to break loose from the heavy layer of sand and bottom muck piled on top of her. The tons of sand that the barges had spilled over the hull was all that kept her hidden from enemy frog-men and underwater sonar.

"She's struggling," Commander Yagisawa said, "like a whale trapped in a landslide."

Every sailor was tired, slightly nauseous, dehydrated, tense, a bit dizzy, and suffering from oxygen starvation. The dead air trapped in tiny alcoves repeatedly drove some men into the main aisle gasping like fish out of water. Even the mixture of oxygen and compressed air released at a steady rate added ear and toothaches to their discomfort. Yet they all urged the submarine to rise.

As if responding to their will the S-67 broke away from the suction of the bottom like a giant plunger being lifted off a slick surface. The seasoned crew staggered, rocked, and leaned with the motion of the ship as the deep currents of Shibushi Bay cradled the hull and carried her along the bottom. The chill and the sting of the poorly oxygenated air was laced with extra body heat and the sickeningly sweet smell of nervous excitement as they came under attack. Depth charges exploding nearby tossed the submarine about. The strain of fighting for yet another breath of life released hidden resources that helped each man do his task.

"Steady as she goes," Commander Yagisawa said. "All we need is a few minutes more."

A thundering explosion popped outer seams and blew out the overhead valves that controlled the hydraulic pressure to the diving planes. The master mechanic suffered terrible burns to his face and shoulders shutting down the ruptured pipe that fed live steam into the compressed air tanks used to flush the torpedo tubes. But nothing disturbed the U-boat's carefully drilled surfacing routine. The S-67 skimmed along just beneath the surface at six knots. The amber boil that swelled up forward of the hidden conning tower marked her as an intruder moving briskly toward the center of delphinium square seventeen. On command, the gun crew gathered beneath the escape hatches while the executive officer raised the periscope and readied it for use. Swiftly, the captain stepped up to the scanner, fixed his eye to the monocular, walked the viewing box through a full circle, and brought the periscope down.

"Men are climbing down on cargo nets," Captain Nakao said. "The landing craft are so numerous that the enemy destroyers are forced to twist and turn like ambulances in a traffic jam."

Each man felt the lift and the tingle that charges every nerve as he crosses the threshold of battle. Yet everyone who heard the captain's voice knew that his fate was sealed. The officers and ratings doubled their devotion to task and took the news in stoic silence. Only the gun crews spoke and massaged their muscles as they prepared to go into action.

"You will have more targets than you can count," the Master Gunner Socho advised. "But even your machine-guns are to shoot at nothing but war ships."

"The shells from our deck cannon can sink a destroyer," the gun captain declared. "And except for a cruiser's eight inch guns, they pose the greatest threat to our mission."

The submarine's forward and after hatches sprang open amid a shower of descending seawater. The machine-gunners and the deck-gun crew rushed up the ladders with the agility of trapeze artists climbing to their platforms. Behind them, the blue, dank, stale, and fetid air that escaped from the hatch made room for the moist sea breeze that swirled down the opening and wafted through the crowded control cabin.

"Leave the hatches open," the captain ordered. "They bring us all the sweet smell of life."

Near misses brought in great cascades of seawater. Eight-inch shells that bored green tunnels beneath the submarine exploded with a force that drove great waves of water up over the deck. The wash poured down through the open hatches. A salvo that bracketed the hull twisted her diving planes and buckled her outer fuel tanks. The geysers that rose high above the conning tower drenched the gun crew in white water that washed the loader overboard. Filling in, the Master Gunner fed shells into the breech as fast as the petty officer could track, aim, and fire. Still the cruiser bore down on them with her curved bow projecting menace like a raised scimitar.

"This is cutting it too close," Gunner's Mate Masataki Enamoto declared."

Another torrent of seawater swept over the hull and funneled down the open hatches in a flood that left the corridors awash. Yet the mixture of brine and sweet air that spread into each available corner of the submarine was more welcome than breath itself. All but one man aboard sucked in deep gulps that made his face glow.

"I can feel the gods invade my soul with these last breaths of fresh air," Seaman First Class Keisuki Takarabi sighed to a comrade. "I would hate to die alone."

Yet no voice, fresh air, or sea spray got past the watertight door that sealed off the forward torpedo room. Inside that battle-rigged compartment a giant of a man kept watch over a ceremonial candle that cast its yellow flame on the curved and sweat soaked bulkheads. With each toss and lurch of the hull the young warrior raised a leg and restructured his balance with a sharp stamp.

"Uuuggh uh," Master Kempei Mukai grunted to himself. "Wait for the signal."

Carefully, the champion Sumo wrestler took off his saffron robe and black ceremonial sash. Once they were folded and set neatly on the deck he snuffed out the candle and doused himself in fresh water as the red warning light began to flash. Barely audible, the coarse filaments in the signal light gave off an almost imperceptible ping with each flash. Focusing on that, the giant wrestler composed himself for the final act. Naked, except for the thick band of cloth that circled his ample waist and swept around between his powerful legs, he stood back to give his stomach breathing room. Weighing in at four hundred fifty-two pounds he did a dozen deep-knee bends and long meditative squats that soaked his skin in sweat. Then he bowed to the heavy missile hanging suspended in a torpedo cradle. With each heave and roll the thick-bellied blockbuster twisted and swung like a seal fresh out of the sea. Breathing hard, the wrestler addressed it in reverential tones:

"In the peal of the bell,
Echoes the impermanence of all things.
Thus, even the mighty become
No more than dust before the wind."

Composed for the final stroke, Sumo Master Kempei Mukai took the curved fire axe from its box and felt it for heft and balance. A swing of the blade gave him the feel of handling the tool with grace in cramped quarters. Alert, he watched until the battle lamp gave off a soft but steady red light. In that stillness the all-metal compartment and the solid flesh of Yokozuna Mukai took on a ruby glow. From his ankles to his neck, each muscle flexed and held firm until his thick legs, wide waist, massive chest, and stout arms all tensed as tight as a hawser hauling up a ship's anchor.

"Now," the massive giant breathed softly. "Eeeyai ah."

A final turn brought the axe around in an unencumbered swing that struck the nose of the missile a sharp but measured blow. His straight spine, the careful stroke, his composed face, and the short ponytail of combed hair that hung down his neck suffused his entire being with <u>hinkaku</u>. The measured shock of metal contact traveled the length of the shiny steel casing and triggered the impact fuse in the tail. The gun-barrel detonator fired its charge down through the center of the nine thousand-pound weapon and exploded the captured American atom bomb.

CHAPTER ELEVEN

Terrorism is the use of a-moral force
Against immoral power,
Which is a lesson
The Arabs and Israelis have down to a science
And the Irish have etched on their souls.

The atomic explosion vaporized the Sumo wrestler as time and substance collapsed in the instantaneous outburst of energy. The brilliance of a thousand suns shredded his skin, evaporated his blood, and disintegrated his bones. The harsh, blast melted the surrounding heavy bulkheads and dissolved the steel shell of the compartment into a wall of expanding white heat that consumed everyone aboard. In a billionth of a photoflash, the flesh of the twenty-six man skeleton crew vanished from bones that became wisps of calcium in the holocaust.

The Japanese sonar striker tracking the screws of the attacking cruiser flew back with his swivel chair as his body exploded. The sonar master calling out the shortening distance of a full spread of approaching torpedoes from a destroyer nearby choked on the heat that burned his tongue to a crisp. The chief engineer adjusting an overhead valve had no flesh on his fingers by the time the bones disconnected. The captain addressing the periscope became a part of the cup enclosing the eye-piece as flesh and rubber fused. Each man etched a momentary shadow of his existence on to nearby steel surfaces even as the submarine suffered a spontaneous melt down.

With the roar of a volcanic eruption, the dissolved Japanese submarine merged with a great geyser of boiling ocean water as it turned into a froth of foam. The nuclear explosion spread a dome of unearthly yellow light and bronze streaked heat out over the ocean for a mile in every direction. The shock wave that accompanied the blast tore the hundreds of tiny American landing craft from the sea like leaves swept up in a hurricane. The small troop carriers, the LCIs swarming with infantry, the LSTs loaded with tanks, and the huge troop transports all rose up and tumbled into nothingness in the heat and the firmament that churned the atomic mist hovering between the deep and the sky.

Marines in full combat dress had the flesh peeled back from their foreheads, cheek bones, and jaws as they died with freshly exposed skulls and hands turned into charred burls and claws. The corporal and his squad, the helmsman and his crew, as well as the major along with an entire company, all suffered horrible extinction. The blood swelled up from inside and burst out through charred skin festered with boils. Thousands on thousands of Marines, sailors, and soldiers broiled to death in that lethal foam.

The giant fireball that consumed the flotilla of landing craft swallowed a dozen warships it sucked up from the sea. The spread of advancing torpedoes melted away and exploded all at once. The attacking cruiser and the accompanying destroyer bearing down on the Japanese submarine rose up like prancing steeds and dissolved. The sixteen-inch thick armor plate that enclosed the citadel of the battleship New Mexico melted down into an outer cover of liquid steel that turned the ship into a superheated oven. Several light cruisers as well as four fast fleet destroyers simply ceased to exist. The scarred bodies of Marines hardened by combat on Saipan, Tarawa, and Guadalcanal burst apart and burned by the thousands.

The fire-storm that engulfed the rest of the troop ships and their nearby escorts roared like a gigantic open hearth furnace. Wild waves of orange and white heat caught soldiers and sailors in midstride and fixed the shadows of their vaporized bodies on steel bulkheads charred black by the blast. The entire invasion force marshaled for the initial assault on the beaches was cremated in molten hulls turned into smoldering incinerators before they sank.

All around the spreading ring of carnage, thin-skinned destroyers and armor plated light cruisers erupted in cascades of explosions as fires inside their gun turrets and powder magazines blew the warships apart. The battleships exploded with such force that huge sixteen-inch gun turrets rose hundreds of feet in the air with their crews inside. A witness, disemboweled by the blast, offered up a spontaneous sentiment with his last breath.

"I have seen the wrath of man," the coxs'n whispered. "I need not fear the wrath of God."

The blast wave that leaped across the line of sinking battleships swept badly scorched merchant seamen into the ocean. Relentlessly, it drove row after row of cargo ships over on their sides like a convoy struck by a typhoon. The nuclear wind behind the shock wave sandblasted men and ships with hot granules that penetrated flesh and paint to set bones and hulls afire. The chains holding down smoldering howitzers, smoking Sherman tanks, and blazing supply trucks gave way. The sprawling deck cargoes carried everything in their paths as they went overboard and plunged into the sea. Below decks, shifting cargoes cracked and crushed stunned freight handlers like raw eggs in a basket of bricks. On the sea, the hot light that raced out ahead of the surging blast blinded look outs aboard the cruiser designated as the admirals permanent flagship twenty miles away.

"The sun is rising in the west, out of the sea," Fleet Admiral William F. Halsey rasped as his eyes melted and his bronzed face puff up with fatal flesh burns. "And it has swallowed the whole damned fleet!"

"You warned the general about Shibushi Bay, Admiral," Lieutenant Commander George Tomkins shouted despite the hot flash that dissolved the lenses of both eyes. "But the pig-headed fool insisted that a small gulf, shaped like a deep bowl, was just what he wanted for the opening of an armed yet sheltered invasion on a broad front."

The shock wave expanded its lethal ring for thirty miles all around. Held in its cruel central grip, shattered remains of the invasion fleet rose like a shimmering crystal chandelier to destroy the planes skimming over the beaches. A Grumman Avenger banking into the atomic storm had its greenhouse smashed. The Sperry ball turret rolled out of its socket with the gunner inside just as the wing folded up and the torpedo bomber tumbled backwards in a horizontal spin. The blast tore the wings off dive-bombers and fighter planes and sent them plummeting into the ground like rockets. A trim SB2C Helldiver let loose its bomb and completed its pull out just as the wicked clear-air turbulence struck. The shock knocked the plane over backwards and tumbled it nose over tail until the heat set its fuel tanks on fire and the explosion blew it out of the sky.

All around the bay, the blue and pink cloud of flame that advanced behind a purple wave of compressed air knocked down the bombers returning to refuel. That roaring wild wind also destroyed three squadrons of Helldivers heading in to attack. Planes thrust forward like surfers on a wave smashed into the tails of squadron mates thrown into a stall by the same iron hand of heat. And the rigid dome of compressed air reaching for the heavens wiped out the fighter planes flying top-cover. Struck and pummeled from beneath, a Grumman F6F Hellcat flipped over and floated atop the updraft for five thousand feet before exploding into a shower of bits that continued to rise.

In moments, the number of American lives lost, ships sunk, and tanks and planes destroyed in the Pacific doubled. More slowly, the living gathered their strength for a struggle that had only begun.

"Emergency steerage," Admiral Bill Halsey ordered just before he collapsed and died. "Due west into the maelstrom."

The cruiser, Tuscaloosa, shorn of its bridge and dragging a mangled superstructure, deliberately turned toward the source of the blast. As the senior officer still alive in the wreckage, Lieutenant Commander George Tomkins was determined to bring his ship to the aid of any survivors.

"Steady as she goes," George Tomkins directed despite his blindness. "Prepare to lower life boats."

Unheard and unattended, the muffled voice of the dying admiral's aide continued to issue directions until the breath in his mangled and scorched lungs expired. Nearby, sailors dragging along their crushed limbs and tattered strips of charred flesh moved slowly to comfort the dying. Men soaked in their own blood and barely able to stand fought raging fires with hoses that writhed in their grip like angry boa constrictors.

"Before the water from the hose travels twenty feet it turns to steam," a scorched fireman complained as he collapsed. "It's like pissing into a blast furnace."

Aboard merchant ships, wipers and electricians became boiler tenders and helmsmen on vessels wallowing in the heavy seas that broke over their sides. All through the ships still afloat, men shouted, cried, pleaded, swore, and worked in dogged silence as they fell back on habit in the struggle to gain control over the chaos that ruled their tiny sea-going domains.

"Who left these empty davits unsecured?" Third Mate Bucky Walker demanded. "The block and tackle alone can take a man's head off in a blow like this."

Out on the fantail of a crippled destroyer escort, the fifty-year-old chief petty officer up from below hacked at the tangled rigging that cluttered the buckled deck. As soon as the hatch leading down to the engine room was cleared and open, he rushed below to fight the fires. Like so many aboard sinking ships, he scurried about with a demonic energy fueled by scorn.

"If those lousy Japs don't watch out," Chief Walter Danby muttered, "they're gonna make us mad."

The same fierce determination surfaced wherever men found their ship in trouble. Aboard the aircraft carriers, yellow and green shirted plane handlers shoved wrecked planes overboard and cleared the flight decks for take-off and landing operations. Wherever the devastation reached, deeply ingrained customs dictated automatic responses to danger. Working the crank of the klaxon horn, the safety officer covered the listing deck of a burning fast fleet carrier with a squawk that hovered between a croak and a turkey gabble.

"All hands keep clear of spinning propellers," Ensign Andy Ralston warned nonsensically over the loudspeaker. "Nobody crosses the deck during landing or take-off operations."

Everywhere, battered, burned, broken, and dying sailors struggled to shake off the effects of the initial blast and fight for the life of their ship. Yet over twenty miles to the north of the suffering armada, the two Navy dive-bombers chasing the Korean whaler and the Japanese glider were just being engulfed by the monstrous windstorm.

"We're in for it," Max Bryson warned. "The beach has rolled up into a wet sandstorm."

A torrent of loose sand and torn up ground cover tumbled over the sheltering crest of Toi Point. The rainbow of eerie light blinking on and off in the giant mushroom dome rising high in the air gave a yellow and green glow to the mist racing over the ground. Momentarily shielded from the advancing destruction, the radio-gunners in the rear seats of their Helldivers swiftly came up with evasive action.

"Get rid of the bombs," Carson Braddock urged. "They're dragging us down."

A great curl of grit-laden air rolled over the mountain and covered the chartreuse mist. The rapidly moving turbulence darkened the sky like an eclipse. The slashing wind flipped the Helldivers over on their sides and slammed them down toward the sea. Instinctively, both pilots worked the stick hard and advanced the throttle to emergency power so the torque would help pull the heavily loaded dive-bombers through the involuntary snap roll.

"Fire off the rockets and dump the napalm canisters," Max Bryson insisted. "The extra weight acts as an anchor."

In the rear cockpits, the paired thirty-caliber machine-guns threatened to break free from their steel tracks and the belted ammunition spilled out of the stacking cans. Caught with their seat-belts unfastened, the gunners held themselves in by curling their arms under the modified Scarff-rings and gripping the wayward machine-guns from underneath.

"I'd rather do a barrel roll on a toboggan," Carson shouted to himself. "With a pregnant hippopotamus strapped to the bottom."

Neither pilot managed to lighten the load so the looping roll-out cost them nearly a thousand feet and brought both planes around just above the spume of the breakers. Soaked in spray, sandblasted by debris, scratched, and slashed from the twisted belts of ammunition, the gunners wiped their goggles and reestablished radio-contact as they caught their breath. The soot and grit that covered their faces made them look as grimy as sandhogs wearing goggles. The radio interference forced them to speak in clipped phrases.

"That Jap glider pilot—is making it ashore," Carson Braddock gasped. "But that fucking downdraft—slapped his sailplane—into the surf—like a swatter clobbering a dragon-fly."

"You don't need to worry—about that wooden whaler—going to sea again," Max reported. "The high surf—and that God-damned tidal-wind—washed her up on the rocky ledge—above the beach."

Both planes climbed away from the coast and fought the dust-shrouded turbulence that poured over Toi Point. The radio-gunners straightened up their cockpits and switched the cog-wheeled tuners on their ANARC 13 transceivers to a short-range frequency for clearer transmission and reception.

"Speak up—for Christ's sake," Max's pilot demanded. "The static is worse——than chattering chipmunks—fucking on a metal roof."

As the pilots and radio-gunners looked up from their tasks, the sky ahead opened out into a layered panorama of vividly stratified clouds pierced by an angry column on the rise. Solid and violent in its thrust toward the stratosphere, the great shaft of atomic debris stood out as a monstrous pillar of the heavens themselves.

"Oh sweet mercy," Carson murmured. "That churning mushroom cloud must be pushing up through fifty thousand feet."

"The shaft has got to be two miles wide," Max supposed. "And the thunder head is boiling with purple, green, and jet-black clouds filled with flashes of pink and yellow florescent fire."

"Keep away from that monstrous funeral tower," Carson advised. "There is nothing but death by Hell-fire inside."

On his rear seat gunner's warning, Carson's pilot banked their Helldiver away and led the other plane around the black rain that fell from the atomic cloud. Up wind from the nuclear storm, the two dive-bombers dropped down over the bay and circled the remains of the devastated invasion fleet.

"Jesus," Carson sighed. "We missed being part of that by a hair's breadth."

As the surface of the sea settled, the bright morning sun sent long lime and amber shafts of light through the water. The soft beams broke up as they descended and covered the bottom with bronze bands separated by wavy green lines. The striped illumination that drifted across the bottom picked out each of the sunken warships and made them look like neatly ribbed skeletons on a sandy beach. But the shimmering glow that fell on the vessels still afloat was what held the fliers' attention.

"Burning wrecks, overturned hulls, sinking derelicts, and hulks battered beyond recognition," Max catalogued. "I have never seen such total devastation."

"There are more bodies floating around down there than I can count," Carson lamented. "And not a raft or a life boat in sight."

Initially, the wreckage and the carnage spread out across the bay concealed all signs of life and movement like a bunch of wood-chips hiding termites. As seasoned observers, however, the aircrewmen's eyes peered into the corners and the edges of the disarray even before the young fliers set their shock and their dismay aside.

"Counting ship's company and soldiers in landing craft," Carson Braddock surmised, "there must have been a hundred fifty thousand men in the initial invasion fleet."

Peacock swirls in the green water drew the aviators' glances to the twisting wake of a landing craft making headway under its own power. The pale splashes of a swimmer striking out toward a floating spar thrust a touch of drama on to the littered sea. But the flashes of several explosions in quick succession drew their eyes to the fighting going on in the hills beyond the beach.

"Oh, shit. That's got to be heavy artillery," Carson commented. "And it looks like it's all one sided."

"We've got a whole fuckin' division of ParaMarines in there," Max declared. "Those poor bastards don't have anything heavier than mortars and anti-tank guns. I shit you not."

"We seem to be the only ones still flying," Carson observed. "I guess it's up to us to give our troops a little air-to-ground support."

The wide-winged Helldivers banked in-shore together and

climbed up over the closely packed array of steep hills that rose behind the beach. The patches of white smoke drifting over the trees showed where the Japanese field guns were positioned.

"Give us a minute before you attack," Carson advised his pilot. "That snaproll created a bloody mess back here."

The radio-gunners worked hard untwisting their ammunition belts, re-laying them in the feeder-cans, and clearing their machine-guns with test bursts. The pilots armed the rockets slung beneath their wings and opened the bomb bay doors in the bellies of the Helldivers. Primed and trimmed for low-level assault, the dive-bombers nosed down on the enemy guns.

"The Japs don't have a single anti-aircraft gun protecting their heavy batteries," Max Bryson declared. "The bastards must have known that just about all of our planes would be swept from the sky."

"I don't see our guys getting any reinforcements much before Gargantua turns gray." Carson Braddock concluded. "They are heavily outnumbered with their backs to the sea."

The grit-scoured dive-bombers fell on the Japanese heavy artillery like a pair of tattered hawks dropping down on ground hogs. The Helldivers' twenty-millimeter cannons cut down the enemy pointers, loaders, spongers, and rammers as the planes released their bombs and napalm canisters. The four anti-personnel bombs overturned two of the Kawasaki ten-ton gun carriages and tore off the breech on a third Arisaka howitzer. The M-47 A-2, one hundred pound canisters of jellied napalm, set off dozens of powder sacks laid around the firing station like sandbags. The massive explosion shot streams of liquid fire high in the air and blew the Mitsubishi tow trucks over on their sides.

"Our men have to withdraw to the beaches," Carson insisted. "Quick."

Shooting into the grease darkened smoke and the bright orange flames, the Navy rear-seat gunners picked off burning soldiers and gun-handlers escaping from the blaze. It was a swift and flawless attack that wiped out the enemy guns in less than four minutes.

"Lord knows what they'll do when they get there," Max replied.

"The whole bay is a wasteland."

The scuffed Navy Helldivers circled the destroyed gun position once and withdrew with their propellers at flat pitch. The racket seemed to come from their shadows racing up and down the recently denuded hills like broad winged eagles intent on flushing a hidden quarry out into the open. Instead of running, however, the seasoned Japanese ground troops froze in their tracks and refused to look up as the planes flashed overhead. As soon as the danger passed they continued their advance on the bomb-damaged farmhouse near the junction. Methodically, the officer and the non-com in charge worked their men into position with hand signals.

"As soon as we take this outpost, Sergeant-san," Colonel Matome Tadashi ordered. "Bring up the tanks."

"It will be done, Excellency," Sergeant Major Yokio Yamashita affirmed. "Between the advancing armor and our infantry charges, the main body of enemy troops will be squeezed together and driven toward the shore like herring in a fisherman's funnel."

The sergeant major's whistle sent a barrage of mortar fire into the farmyard as the Japanese foot soldiers broke from the woods. American snipers shooting from the half-collapsed roof of the barn dropped a dozen of the colonel's men before the attackers reached the shelter of a rough-hewn stone wall. Charging ahead, a nineteen year old Burma Trooper took a hit in the chest and a round in the hip that doubled him over yet he managed to carry his eighty pound box of hand grenades up to the farm yard gate before he died. Mortar shells and hand grenades set the barn on fire and drove the American Marines down into the cobblestone yard where they shot it out from behind the corn crib, a dead mule, and an empty hay wagon. As Colonel Tadashi brought the rest of his men up behind the stone wall the Yanks pulled back into the shattered main farmhouse. Breathing hard from the long run, Sergeant Major Yamashita covered his squad with his sub-machine-gun as the riflemen slipped over the unmortared wall. He worked in clip after clip and shot up an enemy machine-gunner and his loader as they dragged their heavy weapon and ammunition boxes toward the house. His expert use of the weapon brought high praise.

"From now on we ought to call you The Chopper instead of me, sergeant-san," Colonel Matome Tadashi declared. "Those poor bastards never knew what hit them."

As he spoke, the colonel stood up and made ready to mount the low wall. Strong, thick-bodied, carrying a bit of stomach, yet lean, compact, and well into his fifties, he lacked the spry scramble of the younger men. Without warning, the sergeant major brought the short barrel of his sub-machine-gun around like an axe and struck the colonel a blow across the stomach that doubled him up on the spot.

"Sorry, most honorable Excellency," Sergeant Major Yokio Yamashita apologized. "These Yankee-dogs are good. You must roll over as flat as a patient on a stretcher or not at all."

Without giving the colonel a glance, the sergeant major swung his sub-machine-gun around and covered the action. The burst of enemy gunfire from inside the house whistled around his ears as he opened up on the American who leaped out through the ground floor window. But his concern for the colonel broke the sergeant major's concentration. Even though he opened fire with his weapon resting atop the wall the bullets zipped and bounced all around the American corpsman charging out into the courtyard. Dodging with the agility of a panther under fire, Corpsman Casey Dworkin grabbed the wounded gunner by the shoulders of his battle jacket and dragged the man inside amid a shower of gunfire that chipped the stone and stucco doorway all around. Then to the amazement of his comrades he darted out again and brought the loader in on his back.

"I swear I don't know how you do it," Gunnery Sergeant Marty Mann declared. "A rifleman couldn't cover ten feet out there without being hit."

"Maybe you should all put on red-cross arm bands," Corporal Dworkin replied. "All we do is dance between the bullets."

The corpsman and the gunnery sergeant stemmed the bleeding and treated the bullet wounds with sulfa drugs and sterile bandages from the field kit. The company was divided into three groups. Gunny Mann's downstairs defense unit barricaded the battered doors and blown out windows against hand grenades. Upstairs, Corporal Tony Regni's assault-repulsion squad kept the enemy riflemen hunkered down behind the farmyard wall. In the ruined attic Corporal Vinnie Cantelmo's snipers took stock of the enemy forces moving up beyond mortar and normal rifle range. And to keep them all in touch with each other, the radioman moved up and down the beat-up staircase like an indecisive peeping Tom. The bulky field radio strapped to his back forced him to rest on each landing while he caught his breath.

"Now that da wind storm has died down—I got dem Navy fly-boys on da horn," Private Jackson Grady out of Detroit shouted down the staircase. "They're comin' back—to dust up da Nips again."

Incoming shells, outgoing mortar rounds, and the pounding of the machine-guns filled the disheveled farmhouse and bomb damaged barnyard with a terrible din. Over it all the sharp crack of rifle fire rang out like an angry bark. Intense small-arm fire from the upstairs windows forced several Japanese riflemen to take shelter behind the chicken coop. Each round of sniper fire from the attic dropped a Japanese soldier climbing over the wall. And those Japs that made it into the yard fired at the house from the corners of the pigsty and the donkey stable.

"Hunker down," Private Grady warned. "Here comes Navy air."

The intense struggle for command of the yard drowned out all other noises until the two Helldivers skimmed in over the trees. Suddenly, the roar of their engines smothered the farm in a blanket of destruction. The five-inch rockets they fired into the cobblestone yard drove the enemy soldiers away from the burning storage bins and sheds.

"Concentrate on the Japs in the farmyard," Carson told his cousin. "I'll get the ones behind the wall."

The aerial gunners strained against the forces of the shallow pull out and the tight turn that kept their shooting radius short. As their planes banked and swung around just above the trees, Carson Braddock and Max Bryson fired into the enemy positions. Long bursts of aerial machine-gun fire cut through the ranks of Burma soldiers crouched behind the stone wall. Short bursts picked off half of the foot soldiers running for the trees. The string of bullets that chased an enemy corporal away from the corncrib suddenly hammered across his shoulders and whipped his limp body around. The Japanese soldier's arms flew out as he turned like a loose-limbed dancer in a spin. His collapse and skid across the cobblestones brought a cheer from the farm house.

"A well done from Fox Company, Navy," Gunny Mann shouted over the field radiophone. "Now pay attention. We need more ammunition, medical supplies for our wounded, and some food. Otherwise we can't hold this outpost until the invasion forces reach us. Over."

The request took the two radio gunners by surprise. Deep in enemy territory and out of touch with what remained of the fleet, the paratroopers had no way of knowing what had taken place off shore. All they knew of the atomic explosion was the fierce shock wave that had rattled the farmhouse so hard half of it collapsed. It fell to the fliers to break the news.

"Forget it," Max advised over the scratchy airwaves. "The backup units that weren't cremated in mid-air or demolished off shore were called back. Right now there's nobody on the beach."

"The invasion is off," Carson confirmed. "The entire assault force has been wiped out. Your additional supply drops have been cancelled. Fox Company is on its own. Over."

The news and the advice made no sense to the gunnery sergeant who had seen his men through six island invasions. Even in the darkest hours the Marines of Fox Company had always known that they were not on their own. Suddenly, the messengers flying overhead became an irritant the gunnery sergeant major could do without.

"Either get us some help in a fuckin' hurry or get your cock-cradling asses out of here," Gunny Mann insisted. "A joke like that we don't need."

The shellfire creeping in toward the farmhouse let up and the rumble of mechanized equipment filled the air. Looking for help, the snipers in the attic swung their binoculars away from the battle and scanned the five-mile belt of scorched earth that followed the crescent of the bay. Both groups reported their findings to the breathless radio operator working between floors. He, in turn, relayed the bad news downstairs.

"We got Jap medium tanks coming over the hill some three miles up the road," Jackson Grady called out, "And the boys on the roof tell me that the whole God-damned invasion fleet has been replaced by a lot of burning garbage scows."

Shells from the distant tanks tore the remains of the roof apart and forced the snipers and the observers to abandon the attic. Three fifty-seven millimeter shells from the nearest fourteen ton Chi-Ha burst through the ruined outside wall and bloodied the squad on the second floor. Fragments of hot steel tore a strip of scalp off a junior radio operator's head because his earphones made it awkward for him to wear a helmet. A partially spent round smashed through the shoulder of the machine-gunner from Canton, Ohio, and sent splinters of bone through his lungs. Debris from the round that exploded against a mirror covered the back of the corporal from Fernly, Nevada, with a mixture of shrapnel and glass that turned his flesh raw with wounds.

"They're getting our range," Gunny Mann told his leading corporal. "We've got about five minutes to make our move."

Alarmed, Corporal Tony Regni sent a runner across the road to make sure that Colonel Michael Jeffers' anti-tank gun had a clear field of fire once the enemy got within a mile of the farm. As he went back on the radio to send for naval gun support he received an unexpected call over the combat frequency.

"Fox Company. Fox Company. Do you read me?" the voice inquired. "This is Top Cover Leader. Come in. Over."

"Top Cover Leader this is Fox Company," Gunny Mann answered. "Make it quick. We are under tank attack. Over."

Two-inch shells from the Japanese Chi-Has worked away at the thick but badly damaged stucco walls on the ground floor of the Japanese farmhouse. Their staccato pounding shook the building like a demolition crew swinging a dozen sledge hammers. Seen from the air, the spread out enemy tanks seemed to move as slowly as a half dozen horseshoe crabs surrounding a stranded jelly-fish.

"O.K. Fox Company. Here it is in a nut shell," Aviation Radioman First Class Carson Braddock stated in a deliberately deepened voice. "Your company has been ordered to lead the withdrawal to the beach."

"You, and whatever other companies you can scrape up, must dig-in behind the driftwood logs," Aviation Radioman Max Bryson added with a gravity that tacked on a few extra years to his voice. "You must create a corridor so the entire division can be evacuated under enemy fire."

The changes in delivery distracted the gunnery sergeant for a moment. The blood on his hands from bandaging the radio operator's scalp wound made the field radiophone slippery. Between the static and the incoming rounds he lost track of just who was on the line.

"By who's orders?" Gunny Mann demanded. "On what authority?"

"By order of the senior surviving tactical commander," Carson Braddock declared. "The top-dog with the big picture. No one else can decide whether you should stay or go."

"He damned-well better outrank Colonel Jeffers across the road," Marty Mann stipulated. "Iron Mike don't like to retreat. No how."

The challenge drove the two naval aircrewmen to trade glances across the airspace that separated their dive-bombers. The exchange of a thumbs up signal was all it took for the cousins to continue with the masquerade.

"Then it's up to you to convince him," Max Bryson insisted. "And you better get the word out to the rest of the division."

"The invasion is off. There will be no further support," Carson said. "Radiation from the atomic explosion makes long-distance radio transmission a sea of static. So don't waste your time looking for confirmation from the high command. This is the only order you're gonna get."

"Thanks a lot," Gunny Mann murmured. "It might be easier all around just to persuade the Japs to surrender. Over."

The radio signal faded and left the frequency filled with static. Numbed, the gunnery sergeant was about to hang up the field-phone and finish tying off the radioman's head bandage when the more authoritative of the two voices reappeared.

"Be sure to get whatever is left of your men down to the beach as soon as you can," Carson directed. "The evacuation fleet will meet you there. All ships must be fully loaded and pulling away from shore by noon. Out."

On the radio gunners' hand signals to each other's pilot, the two Navy Helldivers broke away from the farmhouse together. A shallow dive took them further inland from the junction defended by Fox Company and down over the hills that sheltered the main enemy strike force. Partially concealed by their engine-muffling glide, the SB2Cs fired their remaining rockets at the tanks coming down from the hills. The five-inch solid fuel missiles streaked down at the leading Chi-Has like a flight of smoke-fletched arrows. The explosions derailed a turret on the leading tank, stripped the tractor treads off the next one in line, and ignited another tank's diesel engine. As the planes flashed by overhead, each of the rear-seat gunners picked off an enemy tank-man running for the trees. The plane's climb out and the wide turn away toward the bay gave the Navy fliers a chance to get back on the air to each other.

"What evacuation fleet?" Max Bryson demanded. "I don't see any boats coming into the bay. Hell, the carriers haven't even launched any planes yet. Over."

"The Max and Carson Armada," Carson Braddock replied. "We are about to launch our own bathtub fleet. Over."

"You're out of your mind," Max declared. "How the fuck are you gonna do that?"

Dark and dulled by battle smoke, the SB2C Helldivers streaked out across the bay and circled over the few vessels that looked as if they might be sea worthy. Each pilot gauged the strength and direction of the breeze by watching the smoke drifting across the clearly defined ripples. The radio-gunners flying in the rear cockpits had little to do but stare down and mull over the choice that the disaster presented.

We can return to the fleet, Carson mused, *and be heralded for our miraculous survival.* Equally puzzled, his cousin questioned his own instinct. *It might be best if we stayed here,* Max supposed in silence. *And do what?* But reflection was a luxury neither of them could afford. With time and fuel running out, a decision had to be made.

"Right," Carson allowed. "The only sane thing to do is to write off those poor Marines back there and fly home. Fox Company and the rest of the division will understand. I shit you not."

The one cousin's angry, cold-blooded assessment brought the other one around. Even so, both rear-seat gunners studied the scene below in a state of delayed shock.

"By noon our planes won't have enough fuel left to ride shotgun," Max lamented, "even if we could conjure up an evacuation fleet out of thin air."

Chilled as their Helldivers descended closer to the surface of Shibushi Bay, the young enlisted fliers scanned the great expanse of green water coated with a golden shimmer laid down by the sunlight. Relentlessly, they searched for signs of life anywhere on that wreck-strewn bay and came up empty.

CHAPTER TWELVE

Each day, somewhere,
The old world dies
And a new one is born
In the most unlikely Eden.

Off in the distance the remains of the giant mushroom shaped cloud fanned out into layers of glittering ice crystal. Overhead, the jet stream spread its pink radioactive crown across the sky. And far below, the evenly paired, stripped down, and grit covered Curtiss Helldivers leveled off at two-thousand-five-hundred feet above the wreckage that littered Shibushi Bay.

"Not that I like it," Carson Braddock radioed to his cousin, "but this seems the only way."

"As my Dad would say," Max Bryson replied, "in for a penny in for a pound, irregardless."

In the rear cockpits, the radio-gunners made final adjustments to the straps on their parachute harnesses and made sure that the seat packs were buckled to the harness rings. After securing their machine-guns beneath the turtle back hood, they cranked it up to fit against the tail fin. Ready, Carson turned forward and spoke to his pilot over the inter-squadron frequency. His words were clear and firm. But the edge that fear put in his voice turned the demand into a plea.

"The moment you land," Carson Braddock advised, "pull together a strike force to cover the troop withdrawal and our make-shift evacuation. We'll be counting on you."

Alerted by his cousin's nervousness, Max checked the packaged liferaft in the canister just above his head. He secured the remaining smoke bombs in the open rack by his feet as well. A light tug at the

D ring fastened to the harness strap that crossed his chest assured him that the connecting wire would tear his seat pack open and release the pilot-chute when he yanked it in mid-air. Tense, anxious, yet determined to jump if Carson did, he made a strong appeal to his own pilot.

"Go straight to the Old Man," Max Bryson demanded. "Tell him we will need two rescue ships in close to the mouth of the bay. One for the able bodied Marines and the other for the dead and wounded that Fox Company and the rest of the division will be bringing with them."

The pilots drew their Helldivers abreast of each other, throttled back their engines, cracked open their dive brakes, and kicked right rudder. The lumbering dive-bombers eased into a smooth, flat skid that slowed the passage of air over the inside wing.

"Roger," Max's pilot replied. "Double wilco."

"The Captain can be a bastard," Carson declared. "But don't take no for an answer."

Neither pilot had ever had a crewman bail out of his aircraft. They loathed the thought of seeing their radio-gunners go over the side and parachute down into enemy waters littered with wreckage and dead Americans. But since it had to be done they offered their best advice and good wishes.

"Unbuckle before you hit water," Carson's pilot said. "The canopy can drown you."

"In a current," Max's pilot warned, "it becomes a sea anchor that drags you down."

Working quickly, the radio-gunners each dropped a smoke bomb as a wind gauge. Then they threw their firmly packed inflatable liferafts over the side and climbed out on to the root of the wing. The turbulent slip-stream tore at their goggle helmets, flight jackets, orange Mae Wests, and dangling parachute packs. Tightening their grip on the gun-track they hugged the fuselage and crouched on the trailing edge of the wing. The slashing slipstream added to the chill that risk stirred into their blood. Anxiety tore at their organs with razor sharp talons. Below them, the burning warships, floating wrecks, and dead bodies were all fixed in a gold and green ocean. Wherever they looked the surface of the sea was in chaos. Each derelict was an interlocking piece of a mangled puzzle pressed into just the wrong place. On that maddened seascape, the passage of an empty landing craft pushing through the debris looked especially bizarre. Only by concentrating hard could the jumpers keep track of their uninflated life rafts as their Helldivers swung around.

"God damn," Carson Braddock said in a shout that went unheard. "This IS insane!"

Half a mile up wind from the orange life rafts, Carson let go of his grip on the fixed Scarff ring and tumbled backwards off the wing. The sudden free-fall caught at his innards and stole his breath away. Swiftly, his hand clawed his chest and yanked the ripcord of his chute. The explosion of the canopy opening up overhead matched the shock the jolt threw into his stomach.

"Slow me down," Max yelled as he flashed by. "I am tumbling out of contro-o-o-l."

The turns and twirls that swung the sea and the sky together in dizzy streaks of blue and green filled Max with nausea. But a swift tug at his ripcord stopped the turmoil as soon as the white canopy pulled out of the pack. The parachute snapped open with the clap of a blown up paper bag. Stopped all of a sudden from a long free-fall, the harness straps cut into his groin with a cruel bite. The sudden chaffing vanished, however, as he looked up to see the huge nylon umbrella of his parachute crumble and spill away its overload of trapped air. Relieved, but still jittery, he watched the canopy swell out into a ribbed circle of bright cloth that let him fall at a reassuring pace. Encouraged, even though the air around him sizzled, Max was too keyed up to remain quiet.

"Crazy paratrooper." Max Bryson insisted. "Those creeps get to like this sort of thing."

"Don't you believe it," Carson Braddock replied from up above. "They hate it."

The rush of air through the vent at the top of their canopies gave audible breath to their gentle descent. The debris, the dead, and the wrecks beneath them floated on a stretch of sea so clear and smooth that each item seemed suspended in mid-air. The calm that overlay the chaos was just strange enough to drive them back to their idle chatter.

"Hell, it's a volunteer outfit, ain't it?" Max demanded. "They can't all be nuts."

"Each one has the same desire," Carson said. "He longs to be with guys who like to jump."

Fifty feet above the invisible surface, both men undid the buckles of their parachute harnesses and hung from the straps by their hands. Their speed over the water seemed to increase.

"You drop short of the raft," Carson urged. "I'll go long and we'll have her between us."

Max Bryson released his grip two stories up and fell into the glazed sea feet first. He sank like a spear thrust into a pond and the strong scissors kicks that brought him up to the surface left him gasping for breath. A quick look around located the uninflated orange bag containing the life raft a few hundred yards to the east. But it did not take long for him to discover that it was drifting away almost as fast as he could swim. Even so, he broke out in a fast crawl.

Carson Braddock rode his chute down until the toes of his ankle-top shoes touched the gentle swell. As soon as he let go, the water grabbed his feet and he splashed into the sea flat on his chest and face. Coughing and spitting salt-water like a drowning seal, he floated in place and let the packaged raft drift to him. A sharp tug on the lanyard released the gases that split the cylindrical bag open as the cousins inflated the two-man rubber dinghy. The relief of having the raft in their grasp took away some of their anxiety enough for them to kid one another.

"You went in like a cormorant," Max scoffed. "All beak and neck and half-folded wings."

The two young men climbed into the yellow rubber raft and broke out the paddles. The sea water they brought in with them forced them to bail it out by hand.

"Hell, I thought you would never come up," Carson replied. "Esther Williams you ain't."

The oar splashes and the sweat that trickled into their cuts combined with the heat and strain of paddling to turn the tiny raft into a torture chamber before they had gone a mile. The bodies they bumped aside and the ones they passed were all too limp and lifeless to investigate. A Marine with the scorched remains of his battle fatigues burned into his charred body bobbed up and down in the gentle surf like a full-sized quilted doll. Even the steady ground swells slowed them down.

"The rise and fall of the sea is so regular," Max said, "it's as if the earth were breathing."

"Or sobbing," Carson suggested. "Sobbing her exhausted heart out."

Between the heavy layer of low smoke and the slick green water, murmurs and moans of human suffering slithered across the still surface like long snakes of mortal pain. Yet it was the churn of an unmuffled engine approaching through the acrid mist that caught the rafters' attention.

"It sounds like one of those amphibious trucks," Carson declared. "But how the Hell can an empty DUK hold a straight course with nobody at the helm?"

"We will only get one chance as she motors by," Max concluded. "So we've got to be near enough to pluck the feathers off this ugly duck's back."

Both aircrewmen paddled furiously as the olive green personnel carrier broke through the surface haze. Each of its four heavily tired drive wheels kicked up a spume of white water tarnished with oil and debris. Since she carried no troops, the high freeboard and the level gunnels made the two and a half-ton vessel look like a short and fat dugout as it bore down on the raft. At the last moment, Carson Braddock leaped up from a crouch and grabbed the cloth fender that hung draped across the bow. The kick from his vigorous lunge spun the tiny raft around on top of the bow-wave and forced Max to catch hold of the mat suspended along the side of the hull amidships. Kicking and clawing at the ribbed freeboard, each sailor managed to keep his feet away from the tractor-tired wheels as he climbed up over the side. Winded, they sprawled out on the charred grate that held them above the murky water sloshing around in the bilge. In a minute, they rose up and took notice of the figure at the helm.

"OH LORD!" Carson agonized. "The poor bastard is half skeleton and half pot roast."

Gently, Carson Braddock eased the dead coxswain's stiff body away from the bent steering gear. The fingers clutching the spokes of the wheel broke as Max Bryson pried them loose.

"The heat was so intense it turned him into an instant flesh and bone statue," Max observed. "And yet it did not stop the engine, ignite the gasoline, or burn the rubber tires."

"That's because all the vitals are on the water line," Carson declared. "And the tires are constantly bathed in the sea."

Max wrapped the sailor's charred and leathery body in his own flight jacket and weighted it down with spare engine parts from the repair locker. Together, the fliers eased the coxs'n overboard and watched the remains sink through several layers of tight water swirls.

"Sorry we couldn't keep you aboard mate," Carson apologized. "The hands we need to bring off this evacuation will have to put death behind them."

"Besides," Max added. "Most of your shipmates are down there waiting for you."

A swift swing away from the sinking corpse, a few "S" turns, and a quick reverse gave Carson the feel of the clumsy craft. For a while they steered the DUK through the floating wreckage looking for survivors. A brief stop alongside a sinking mine sweeper yielded a few thousand rounds of ammo and an air-cooled fifty-caliber machine-gun that Max slotted into a weatherboard hole on the DUK's port bow. As they combed the edge of the blast area the landing craft moved through green and purple streaks of bunker oil that shimmered with pink in the bright morning sun. Each probe of the landing craft's boat hook separated a bobbing body from the soft and slick surface that surrounded it. The blond sailor with his face and flesh peeled back right down to the clean white skull had the remains of his powder blue chambray shirt wrapped around his neck like a threadbare silk scarf. Deftly, Max Bryson hooked the shredded cloth and gently laid it over the naked skull.

"Circle to port and come around," Max Bryson ordered. "That oil soaked carcass with the greasy rag-mop for a head is alive. I saw it move."

At the touch of the boat hook the grimy mass of stain and cloth rolled over and took hold of the wooden shaft. The jowled face and hairy chest were followed by torn dungarees and awkwardly kicking feet as Max helped the aging sailor up over the side and into the landing craft.

"I was playing dead," Chief Machinist Mate Walter Danby said. "In case you was a Jap."

"You are the first man we have seen," Max offered, "who isn't a burned roast or shark bait."

"I was below, in the engine room, when my destroyer escort went down with armed depth charges tied down on deck," Chief Danby explained. "At ninety feet the whole fuckin' fan-tail exploded and I rode up to the surface in a great bubble of air."

The chief machinist mate wiped his head and face with the tail of his suntan shirt. Then he twisted the seawater from the bottom of the garment before tucking it inside his pants. A swift tug at his loosely laced shoes had them off, emptied, and ready to be eased back on to his feet. Throughout the whole operation, however, he never took his eyes off the young fliers. Their very presence amazed him but every word they uttered gave him hope.

"We are looking for someone who can run one of those large landing crafts we saw from the air," Carson stated. "Any suggestions?"

"Get me a couple of deck hands and a bosun to take the helm," Chief Walter Danby declared, "and we're in business."

"All right," Carson shouted. "Things could break our way yet."

Encouraged, Aircrewman Max Bryson took off his flight jacket and raised it as a scruffy battle pennant on the DUK's stubby mast. Carson Braddock gave the vessel full throttle and headed out toward a graveyard of derelicts floating nearby. Swollen bodies rolled under the blunt bow. Charred corpses came apart against the thick tread of the fat tractor tires that turned them under. Dead men slid off the thick bow-wave often enough to give them the feeling of plowing up a graveyard. But the prospect of getting some of the trapped Marines out alive urged the young sailors on at the full six knots the vessel could manage. And that caused a problem.

"How long ya gonna waste fuel in enemy waters," Chief Danby

scolded. "Slow down a couple of knots and you'll double your range."

"Aye-aye, Pops," Carson replied. "Out here even Jap gas stations are few and far between."

At four knots, the twenty-six-foot long DUK churned up a gentler wake as it nosed down littered corridors and wound between capsized warships and smoldering hulks. An hour in the late summer sun made the dead float a bit higher than the living. That made survivors easier to spot.

"I've seen corpses before," Carson said. "But this carnage saps the very life out of you."

The all but naked bosun wearing nothing but shorts and socks caught their attention by poking his head up through surface litter like a curious sea otter. Nearby, the welts on the boiler tender's back showed through his wet shirt like black and blue lash marks as he struggled to swim away from capture. A mile away, the young seaman with a clawed chest propelled his upper body high above the crest of each swell so he could be seen over the wreckage. And the carpenter's mate floating upright in a kapok life vest yelled himself hoarse before they got around to picking him up. In addition, the half-drowned soldiers and Marines they pulled out of the water volunteered to help as soon as they drew a few lungs full of fresh air. Pleased with the haul, Chief Danby scanned the bay some distance from the center of the blast and picked out a vessel that looked ship-shape.

"Bring us up alongside that Landing Craft for Infantry with all its paint scorched and peeled on the seaward side," Big Walt Danby suggested. "Judging from her drift, the smoking cargo net, and the visible Plimsol line, she's empty and water tight."

"Find us a gentle beach." Bosun's Mate First Class Sandy Kitchner proposed. "We'll nose in through the surf and run the troops up the bow's port and starboard disembarking ramps."

The slab sided LCI was just under one-hundred-sixty-feet long. And the thin-skinned freeboard was topped by a tall deckhouse. The small fires still burning around her wheelhouse warned of dangers below. Still, the shimmering heat waves that hovered above her small twin stacks was all the encouragement her new captain needed.

"She's still got a head of steam," Chief Danby insisted. "Let's get this show on the road."

"Marines come with me," the Boiler Tender First Class ordered. "You can put some seawater on those fires as soon as I get the pumps started."

The mixture of Marines and sailors eyed the scorched cargo net as the tiny DUK drew up alongside the large landing ship. The swells and troughs that rolled easily along the buckled and dimpled hull of the larger vessel raised and dropped the small landing craft up and down like a yo-yo. Turning hard over at the helm while Max managed the throttle, Carson jammed the port quarter of his boat firmly against the ship's hull as the crew leaped up on to the cargo net. The swell that washed over the DUK's bow and swept across the net broke the grip of Seaman First Class Darcy Towers from Sinclaire, Wyoming. As he teetered backward, the bosun caught his arm and pulled him forward for a fresh handhold on the free hanging net.

"Organize a small relief party to take care of any hands still on board," Bosun Sandy Kitchner ordered. "Deep-six all the dead that ain't baked to the deck and give me the dog-tags."

Slowly and laboriously, the sailors and Marines climbed up the large rope squares of the hemp cargo net. Carson eased off on the wheel and took the DUK out of the shadow of the landing craft's hull. Feeling exposed, Max field-stripped the fifty-caliber machinegun he had mounted on the gunnel and lubricated the entire firing mechanism from the tiny grease pot he found in the drawer beneath the compass. He worked each movable part as he reassembled it. Then he dried and greased the belts of fifty-caliber ammunition with great care as he laid the leading round beneath the breech cover and slammed it shut. A surprise practice burst swung everyone's head around and brought the new commanding officer of the LCI out onto the bridge-deck. After exchanging brisk nods of reassurance, he waved the DUK off and stepped back inside the wheelhouse.

"Captain Danby thinks she's OK," Max said. "Now all he need is some passengers."

"Right," Carson said. "A Jap gunboat should be out here to pick over the wreckage soon."

Moving in toward the beach, the clapboard sided DUK wallowed through the outer line of breakers like a walrus on the hunt. A swift look at their watches convinced both fliers that they still had time to comb the water for survivors. A quick turn about sent them charging back through the breakers for practice and then out into deep water again. Awkward as it was, the thick wheeled DUK trod the waves like an ocean going jeep. A mile off shore the ground swells changed from blue to golden green as the sunlight reflected more directly off the sandy bottom. But the beauty was soiled by great patches of half bloated corpses tangled up in the floating debris.

"Easy, Skipper," Max cautioned. "We've got wounded two points off the starboard bow."

The DUK slowed to a crawl as Carson nosed the small landing craft into a pocket of cruelly mangled men moaning and moving about like small clusters of crippled water spiders. The legless Marine keeping his dead buddy's head above the waves while the salt water bleached his torn flesh pleaded to be left alone. The scorched and scalded officer lost so much skin when they tried to haul him aboard that his faint screams just faded into gasps as life and breath drained away.

"It's hard to know what to do," Max said. "Most of these men are beyond any help at all."

A quarter mile further from the beach the DUK came across a cluster of badly burned Marines clinging to a log-jam of twisted debris like half-drowned cats. The sergeant stayed in the water boosting the privates and non-coms up until the remainder of his squad was in the boat. The corporal helped Max haul the battered and retching sergeant in over the gunnel. He had a gash across his forehead that ocean brine had bleached almost white. The mixture of fat and flesh was swollen enough to look like a burst grapefruit rind.

"How the Hell did so many of you from the same unit manage to survive?" Max inquired. "Up until now we hadn't even found two men from the same ship."

"The shock wave flipped our Higgins Boat like a flap-jack on a griddle," the sergeant explained. "We were the ones under the overturned boat when the heat wave passed over."

Shaking his head in amazement, Carson steered the DUK further out to sea in search of a vessel to put the wounded aboard. In open water he came across a partially crippled quartermaster using his knotted pants as a float to save his strength. A brief chat during the rescue made it clear that he could take command of a sizable vessel if they could find another one in good condition.

"I've handled everything from an outrigger to a sea plane tender," Quartermaster Henry D. Northrop declared. "But the toughest was an eighty foot long propeller driven barge. She was powered by an eight hundred horsepower airplane engine mounted astern. We used her to scoot across Pensacola Bay. In a heavy chop that mother went airborne. I shit you not."

A high-speed search that drenched the passengers in spray turned up another one-hundred-fifty-eight-foot long Landing Craft for Infantry on the verge of going under. The battered sides and twisted wheelhouse of the LCI made it look like a beat up old crate that was about to fall apart. But garrulous "Hank" Northrop insisted that he could keep her together inside the bay.

"She ain't no queen," the forty-year-old Captain said. "But she can make it close to shore."

That was all Carson and Max needed to know. They unloaded their injured passengers on to the LCI and sped off in search of more survivors. In less than half an hour, the quartermaster and the sergeant's rifle squad had the LCI limping along. Just as swiftly, the DUK had put nearly three hundred additional wounded survivors aboard. In rapid order, the landing craft turned into a hospital ship. As soon as she got under way, however, she attracted unwanted attention.

Japanese spotters up in the hills had their mobile artillery send five-inch shells raining down around her in a ring of thunderous explosions. Bombs from heavy mortars along the shore kicked up waterspouts that drenched her decks as she maneuvered to picked up even more wounded. Still, the quartermaster at the helm kept the LCI sailing a tortuous course through the shallows as his lookouts spotted isolated knots of survivors. Bandaged, bent, pale from pain, and braced up against the wheel, the ageing captain of the LCI looked like a mummy reluctantly returned to life.

"You're on your own," Max shouted from the DUK. "We have to contact our troops on the beach before the Japs can move any more men and tanks up against them."

"Good luck," Quartermaster Henry Northrop shouted. "We will stand by to pick up strays."

The exchange was drowned out by the roar of carrier based aircraft passing overhead. The Grumman fighter planes and the long nosed Vought Corsairs rushed across the beach at masthead height. All along the hills five miles behind the shore-line they rose in graceful wing-overs and dove to the attack. As they dropped behind the hills the cousins returned to the rescue operation.

"It's too risky," Carson yelled. "We won't be able to help you if you founder or get hit."

"Even the dying want to help," Captain Northrop insisted. "Besides, you need a back-up."

Touched by the sentiment and encouraged by the quartermaster's dedication, Carson steered the DUK in toward shore. The heavily-tired landing craft thrashed across the undulating surface of the bay kicking up a wheel driven spume that dwarfed and soaked the squat vehicle. Under ever increasing enemy artillery fire Carson Braddock and Max Bryson gave no thought to drying out or saving fuel. Making almost ten knots as it picked up speed from the ground swells the DUK headed for the beach like a hippo in a hurry.

CHAPTER THIRTEEN

Heroism in battle
Is like fireworks,
Spectacular but insubstantial
Since the real gains are made
Step by blood soaked step
Thanks to the unsung warrior.

The mini-fleet of salvaged rescue vessels picked its way through the wreckage that littered Shibushi Bay. Inseparable from their unsteady wakes, the hulls of DUK-18, LCI-57, and LCI-32 looked like flat arrowheads fastened to cruelly twisted shafts. Overhead, the blue bellied Hellcats and bubble canopied Bearcats from the most distant aircraft carriers streaked in toward the shore ahead of the mighty roar of their air-cooled radial engines. Inland, the Navy fighter planes struck at enemy tanks with wide banks of fiery rockets and cascades of armor piercing bombs. As a follow-up, a full squadron of long nosed Marine Vought Corsairs hurried in toward the beach at masthead height. All along the hills five miles behind the shore, they rose in graceful wingovers and dove to the attack. The surprise assault turned a dozen motorized Chi-Has into metal crematoriums. Wheels down and landing flaps extended to slow their approach, the inverted gull wing Corsairs descended on the Japanese infantry like huge birds of prey. The napalm canisters and fragmentation bombs they dropped filled the air with great clouds of oil blackened smoke. The smoke clouds were lit up to a burnt orange and rusty charcoal hue by the flames that burst out from the instant ground fires that they started. The attack devastated major units of the Japanese attack force pushing toward the beach. The advanced patrols of enemy troops caught in the path of the drop were swallowed up like terrified animals in a forest fire. Nevertheless, Colonel Tadashi's ground assault continued. His seasoned troopers made a determined drive to populate the beach with snipers hidden in scooped out oyster holes. By keeping well separated and crawling in on a wide front, quite a few of the snipers avoided the worst of the American aerial attack. But planes from half a dozen aircraft carriers continued to attack in depth. The American fighter planes were followed by waves of dive-bombers and torpedo planes that stopped the major enemy advance and scattered any survivors not already protected by their sand bunkers. The airborne rockets and anti-personnel bombs thickened the light breeze with clouds of red dust so dense that the ground and the shoreline were blotted out. Japanese soldiers choked, staggered, and fell in the murky mess only to have their own tanks run them down in a mechanical stampede. Yet the enemy was not the only one to suffer from the thick clouds of red dust that rolled down the hills toward the sea.

Before a warning could be sounded, three American fighter planes skimming in off the sea in tight formation crossed the "death zone" in less than a minute and plowed into the sand dune that sheltered the scorched tree line. The flight leader flew his inverted gull wing aircraft into a fifty-foot high mound of white sand so dense that the impact drove the engine back through the cockpit with the force of a printing press. Each of his companions caught the side of the dune with a wingtip that sent their planes into the mangled forest doing a flat spin that cut scorched tree trunks down for a hundred yards. To prevent further losses, a Vought OS2U Kingfisher the color of a dirty clamshell dropped down until its massive main pontoon was only a few feet above the sand. Throttled back, the single engine scout plane flew back and forth along the twenty-mile curve of beach on the verge of a stall. As a slow but steadily moving spot of white, the mid-wing rescue plane gave the incoming pilots a visual fix on the shore. In addition, the lumbering scout plane radioed instructions to the senior flight commander who was coordinating the aerial assault.

"If you come in below our flight line you're dead," the Kingfisher's radio-gunner warned, "so buzz us like a hawk snatching a pigeon in mid-air. But keep your napalm canisters outa my greenhouse."

With each sweep along the shore the clamshell white Kingfisher attracted rifle and sub-machine-gun fire from the surviving Japanese soldiers dug in to confront any American troopers who stumbled ashore. Hits from the twenty-five caliber Japanese rifle bullets punched through the steel skin of the pontoon and the cowl of the Kingfisher with the ring of a flat dinner gong.

"The bastards fire and vanish before I can shoot back," the inexperienced rear-seat gunner complained. "At this rate it's only a matter of time before one of us gets picked off."

"The carriers have got to send in another wave of heavies to soak the beach six feet deep in flaming napalm," the exposed pilot advised. "The entire beach is infested with Japs who pop up out of their holes like ground hogs on a hot spring day."

The plea brought three more squadrons of TBF Avengers skimming in over the water with their bomb bay doors wide open. The rockets, bombs, and napalm canisters that the thirty-six planes dropped left a carpet of scorched sand from the shore to the tree line. The blast, shrapnel, and fire killed half the Japanese troopers dug-in beneath the surface. Concussion collapsed the sand walls on top of most of those still struggling to breathe inside their makeshift bunkers. The few survivors suffered dizziness, nose bleeds, and burst eardrums from the severe shock waves and pressure cones that rippled through the sand. It was often strong enough to pop the garbage can lids off their soggy oyster holes. But it was still indiscriminate bombing. As a result, the Marines making their way to the beach suffered from the "friendly fire" almost as much as the enemy. In the mixture of airborne soot that covered the battle zone, the smoke pots, ground flares, and orange panels that marked Fox Company's position were hard to see. Again and again, squadrons of Grumman Avengers, Curtiss Helldivers, and twin engine Grumman F7F Tigercats laced the charred tree line behind the beach with tons of napalm. The curtain of oil and gasoline flames that covered the escape corridor was repeatedly renewed even as long lines of bedraggled troops emerged from cover. In a desperate effort to escape the smoke and flames, the leading columns of the First Marine division rushed into the water and started wading out to the landing craft. Eager to help, the LCI serving as a hospital ship started in toward the breakers that curled and collapsed before skimming into the shallows as thinly layered shelves of powder blue surf.

"Warn LCI-32 off," Carson Braddock ordered as he drove the DUK up the beach. "Those outer breakers will snap her in half like a brittle twig."

"I can't," Max Bryson replied. "The flares went off when the heat wave roasted the cox'n."

"Do something," Carson demanded. "Or she's a gonner for damned sure."

Max Bryson raised the barrel of his fifty-caliber machine-gun to an elevation of forty-five degrees and fired off a long burst that went out beyond the breakers. By watching the smoke from the tracers, he walked the rounds over the water until the splashes cut across the LCI's bow.

"Less guts is better," Max urged. "We don't need a hospital ship crippled in the shallows."

Moments later, the enemy guns in the surrounding hills lobbed another barrage of shells at LCI-32. The cannonade of five-inchers hit and burrowed deep into the shallow bottom of the bay before they exploded. The mixture of water, mud, sand, shrapnel, and seashells that rose up issued a vivid warning. The shattered victims that the explosions threw aloft made the bay look as if the shallows were mined. And that was a possibility that the captain of the LCI could not ignore. Rather than risk what seemed like almost certain destruction, Quartermaster Henry Northrop turned LCI-32 away from the beach. Dismayed, the hundreds of troopers already in the water began to mill about like frantic minnows in a bombarded pond. Their plight soon caught the eye of Fox Company's second in command.

"Get those men out of the water and under cover," Gunnery Sergeant Marty Mann ordered. "It's too soon to go for the boats."

"Tell the sergeants to wait for the other boat to belly up to the beach," Colonel Iron Mike Jeffers insisted. "Then have the corporals run the men out on the double. I want LCI-57 loaded with all the able-bodied troops she can hold and pulling out to sea before the

Jap artillery can get her range. Is that clear?"

"Yes sir," Corporal Tony Regni affirmed. "What about the lame and the wounded?

"Send the colonel's orders and these instructions by your best messenger," Gunny Mann directed. "Each unit is to hold back a small able bodied patrol to take the injured and the available dead out to LCI-57 as soon as she clears the breakers. Remind them that the Marines don't leave nothin' but enemy dead behind."

Satisfied that the departures were properly organized, Colonel Michael Jeffers had his radioman re-direct the attacking dive-bombers away from the exit corridor and on to the enemy artillery back in the hills. A fresh wave of concentrated strafing and bombing slowed the enemy advance toward the beach. Japanese troops took eighty-percent casualties as they tried to overtake the Marines crossing the five-mile wide belt of scorched earth behind the high line of driftwood that rimmed the shoreline. That breather gave Fox Company time to dig-in along the exit corridor.

"I quote the Marine's Bible," Iron Mike said. "The first into battle shall be the last one out."

Barely within earshot, the sluggish and battle worn companies of the division gained strength and speed as they came within sight of the beach. Wherever an enemy soldier appeared in hot pursuit Corporal Vincent Cantelmo gunned him down with a hand held Browning Automatic Rifle. Encouraged, Gunny Mann's sidekick set the early arrivals to work shoring up their position.

"I want a forward battle line that eats enemy tanks for breakfast," Corporal Tony Regni demanded. "Give me a drop-back position so strong we can turn crocodiles away bare handed."

Despite the desperation of a ragged retreat under enemy fire, each unit had a leader who quickly sized up the situation on the beach and spoke for the surviving members of his company. To a man, the sight and the sound of the tiny fleet coming to their rescue gave them hope. Energized, some of the wounded hurried through the protected gauntlet at a brisk trot. Bustling out on the beach, the officers and leading NCOs called out their condition on the run.

"Baker Company," the first sergeant declared. "A Jap colonel and his sergeant major had about a dozen men hidden in a gully about a mile from here. They wiped out our scouts and advanced patrol. We have no officers left."

The major leading Charlie Company had a badly broken arm dangling from his shoulder socket. Nevertheless, he hovered around the men carrying the wounded like a sheep dog tightening his flock. Unable to separate him from his men, Corpsman Casey Dworkin set, splinted, and cupped the major's bad arm in a crude sling on the move.

"Get him to the beach quickly," Corporal Dworkin insisted. "He should be lying down."

As Able Company passed through, the bodies of the dying swung, bobbed, squirmed, and bounced in their blood soaked canvas slings. The few plasma bottles hanging from cleft sticks gave the column the look of a religious procession in search of a cure. Dog Company had no officers or sergeants left but the senior corporal moved back and forth checking the wounded while a private first class set the pace. Despite the protective shield provided by Fox Company, however, return fire from the advancing enemy still took its toll inside the escape corridor.

"Enemy traffic on the perimeter," Tony Regni shouted. "And it's getting worse fast."

A Japanese mortar shell went off under the feet of two riflemen from George Company. The blast threw their mangled bodies up into the raised up root system of an overturned cedar tree. Blind cannon fire from an advancing enemy tank wiped out three men of Easy Company's Tommy-gun squad bringing up the rear. Direct hits from the fifty-seven-millimeter cannon shells didn't leave enough to be carried out on to the beach. The swift enemy build up drove the colonel to put all of Fox Company on high alert.

"Heads up men," Colonel Jeffers demanded. "As soon as the enemy brings up enough strength we'll have a Banzai charge on our hands."

"Keep your spare clips of ammunition, your grenades, and your bayonets handy," Gunny Mann advised. "When they charge in a human wave backed up by another and yet another you don't want to be fumbling around for your vitals."

"Remember, the crowd on the beach is counting on us," Corporal Cantelmo urged. "If the Japs break through they'll finish them off like weasels in a hen house."

The deluge of enemy artillery shells and mortar rounds raining down off shore punctuated the cries of the Marines with explosions. The blasts that penetrated the shallows and threw up dark showers of muck gave off the muffled and dreadful rumblings of an under water volcano. Farther off shore each Dresden blue shelf of rising surf was hit with heavy artillery shells. Their huge eruptions tore through the ranks and sent broken bodies rising high on dirty waterspouts. Wherever they fell, men wallowed under the impact of the grit filled water. Concussion from the shells that burst all around the landing craft frequently broke the backs or burst the lungs of swimmers as they struggled toward the breakers. The five-inch shells that went off in the deep water beneath the bow of LCI-57 threw up a mist that held a rainbow high over the black smoke pouring from her stacks. A near miss dimpled the high freeboard with added pockmarks. But the steel shower lacked a punch strong enough to penetrate her scorched hull.

"Good girl," Captain Northrop said as he eased LCI-57 through the barrage. "You're a sturdy old tub."

Quickly, the landing craft moved in among the wading troopers. Except for the carnage it caused, the chatter of the incessant gunfire and steady eruption of geysers all around her did not significantly disrupt the loading process. Wherever a shell landed, nearby companions took hold of the dazed, the wounded, and the dead. The tiny groups that floated their buddies out to the breakers were not slowed by their burdens. The quickest and the strongest hung back and helped their comrades climb up the departure ramp where the ships-company took over.

"I've never seen such a body of Marines swimming out to a ship before," Seaman First Class Oliver Cranshaw observed. "They're packed tighter than a school of anchovies."

Nodding assent, Bosun Sandy Kitchner let his seasoned eyes scan the shallows to make sure that only dismembered bodies were left behind floating in the surf. Then he turned and sized up LCI-32 standing off the breakers waiting to receive the badly wounded still ashore.

"Pity the poor bastards that get aboard that tub," Bosun Sandy Kitchner groaned. "With a narrow and rickety ramp hanging down on each side of the bow she floats like a Siamese pelican."

As the wounded were eased into the surf, only two barriers stood between the enemy and the sea. One was the blistering heat shield created by the solid wall of flames sporadically renewed by the navy planes overhead. The other was the thin line of Marine paratroopers dug in behind the driftwood that was scattered all along the high water mark. Their camouflaged helmets and rifle barrels formed a staggered picket line.

CHAPTER FOURTEEN

What sets warring nations apart
Is their beliefs.
What unites enemies in combat
Is their courage.

In the heat and choking cinders that covered the beach of Shibushi Bay, the survivors of Fox Company were forced to pull back to the very edge of the exit corridor to keep the enemy from bursting upon them all at once. Even then they had little warning.

"Oh shit," Gunny Mann cried. "Three Japs just broke through the wall of flame."

"I got the smoking bastards," Marine Corporal Vinnie Cantelmo shouted. "They look like baseball pitchers with pretty good arms."

Concealed in a pile of smoldering logs hot enough to burn holes in his camouflaged fatigues, the Marine corporal sighted on the nearest runner. A short burst from his Browning Automatic Rifle caught the Japanese corporal from Sapporo in the stomach. The blood that frothed from his mouth hid his face as Vinnie locked in on the next sapper. Five rounds slammed into the chest of a fisherman from Shikaku just above the heart and spun him around twice. The third grenadier ducked and dodged through two bursts until Vinnie zeroed in. Half a dozen shots smacked the factory worker from Yokohama so hard in the head, legs, and shoulder he staggered like a drunk. Yet, before he dropped, each man threw a live grenade. The two that tore Vinnie's log shelter apart drove a dozen large splinters into his left arm and tore a hole in his waist. But the third one posed a serious threat to the airborne Marines dug in above the high water mark.

"Heads up," Corporal Tony Regni warned. "One dynamite

baseball on the loose."

The longest toss propelled the tiny bomb into the roots of a driftwood tree trunk where it dropped through the wooden fingers like a marble on a peg-board. The explosion caught the trooper who was reaching for it full in the face and chest. The swift and utter finality of the death of the twenty year old Marine from St. Cloud, Minnesota, denied him further attention.

"We've got an enemy tank using the black clouds of napalm as a smoke screen," Colonel Iron Mike Jeffers shouted. "Let's get a bazooka on it."

Gunny Mann fed the finned rocket into the rear of the steel tube as the pointer took aim. As soon as his loader was clear, Corporal Regni triggered the stovepipe launcher and sent the missile away. Riding at the head of a bright tail of flame and smoke, the wobbling rocket drove through the smoke screen and struck the light tank just above its treads. The missile penetrated the thin armor plate and spent the bulk of its explosion inside the doomed machine. The smoke that escaped through the joints in the armor was filled with steam that squealed as the ammunition inside exploded and blew the lid off the top of the turret.

"Hot Damn!" Gunny Mann exclaimed. "Those suckers boiled like live crabs in a kettle."

The barrage of Japanese shell fire and mortar rounds that fell upon Fox Company kept all eyes alert for a determined suicide charge. But even without turning his head, each man pictured the beach emptying out behind him as the last of the division's walking wounded entered the water.

"The Navy's pulling away behind us," Corporal Vinnie Cantelmo complained. "And the Japs are coming on like Gang Busters. We're stuck here worse than pigs on roller-skates."

The half-blind enemy bombardment and the ashes from the shrinking wall of protective flame swept across the driftwood battle-line. The bleached logs and tangled root systems cracked and erupted with the explosive snap and blistering heat of a forest fire ripping through a stand of hemlock. But neither Fox company's wounded nor the dying asked when their unit would break off and get out. It was enough to know that Iron Mike, Gunny Mann,

Corporal Regni, and the Doc, Casey Dworkin, would be the last Americans off the beach. To make their presence felt the leaders kept up a steady stream of chatter as they cruised the shrunken battle-line.

"The Navy won't desert us, men," Colonel Iron Mike Jeffers declared. "See that DUK that's shuttling between shore and the nearest LCI. It may look like an orange crate with wheels but that's our own special battle-taxi for damned sure."

"When you leave the line," Gunny Mann said, "make sure to toss out a couple of hand grenades and run for the water like deer. Not like shit. Like deer."

The gunnery sergeant and the colonel moved up and down the driftwood line checking each bunker for damage and ammunition reserves. Wherever a man was wounded the two Marines manned his post until the medic could patch him up. The private with a bullet in his chest had the gunnery sergeant plug the hole with his finger so he could smoke a last cigarette.

"Give me the count, Doc?" Gunny Mann demanded when the corpsman arrived. "How bad have we been hit?"

"Over seven hundred of the dead were too mangled for the other companies to carry out," Corpsman Casey Dworkin reported, "But they brought out some five hundred wounded."

"How about Fox Company?" Corporal Tony Regni inquired. "What's our condition?"

"Eight dead and two dozen critically wounded have been evacuated, "Doc disclosed. "That DUK shuttling back and forth from my Surgery to the LCI is a floating ambulance."

The emergency aid station that the Marine corpsman set up inside the driftwood line was cut off from a view of the fighting. The thin, wavy, and luminous shield came from a parachute canopy that was strung from the water worn root stems. Between the shelter of the bleached tree trunks and the breezy openness of the sun-drenched canopy, the tiny surgery had an air of cleanliness. Even so, the bloodstains and the gristly remains of hasty surgery could not be ignored. The dead stretched out on logs and the gore on Doc's apron testified to the ferocity of the struggle.

"What about the rest of the men on the line?" Corpsman

Dworkin asked as he took the cigarette from the dead Marine's lips. "How fit are they?"

"Half are wounded," Gunny said. "But each one is paired with an able bodied companion."

"They can make it down the beach like they was in a three legged race," Corporal Regni explained. "But even God don't know how the worst wounded will stay afloat in deep water."

The gunfire from the dead zone's shattered tree line suddenly picked up. The sound of tank treads crunching over rock and scorched timber grew louder. The sharp "clack" of the Chi Ha's fifty seven millimeter cannon cut through the chug and clatter of the small arms fire like the yap of a terrier barking at a freight train.

"I may never command another division again," Colonel Michael A. Jeffers muttered. "But I couldn't find a better outfit if I had my pick from Sparta to Judgment Day."

Moved by the compliment, his Gunny could only nod as a couple of his men were cut down trying to fall back to shelter. The enemy had several new machine-guns and they ruled the moment.

"It's time to go, Mike," Gunny Mann declared. "The worst of the wounded are loaded and LCI-32 has her ramps up. Christ, that over loaded fold-a-boat could broach-to any moment."

Suddenly, the high pitched chatter of a Japanese machine-gun was out of place. It sounded rather like a clatter rebounding off a stone wall. The noise was coming from the wrong direction. With the sea at their backs the men of Fox Company had given little thought to being outflanked. No one had paid any attention to the bodies in the burned out oyster holes that littered the beach. Yet, instinctively, the battle-seasoned gunnery sergeant and the Marine corporal felt the cool chill of fright on the back of their necks. It felt as if they had been splashed with a harsh skin bracer.

"Hit the dirt!" Corporal Tony Regni shouted. "We got unwanted company."

A vicious burst of gunfire swept along the driftwood line from several positions down the beach. Shocked at being attacked from the shoreline, the Marines scrambled up over the nearest logs and shot back from between the rows. The enemy soldiers who pushed the lids covering their oyster holes high enough to get their rifles into firing position made good targets. A dozen bursts from Corporal Vinnie Cantelmo's B.A.R. wiped out the nearest snipers. Fox Company's other gunners blasted the holes hard enough to send the garbage can lids rolling down the wet sand. But that ended quickly when the Americans found themselves under attack from yet another angle.

"Gunned down by Japs in front and shot at from Japs behind," Tony Regni declared. "You'd think we were white Russians in a Shanghai whorehouse."

Two hundred yards away, half a dozen Japanese soldiers were piled on top of one another like sandbags. The men who made up the human shield added their rifle fire to the heavy machine-gun that chugged away just above their helmets. The chop and clatter of the enemy weapons and the flick of bullets in the sand followed the colonel, the gunnery sergeant , and the corpsman as they led the rest of Fox Company to better shelter. Out of over a hundred rounds, only three found their mark. And they all hit the same man. The shot that caught the private in the shoulder stood him up. The next one opened up his stomach. And the last one severed Earl Kendrick's spine. Without a word the blond haired flame thrower operator from Colorado crumbled into a heap and bled to death through the fingers that tried to stanch his wounds.

"Son of a bitch," Iron Mike lamented. "Those Jap sand crabs make our air cover useless."

Using the tangled driftwood logs for cover, Gunny Mann took three men and started crawling toward the enemy's improvised machine-gun nest. Before they had covered fifty yards, high explosive shells from a pair of Japanese tanks turned the logs around them into splinters. The two green and gray Type Ninety Seven Chi-Has bore down with their short barrelled fifty-seven millimeter cannons and their light machine-guns blazing away.

"Jee-zus Kee-ryst," Corporal Cantelmo shouted. "One of them Chi-Haa-Haas is ranging in on the Landing Craft picking up the last of the division."

"If the other tank turns its cannon on that floundering LCI," Colonel Jeffers warned, "we could lose the wounded in deep water."

Without looking back, Iron Mike summoned up a bazooka team led by Vinnie Cantelmo. The wounded eighteen-year-old corporal crawled forward cradling a B.A.R. in his good arm. Expertly, he dimpled the light armor plate on the enemy tank's turret while the others clambered over the driftwood barrier. Scuttling after them with a limp arm dragging in the sand, Corporal Cantelmo shielded his Browning Automatic Rifle with his blood smeared chest and shoulder. The improvised anti-tank team joined the colonel behind a logjam of bleached cedar roots. The entire root system was turned up toward the tanks like a pair of gigantic hands.

"Those Chi-Has are mean bastards, colonel," Corporal Vinnie Cantelmo declared. "You can knock their treads off and they just sit there and shoot up everything within gunnery range."

"Let's take those sardine cans head-on, corporal," Iron Mike decided. "Their thinnest armor plate is between the treads and below the turret. One shot right down the throat will do the trick."

"You make the fucker cough, Mike," Vinnie Cantelmo proposed, "and my boys will yank out his tonsils so hard the bastard'll spit up his balls."

"You got a deal, Vinnie," Iron Mike said. "This time don't cover me."

With a spry leap, Colonel Jeffers jumped clear of the roots and stood straight to hurl two hand grenades into the path of the leading tank. After they exploded in harmless puffs of dirt, sand, and ash, he dropped to the ground and rolled away from the Chi-Ha's machine-gun fire. The bullets followed him in a stitching pattern that showered the forty-five year old officer with sand.

"Look at Mike go," Private Andrew Gillis urged. "Twistier than a snake on a hot griddle."

"Damn," Private Jesse Winters said. "The Old Man sure knows how to get their attention."

The light Japanese tank slowed down in order to give the gunner shooting through the tiny hatch between the treads a chance to pick-off the colonel. As the Chi-Ha's machine-gun bullets chased the squirming officer the fifty-seven millimeter cannon in her turret began to swing around and drop down for a point-blank blast.

Methodically, Andy Gillis slid the nineteen-inch long missile into the rear of the thin metal tube that Jesse Winters held on his shoulder. As pointer, Jesse absorbed the extra three and a half pounds the rocket added to his stove-pipe without wavering or altering his aim.

"Come on, Tojo," Jesse urged. "Take the bait."

A clatter of loose tread plates and the screech of steel brakes sent the Japanese tank through a tight turn. As it picked up speed moving down the beach, the treads clawed and crunched toward the colonel's prostrate body.

"SHOOT, FOR CHRIST SAKE," Iron Mike demanded. "I can feel the fucker's breath."

With a swish of orange flame and a tail of curled smoke, the self-propelled rocket streaked toward the Chi-Ha's front end. It struck just above the small viewing hatch between the two tracks. The hollow charge smashed through the steel shell of the vehicle and the half pound of pentolite split the turret plates open a crack at the sides.

The blast inside the steel cabin blew the driver's body apart and sent his blood gushing from the machine-gun port. The black smoke that billowed from the escape hatch in the belly and oozed out of every crack, split, and crevice all around, signaled the fiery death of all five men inside. The young Japanese gunner who opened the top turret burst into flames like a kerosene torch as soon as he hit the fresh air. The billowing smoke and bright flashes that rose out of the top of the turret made the squat Chi-Ha look like an erupting volcano.

"Bulls-eye," Iron Mike yelled and scrambled for the shelter of the roots. "Not only did you get the fucker's tonsils and his balls, you got his bloody ass-hole as well."

The moment of triumph was sweet and brief. Almost by reflex, the colonel hurried back to his wounded companion and sized up his condition.

"Don't look now," Vinnie advised. "That other armor plated flivver is after bigger game."

"Then the least we can do is slow the bastard down," Iron Mike stated. "If you're up to it."

Alarmed by the corporal's loss of blood, Iron Mike dusted the wounds with sulfa powder and pressed a battle bandage over the nasty hole in the young man's side. Heavy machine-gun fire from the surviving enemy tank kept the four-man team pinned down. But an opening on the upturned root system gave them a shot at the tank as it sped by.

"Let him have it," Iron Mike ordered. "Blast the fucker's treads off."

Private Andy Gillis and rifleman Jesse Winters loaded and fired the bazooka like hunters picking off a buffalo with a cannon. The fifty-nine millimeter missile dragged a fiery tail with it as it exploded against the tank's forward drive wheel and broke its tractor-tread apart. Unable to move forward or back, the fourteen ton Chi-Ha pivoted around on its ruined tread and opened fire on the half-hidden bazooka team. After a barrage of shells that set the driftwood shelter on fire, the Japanese tank turned its attention on the amphibious truck coming out of the water.

"Oh oh," Gunny Mann noted. "That DUK ain't no floatin' ambulance no more."

Amid shell bursts that lined its path, the mottled DUK-W climbed up the wet sand shedding sea brine like a charging crocodile. But bursts that the aircrewman fired back from behind the air cooled eleven mm gun mounted on the bow were no match for the tank's cannon.

"God damn," Max Bryson muttered. "How many rounds can that steel pillbox have left?"

"No more than fifty-odd," Carson Braddock supposed. "He's popping off faster than a dozen bishops in a whorehouse."

Aviation Radioman First Class Carson Braddock made a series of evasive turns as he steered the heavy-tired DUK over the soft sand. Despite the tank's persistent shelling, Max Bryson used his tracers to walk a stream of fifty-caliber rounds into the improvised Japanese machine-gun nest peppering the driftwood line. Moving up from the water and a bit behind, the DUK caught the Japanese troopers firing on Fox Company's driftwood bunker off guard. But their recovery was swift.

"Swing the gun around to face the waves," Corporal Goro Itagaki ordered. "A beast has risen from the sea."

As the crouching Rats of Pusan turned their weapon around a short burst of Max's eleven millimeter slugs ripped apart the kneeling figure feeding the long belt of ammunition into the Japanese machine-gun. The feeder's back split open like wet red-cedar hit with an axe. The slugs that caught the gunner in the chest blew his lungs out through the closely grouped exit holes in his back. A long burst of fire at close range chopped up most of the riflemen sprawled around the weapon. Another hammering of half-inch slugs split the bodies open as the slain riflemen pitched and rolled in the blood soaked sand. In the entire squad, only the enemy corporal was quick enough to flip away. Swiftly, he leaped to his feet before Max could gun him down. As the enemy soldier turned and brought his sub-machine-gun around, Carson raced the engine of the cumbersome landing craft and struck him in the chest with the bow. Corporal Goro Itagaki went down with the crunch of a dry corn stalk. The thick ridges on the fat tractor tires broke his back half a dozen times as Carson geared down and let the weight of the vehicle grind him into the sand. A wave from the paratroopers emerging from their driftwood hideout showed Carson where to find temporary shelter from the enemy tank and make his first pick-up. Relieved, the top NCO of Fox Company gave an appreciative welcome.

"You guys come on like Geronimo," Gunnery Sergeant Marty Mann declared. "Where the Hell did you learn to drive like that?"

"Vancouver, British Columbia," Carson Braddock replied. "As part of the driving test you have to run down five pedestrians or you don't get your license."

The deprecation was as spontaneous as it was false. Being fiercely proud of their heritage, the cousins took great delight in running it down with a kind of Texan extravagance.

"Actually, you only need three," Max Bryson insisted. "As long as you get them all on the sidewalk."

Wry, brisk, and mindless, the smart remarks took some of the tension off climbing aboard the DUK under fire. The Gunny boosted his men up over the side of the vehicle and the sailors hauled them in like sacks of potatoes. Gunning the engine, Carson swerved the amphibious truck in and out of the shelter pockets all along the driftwood line.

"All aboard," Carson called. "This trolley is on a tight schedule."

The crippled and the able bodied paratroopers of Fox Company hurled hand grenades in the direction of the enemy and piled into the open hull in pairs. As the hull filled up with troops, the unhurt cradled the wounded in tight bundles that made room for those yet to come aboard. Near the end of the line space ran out and men sprawled over the hood and the engine cover. One of the last men aboard paid close attention to the information stamped on the landing craft's dashboard.

"The metal placard here specifies a twenty-seven man capacity," Corpsman Casey Dworkin indicated. "What makes you think this fucker will float with over forty men on board."

"We'll worry about that later, Doc," Carson Braddock replied. "Right now we are too close to that trackless tank for even a near sighted gunner to miss."

The fifty-seven millimeter shell that clipped the top of the DUK's bow opened up a jagged hole the size of a basketball and killed two of the men riding on the hood. The shell that ripped through the hull between the wheels blew several men apart and wounded half a dozen others. Splattered with blood, the angry medic ripped off his red-cross arm band and grabbed a canvas shrouded satchel-charge as he leaped from the DUK.

"Keep that tanks top turret gunner busy," Casey Dworkin demanded. "I'll show you a little broken field running."

Max swept the tank with a steady burst that clattered all over the turret. A half dozen rounds hit the top-turret machine-gunner and spun him around in a body breaking twist. In death he lay draped over the steel radio antenna that circled the top of the Chi-Ha's turret like a fence.

"One down," Max marked. "Four to go."

The next enemy gunner to emerge kept low and squeezed off a short burst that caught the defrocked corpsman in the thigh. Hit and spun off balance at full speed, Casey Dworkin fused the satchel charge and swung the heavy canvas bag by its strap as he fell. Launched like a hammer-throw, the bag sailed through the air in a shallow arc that sent it tumbling and skidding beneath the belly of the tank. The bright explosion blew the Japanese machine-gunner out of the turret-top hatch and set the diesel engine on fire. Each of the enemy soldiers who crawled clear of the black smoke fell to the point-blank rifle fire of the Marines and the paratroopers in the DUK.

"God damn," Corporal Tony Regni shouted. "We gotta stencil those kills on the bow."

Moving quickly yet steering with care, Carson brought the amphibious truck up alongside Doc Dworkin. Even before the dust and the sand settled, the colonel and his anti-tank team emerged from their driftwood shelter and took charge of getting the wounded corpsman to his feet.

"Make room for the Doc," Iron Mike Jeffers ordered. "He's got a medal coming for this if I have to mint it myself."

"All aboard before the Japs storm the beach," Carson advised. "The next stop is that beat-up old LCI waiting for us out in the bay."

A dozen hands reached down and hoisted the corporal over the gunnel as Andy Gillis and Jesse Winters boosted him up from below. The amphibious truck was speeding up by the time Gillis and Winters climbed aboard. A deluge of enemy mortar rounds and shellfire raised the soft sand around the DUK into a traveling storm of grain and grit. The sudden sandstorm ripped the colonel's battle jacket apart. A nearby blast forced Iron Mike to side-step and dodge until his only chance was to clamber up over the stern as the vehicle gathered speed.

"This here-now shag-assed-duck is as crowded as a Lisbon trolley car at rush hour," Iron Mike Jeffers declared. "And twice as welcome."

The gears groaned under the load as Carson steered the amphibious truck on to wet sand washed hard by the retreating tide. Max rode backwards on the hood and aimed short bursts of fifty-caliber-machine-gun fire at anything that moved in front of the shrunken wall of flames.

"Hang on," Max Bryson advised. "It's gonna be a wet ride."

The DUK drove through the light surf in a great spray of water that shrank to a churn of white foam as soon as the vehicle slowed down to float speed. A rifle grenade fired by a Japanese soldier far up the beach exploded a few feet under the water and drenched everyone in spray.

"Use your packs and your clothing to seal up the shell holes in the hull," Carson ordered. "If we ship much more water she's gonna go down."

"Each able-bodied man move outward against the sides of the boat," Max insisted. "The moment we start to ship water you men slip overboard and hang on to the gunnels."

"Toss your shoes, rifles, bayonets, canteens, ammunition clips, and the like over the side to lighten the load," Carson demanded. "But keep your helmets and start bailing like Noah."

Max dumped his machine-gun and belted ammunition into the sea. Yet even after all the weapons and the field radio went overboard the DUK had almost no freeboard. The churn of the wheels propelling them forward with their thick tractor treads threatened to wash in over the stern.

"Caulk every bullet hole and cracked seam with shirts, socks, shorts, or whatever fits," Carson advised. "Pack those holes like you were de-flowering virgins on a high school hayride."

The wounded paratroopers inspected the hull for leaks while the able bodied bailed like a bucket brigade. The push through the light surf brought water in over the sides. But Carson kept the vessel from being swamped by riding the troughs until he found a break in the oncoming waves. The colonel and the corporal marveled at the young aviator's seamanship but the gunnery sergeant took a deeper interest in what he heard.

"I know that voice," Gunny Mann declared. "You're the Navy fly-boy that ordered the evacuation over air to ground radio."

The remark caught two people by surprise. The eighteen-year-old flier at the helm blushed and the middle age colonel gaped. Seeing Iron Mike's shock, Carson Braddock treated it as a joke.

"Now where would you rather be?" Carson responded. "Back there or out here?"

Maneuvering beyond the light inner surf, the amphibious truck rolled with the heavy ground swells and shipped water each time the bow dug into an advancing wave. The enemy shells whistling in from shore forced the DUK to take evasive action that exposed it to the rising sea.

"Whose authority were you acting on, sailor?" Gunny Mann demanded. "What officer issued the original command?"

Pretending not to hear, Carson Braddock splashed the water beneath his feet and motioned for the men riding on the gunnels to ease themselves overboard. Privates Winters and Gillis stretched their bodies across the bow and down along the side of the vessel to serve as human weather-boards. Half a dozen soldiers further astern tightened their grips on the vessel's canvas fenders and slid into the sea. Mesmerized by the waves breaking over the bow, Colonel Michael A. Jeffers took a few seconds to assess the sailor's silence. Once its meaning sank in, however, spoke.

"WAIT A GOD DAMNED MINUTE!" Iron Mike demanded. "Am I to understand that an enlisted sailor ordered this retreat?"

"Yes sir," Carson confessed. "Aviation Radioman First Class at your service."

"That's not quite correct," Max said. "There were two of us. Same rank and same date of promotion. Sir."

The directness and the simplicity of the admissions took a moment to sink in. Stunned, queasy from the pitch and yaw of the DUK as it swerved to avoid heavy patches of debris, and unable to hold his balance, the colonel gradually filled up with rage.

"So it's between you two Gold-Dust-fuckin'-Twins, then," Iron Mike snarled. "A miserable pair of snot-nosed swabbies issued orders as the Senior Officers in Charge of Evacuation."

"Almost. But not quite, sir," Carson insisted. "Yes, we acted as the senior on site commanders. We never pretended to be officers."

"Something had to be done fast," Max explained. "And we were the only ones in a position to see the full extent of the disaster. Our pilots had all they could do avoiding radio-active clouds and staying up-wind from the explosion."

Carson Braddock concentrated on easing the DUK over the rising waves as they entered the vast expanse of the outer bay. While the shore retreated and the green water ahead of the DUK darkened with depth, almost everyone fixed his eyes on the LCI waiting to take them aboard. With only a quarter mile to go, the dark green water and the rising wind off the open ocean drove the rapidly receding tide into choppy peaks. But the colonel and the sergeant major ignored the ocean entirely. Suddenly, all that mattered was the debate.

"They never actually lied," Gunny Mann declared. "That could make a difference."

"NIT-PICKIN' DIFFERENCE BE DAMNED," the colonel roared. "No lousy navy tech-sergeant tells Iron Mike Jeffers when to pull out. I shit you not."

Even the men stacked on top of one another along the gunnels drew a certain comfort from the dispute. Along with the pounding ocean crests that broke over their backs, the argument helped quiet their stomachs. But not everyone was so fortunate. Repeated splashes drenched the critically wounded and the exhausted bailers as well. Chills, anxiety, and fatigue put them at the mercy of the buck and heave of the vessel. Those who were sea sick retched into the water flowing by just a few inches below their noses. The few with the strongest stomachs paid special attention to the wrath that twisted the colonel's face.

"Oh oohh," Corporal Vinnie Cantelmo moaned. "I smell a court martial coming up."

The strain of combat followed by the relief of rescue left a cramp in the colonel's gut. It needed a way out. And since his men were closer than family it fell on the nearest with blind fury.

"You're fuckin' A tweet, corporal," Iron Mike declared. "A full blown, ring tailed, purple assed, General Court Martial for these impersonators in spades."

With each riposte, the sounds of battle faded. Soon the American carrier planes attacking the enemy forces on the beach and the Japanese artillery shells pounding the shallows were far astern. All of a sudden, the small landing craft rocking and dipping like an overloaded bathtub on an empty sea became a very isolated place.

"Now that's one trial I want to attend," Gunny Mann asserted. "In full dress uniform with all my buttons and medals polished until they glow like candle light."

"Oh, you will be there Gunny," Colonel Jeffers insisted. "Your ear is the key witness."

"We are all witnesses, sir," Doc Dworkin declared. "And as much as I love you, Mike, I will be a witnesses for the defense."

The murmur of assent traveled through the seasick section of the company as something between a purr and a grunt. Soaked with spray, the colonel looked around and took in the nods and grins of approval from the rest of Fox Company's grateful survivors.

"Put land lubbers on a boat," Iron Mike noted, "and the first thing they do is mutiny."

The staccato eruption of napalm canisters dropped on the beach took everyone's eyes to the destruction that enveloped the driftwood line. Working as glide bombers, waves of Curtiss Helldivers and Grumman Avengers silenced the enemy mortars and tanks by turning the beach into a shimmering backdrop of flame. Up ahead, LCI-57 eased an extra length of cargo net over the side to act as a fender. Slowly, the ship's engines churned out power as the bow swung around in a tight turn that flattened the water into a calm boarding slick. As the green slick spread and deepened into a twisting morning glory pool, Carson drove the fat wheeled DUK up against the net and worked her in alongside the staircase that was her loading ramp. Quickly, Max threw a couple of turns around the hand rail and hauled his line in tight as the men of Fox Company began the steep climb up to the weather deck.

Slowly, battle strained spirits and worn out bodies started to relax. Tired eyes and haggard faces examined the scorched deck and the twisted wheelhouse of the crippled mother ship with hollow stares too exhausted to take in her condition. She was afloat and that was enough for the men of Fox Company. Even Max and Carson turned all questions of their safety and their survival over to the crew of the LCI as they left the DUK behind. Yet as Navy men they could not help but see the destroyers on patrol around the hospital ship and study the mangled superstructure of the flagship on station at the mouth of the bay.

"Oh my God," Carson Braddock groaned. "The Tuscaloosa is a floating junk yard."

"Any ship hit that hard at Pearl Harbor," Max whispered in awe,

"Just tuned over and sank."

Down at the bow, lacking a bridge, shorn of her guns, and spilling smoke all along her main deck, she could barely creep along under her own power. Yet, as they drew nearer, the young men saw that the U.S.S. Tuscaloosa was raising signal flags from a line stretched between her funnel and the mangled crane once used to hoist her float-plane aboard.

"What do you know?" Carson said. "Somebody is alive after all."

The same fatigue that dulled his sense also wearied his brain. Chilled, soaking wet, and gray around the eyes as well as under the jaw, Carson merely stood alongside his cousin and stared.

Locked in an exhausted stupor and the inner anguish of such a terrible loss of life both men made no effort to decipher the line of signal flags riding on the hastily improvised hoist and flapping in a stiffening breeze. Despite the near paralysis of utter fatigue, however, an inner professionalism asserted itself. Automatically, the young aviation radio operators pieced together the message that the flags conveyed:

Once rescue complete
Fox Company and Aircrewmen
Fly to Manila—Stop
All ships withdraw to Okinawa—Stop
Execute.

CHAPTER FIFTEEN

Total war
Automatically
Excludes the enemy
From the moral community

Naval Combat Aircrewmen Carson Braddock and Max Bryson slept through most of the thousand mile flight from Okinawa to the Philippines. Over Luzon, the co-pilot of their long-range twin engine amphibian woke them up to point out the rice fields farmed by the Ifugao tribesmen. The evenly stepped planting paddies turned the steep terrain into a network of contoured terraces carved all across the green mountainside. Each separate hill looked like an isolated fortress circled by rising battlements and crowned with a tin-roof hut.

"Legend has it," the pilot declared, "that the Ifugao grow the best rice in the world because the mountain rain is purified by a dozen benevolent gods."

The glassed-in gunnery bubbles on each side of the Catalina's narrow fuselage stood out like misplaced eyes on the back of a gigantic bug. The teardrop bubbles offered panoramic views. Awake, lethargic, and wet from the gradual let down into the humid tropic air that hugged the earth, Carson and Max slipped out of their dungaree flight gear as the PBY Catalina descended. Using the bottled water stored in the smoke bomb rack they gave themselves a sponge bath as soon as the amphibian landed on the long runway. The cousins changed into their extra tailor-made summer whites while the plane taxied into the hanger. Somewhat refreshed but still tired, they re-packed their gear and thanked the pilots while the long-range reconnaissance plane started to refuel. The co-pilot showed them where to stow their gear for the flight back and pointed the way off the naval air station.

"Good luck," enlisted pilot Chief Greg Lamont said. "You've earned it."

The cocky tilt of their white hats was accented by the folded-in sides and turned-down wings that crushed the square-ish skullcap hard against their heads. The black neckerchief knotted close up on their throats showed off the three crisp folds ironed to a sharp edge along the length of the flat white collars that fell down their backs. The zipper-tight fit of the blouse and the flare of the bell-bottom pants gave the sailors a smart look as they strode through the gate. The eagle and three blue chevrons that marked their rank and the small radar and aerial gunnery patches on their sleeves added color to their starched dress whites. But it was the silver combat aircrewman's wings and the double-row of colored ribbons they wore over their breast pockets that marked the eighteen-year-old cousins as seasoned warriors to the MP in the Army Jeep waiting to take them to town.

The open vehicle beeped and honked through the pedestrian, bicycle, and commercial traffic that crowded the city street in the early evening. The mixture of hand carts and animal drawn wagons held their ground until the last moment. Then they parted to let the blaring Jeep through just as the driver hit the brakes.

"Talk about stop and go," Carson said. "You must wear out a transmission in a week."

From a distance, the general's residence looked like any other white two-story house rimmed by an upstairs balcony that went all the way around. The extended roofline gave them perpetual shade that served as tropical air-conditioning. Close-up, the fresh paint and the restored windows, screens, and rain gutters distinguished it from every other building on the block.

"Pretty fancy quarters," Max allowed. "For Dugout Doug."

Even inside, the carpets on the polished wooden floors and the finely spun window drapes showed a woman's touch that was unusual in a recently liberated war-zone. Before they could take it all in, however, Miss Shirley Hashimoto stepped out of a corridor room and greeted them. Her sheer silk dress and the absence of undergarments showed her lithe young body off to perfection.

"Sorry for the ride down Market Street," Shirley said. "That's the colonel's idea of a joke."

The noise from the study just down the hall was a mixture of half-drunk baritones trying to sing. A coarse accompaniment came from the raucous shouts of a couple dozen men all talking at once. The guard on duty at the door smiled as the girl gave Carson an affectionate hug. Her touch aroused all of Carson's latent desires. Blushing, she stretched out her hands for Max to hold in welcome.

"Be careful what you say and do," Shirley Hashimoto warned. "Fox Company has been eating and drinking and carrying on in there for the better part of two days."

"Geez," Max Bryson gasped. "I thought the general was against that sort of revelry."

"He is," Shirley replied. "But since Fox Company's heroic stand was the only bright spot in an otherwise disastrous invasion they get special privileges."

"It sounds like a Roman victory celebration," Carson Braddock observed. "All that's missing are the screams of the less-than-vestal maidens."

Shirley Hashimoto wore a loose powder green gown that took its provocative shape from the tips of her breasts and the flat hipbones that kept it from clinging to her legs. The naval officer's cap she wore thrown back on her head added a saucy touch to her outfit.

"It is in a way," Shirley confessed. "As soon as they got here, Fox Company was given a Presidential Unit Citation and they've been celebrating ever since."

A wink got her past the guard as well as a hand in opening the study's double doors. The books on the many shelves around the room were in dark contrast to the painted walls covered with a dusty lime wash that soaked up the light from the naked bulbs embedded in the overhead fans.

"Come in, Navy," Colonel Michael A. Jeffers boomed. "Have a drink and a bite to eat."

The invitation was too good to resist. The sideboard held over a dozen different kinds of beer, more whiskies, and a variety of red and white wines all spread out between patches of food. The abundance of picked over roasts, cheeses, fish, and cold cuts had mouth-watering appeal. The raw vegetables, breads, rolls, and crepes added a regal splendor. Still the different colored spills and drippings were accompanied by scraps from a wide variety of pies and pastries. Indeed, the empty bottles, spilled drinks, and vivid stains that covered the long table's white runner suggested that a troop of apes had rummaged through the feast.

"I haven't seen a spread like this," Max Bryson marveled, "since our last Thanksgiving aboard the Brandywine."

Unable to carry much in his hands, Carson poured himself a tumbler of Jack Daniels bourbon and put a thick slice of roast beef on a sliced Kaiser roll. Max fixed himself a Swiss cheese and smoked salmon sandwich and washed it down with a bottle of Feigenspan ale.

"Yeah," Carson Braddock allowed. "In eight months at sea the only booze we had was panther piss brewed out of potato skins and pineapple rind laced with torpedo juice."

The sailors ate and drank slowly as they made the rounds of old acquaintances. Vigorous welcomes and frequent toasts were over shadowed by slack faces and bloodshot eyes. The well and the wounded were fighting off pain and fatigue with rich food and strong drink. The study looked more like a wild home coming party in a hospital ward than anything else. For all the scarred and bandaged troopers who shook their hands and pounded their backs, however, Carson and Max could not keep their eyes off the attractive young woman talking to the colonel.

"This is my niece, Monica," Colonel Jeffers volunteered. "She still isn't sure she has been liberated from the Japs. So be nice to her."

Monica Ritter was a lean and long muscled eighteen-year-old with large gray eyes and rich hazel blonde hair curled in tight rings close to her face. Her dappled brown cotton shirt had pleated frills down the front and looping cuts up the side that showed off bronzed thighs. As she shook hands, her liquid eyes looked out over a shy smile that would vanish at the sight of a frown.

"My father was teaching at Santo Tomas University here in

Manila," Miss Monica Ritter explained. "As soon as they arrived, the Japanese turned it into a civilian prisoner of war camp."

"Oh, how awful," Max sympathized. "We know that Jap soldiers make viscous jailers."

Max nodded a silent apology to Shirley that made Monica smile. Four years of suffering and abuse gave the pretty young woman a combination of steely distance and superficial maturity that served her well. Using it, she moved in on the sailors as she had been recently groomed to do.

"You haven't heard the half of it," Monica replied. "But just enough, perhaps, to understand why I ought to remove your wings and combat ribbons."

"A good idea," Shirley allowed. "I'll take yours, my dear. Iron Mike plays rough."

The swift and deft maneuver caught Carson and Max off guard. Before the fliers could ask for the connection between the prison camp and the party their decorations began to disappear.

"Oh, don't do that," Carson pleaded out of an unaccustomed confusion. "Please."

"They're an essential part of our uniform," Max insisted. "Especially today."

Ignoring the protests, the girls stripped the wings and battle ribbons from the sailors' blouses and retreated into the bedroom that adjoined the study. The moment the door closed the aircrewmen turned on their hosts.

"What in Christ's name is going on?" Carson demanded. "Without that fruit salad and our wings we are out of uniform."

"We got a date with the top brass in half an hour," Max declared. "And no sea-going bellhops are gonna screw that up."

The Marines singing in the corner stopped in mid-tune and regrouped behind the sailors. Corporal Vinnie Cantelmo broke open half a dozen more bottles of whiskey and the radio operator from Detroit poured the liquor into clean glasses until everyone in the company had a fresh drink.

"Watch your mouth sailor," Gunny Mann warned. "This is a Fox Company tribunal."

Marine Gunnery Sergeant Marty Mann and Corporal Tony

Regni took one end of the soiled table scarf and walked it down to the other end of the sideboard. All the food and the opened bottles of booze piled up together inside the runner. The half cleared table left a wall length slab of polished walnut exposed in front of the sailors. Vinnie Cantelmo used his good hand to take a large Spanish Bible down from the library shelf and place it on the cleared section of the table. And Corpsman Casey Dworkin had two troopers bring up a chair so he could rest his injured leg as he sat down.

"O. K." Max said. "You've had your fun. This charade has gone far enough. Call it off."

Instinctively, the two cousins stood back-to-back for mutual protection. Having finished their sandwiches and drinks they set their glasses down and edged toward the exit. Immediately they both came under intense scrutiny. Despite the corpsman's injuries and obvious discomfort, the colonel rested his foot on an unoccupied section of the rattan seat as he looked the two sailors over. Disturbed by the change, the sailors took their hats out from behind their necks and unfolded them.

"This looks like a kangaroo court to me," Carson Braddock asserted. "We don't want any."

Two troopers with truncheons blocked the double door. The entrance to the bedroom was barred by Gunny Mann and Corporal Tony Regni armed with iron pokers from the fireplace. Out flanked and out muscled, the two sailors stood rigidly "at ease" and faced their accusers. When their strongest former supporter opened the hearing they were shocked.

"Did you or did you not order a full scale military retreat?" Gunny Mann inquired. "Entirely on your own initiative."

"Aw, come off it, Sarge," Carson Braddock insisted. "You know what happened."

The appeal went unnoticed. A look around the room revealed a sea of intent faces.

"That's no answer," Iron Mike declared. "Be advised to co-operate for your own good."

"Let me re-phrase the question," Marty offered. "In ordering the retreat did you or did you not put yourselves above the duly commissioned officers of the First Marine Parachute Division?"

The bald re-enactment of the accusations leveled aboard the landing craft filled the sailors with disbelief. Angry, annoyed, and dismayed, the cousins confronted their former defender with all that was left of their hope for fair treatment.

"Once you were on our side, Sarge," Max insisted. "What changed your lily-livered heart?"

"Being abusive won't help," Colonel Jeffers warned. "I won't instruct you to answer the question any more. So for Christ sake keep a civil fuckin' tongue in your cock-suckin' mouth."

The exhausted paratroopers standing around the room raised their glasses in approval of the colonel's orders. The bleary eyes, the unshaven faces, the slept-in uniforms, and the food and drink stains all over the bandages made the troopers look like refugees from the Bataan Death March. Trapped in a room full of cutthroats the sailors had no choice but to give straight answers.

"Of course we gave our order top priority," Carson confessed. "If we hadn't there wouldn't be a First Para-fuckin'-chute Marine Division. Or a Fox Company either."

"Did you or did you not commandeer a number of U.S. Navy ocean going vessels?" Corporal Cantelmo demanded. "Without a requisition or any other proper authority."

Vinnie had one arm in a sling, his leg was in a knee cast, and his dress shirt was slit up the side to let the bandage around his waist breathe in the warm tropic air. The unopened bottle of beer tucked inside his sling was the last remaining bit of the party atmosphere. Even his carefully polished shoes were in sharp contrast to the grim expression on his pale and haggard face. His angry scowl made it clear that only a serious reply would do. To forestall the clash he saw coming, Max took over from his cousin.

"Our authority was our own informed judgment and your desperate need," ARM1/C Max Bryson explained. "How can you bring off an ocean evacuation without boats to carry the troops?"

"Besides," Carson added, "each craft was a write off the moment the atom bomb exploded."

Corpsman Casey Dworkin waved one hand as he demanded the floor and hammered on his hip-cast for emphasis. His high pitched voice and small frame only added to the luster of the bright ribbon that held the polished silver medal in the middle of his chest.

"As soon as we put to sea there was another infraction," Casey insisted. "Did you or did you not order perfectly good government equipment thrown overboard?"

The Silver Star and the wooden crutches propped up against his chair backed up his question with clear signs of his bravery and his suffering. By giving his dumb question new respect, the sailor showed that such things did not go unnoticed.

"It was either that," Carson declared, "or let the DUK go down like an anchor."

The new seriousness brought more Marines in as amateur prosecutors. Bold and forthright in their rumpled suntan shirts and forest green pants they pressed forward to level charges.

"Did you," Gunny asked, "or did you not give command to the senior man on the beach?"

"Hell no," Max stated. "The colonel was pinned down by a Jap tank and he could never have handled the DUK, anyway."

"Did either of you ever salute the senior officer present?" Corporal Tony Regni asked. "Or acknowledge his rank in any way?"

"For Christ's sake," Carson Braddock scoffed. "This takes the angel-fuckin'-food cake."

Despite attempts to dismiss the investigation, the aircrewmen were troubled. The sweat and strain of standing trial before a group of seasoned battle veterans showed in their eyes, their faces, and their stance. With each reply they looked around at former friends and found only cold stares. The faded tropic tan on Carson's cheeks and forehead was flush with anxiety fever. As he and Max inched closer together they instinctively brushed shoulders to make sure their backs were covered.

"All right, men of Fox Company," Iron Mike stated. "You have heard the witnesses for the defense. How do you find the accused?"

The two dozen Marines stood or sat in silence. They all let the question settle until it seemed as fixed and formal as all the words hidden inside the bindings of the books around the room. The leakage from the mixture of food and open liquor wrapped in the soiled table scarf at the end of the sideboard added tropic squalor to the lived-in quality of the room. The scuffs and streaks that the unshaded light bulbs brought out on the dusty lime walls suggested another era. Motionless, the company of bandaged and disheveled warriors looked like a fuzzy sepia-tone snapshot from some earlier war. When they spoke, however, they came to life with a vigor that made the present snap back into focus.

"GUILTY AS CHARGED," Fox Company shouted in chorus. "GUILTY ON ALL COUNTS. GUILTY OF TYPICAL NAVY ARROGANCE."

"You have heard the verdict," Colonel Iron Mike Jeffers stated. "Is there anything you want to say before I pass sentence?"

Carson Braddock and Max Bryson looked around the room at the fit and the wounded. Each Marine stood, sat, or lounged in whatever posture suited him. Yet their faces were masked by the seasoned and expressionless stare that distances a professional firing squad from its victims. Their very remoteness made the aircrewmen's ire congeal with contempt.

"I can understand this kind of chicken-shit from an officer," ARM1/C Max Bryson said. "But I thought you down trodden Leathernecks might give fellow enlisted men a fair shake."

"You bastards better carry out the punishment here and now," ARM1/C Carson Braddock warned. "Because from the moment we get out of this pest hole you will have to deal with the whole God-damned Pacific Fleet. I SHIT YOU NOT."

The angry declaration rang across the room as a malevolent benediction. Gripped but unmoved by its solemnity, the jury remained fixed in an unrepentant stare until the colonel spoke.

"Threats and insults not withstanding," Iron Mike declared, "it is the sentence of this court that you be stripped of your enlisted rank and forfeit all signs and symbols of that noble fraternity."

The guards left the doors and descended on the two aircrewmen like assailants. Working from the blind side, the paratroopers pinned the surprised sailors' arms back. The senior enlisted men took out knives and scissors and went to work on the starched white uniforms. Gunny Mann cut the blue eagle-and-chevron badge of petty officer standing from Carson's sleeve and stuffed the patch into the sailor's chest pocket. Corporal Regni did the same to Max's rating patch. Leaning on his crutches, Corpsman

Casey Dworkin used a scalpel to cut through the stitches that held each man's small radar operator's patch and the aerial gunner's badge on his sleeve.

"Jesus, these are tailor made whites," Carson said. "We paid good money for these outfits."

"We are due at a high level meeting in ten minutes," Max stated. "Have a heart."

To complete the destruction, Corporal Vincent Cantelmo slipped each sailor's black neckerchief out from under his collar and tore it into strips. Privates Jesse Winters and Andrew Gillis pulled the fliers' black Oxfords off and sliced the toe of each shoe with a sharp bayonet. Entering into the mood of the occasion, the radio operator from Detroit slit the sleeves of the sailors' blouses with a straight razor and cut their bell-bottom trousers down their carefully pressed turned-in seam. The others joked and cheered as their buddies undressed the struggling sailors and left them standing in the middle of the room wearing nothing but their socks, shorts, and T-shirts.

"Now that is what happens to sailors who exceed their authority," Colonel Michael A. Jeffers declared. "And don't you forget it!"

Gunnery Mann jerked the well-folded white hats out of the sailors' hands and slammed each one down hard over the spindle of a high-backed chair. As the knob on top burst through each crown a round of shouts, whistles, applause, and foot stamping approval shook the room. But it stopped as the Marine gunnery sergeant raised his hand and pointed toward the bedroom door.

"All right ladies," Gunny Mann announced. "You can come in now."

Shirley Hashimoto and Monica Ritter marched into the study like East Indian maidservants attending a pair of princes. On their outstretched forearms they carried new dress white uniforms folded up in neat squares. The peak caps were perched atop the starched blouses and the carefully pressed pants. The toe of the brightly polished shoes tucked under each cap stuck out like a black boil. Stunned, the sailors grabbed the clothes and put them on quickly to hide their undress and their chagrin. But everything felt wrong. The creases in the pants were turned out instead of in and in the wrong places. As the girls helped them into their jackets the sailors struggled against them.

"I can't wear this," Carson protested. "This is an officer's uniform."

"Will you look at the fruit salad on this jacket," Max complained. "There are ribbons and badges I've never seen before."

Finally the sailors stood still as the girls buttoned the long regulation blouses and adjusted the drape of their new outfits. Neat and clean in perfectly pressed officer's whites, the gold buttons gave just the right formal touch to the extra rows of badges and ribbons that decorated their chests.

"The one below your silver aircrew wings show that you are a paratrooper as well," Gunny Mann explained. "And below that you have the Marine Cops Expert Marksman's Badge plus the ribbon for our Presidential Unit Citation."

"Welcome to the First Marine Parachute Division," Colonel Michael A. Jeffers announced. "You are now honorary members of Fox Company."

Every soldier in the room stood and slammed out his approval with the glass, the mug, the bottle, or the plate nearest at hand. The whistles and cheers turned to groans of envy as the girls embraced the sailors and gave them sheepish kisses. The exchange of good wishes ranged from bone-crushing grips to bear hugs that threw both men off balance. Leaving nothing to chance, the colonel and the gunnery sergeant put both aircrewmen through a head-to-toes inspection.

"Regulation spit and polish is O K for Officer's Candidate School," Gunny Mann ventured. "But a field promotion entitles a man to a little pizzazz."

With his fellow Leatherneck's approval Gunny gave a tilt and forward slope to their peak caps that conferred the right degree of self-assurance. The gold buttons evenly spaced down the hip length jacket accented their lean and fit condition. The knife sharp creases in their pants and the almost patent leather shine on the black Oxfords gave them added class. Satisfied, Iron Mike pronounced them fit for duty with a clap on the shoulder and a warm handshake. The clasp and heart-felt camaraderie let most of the tension flow from the sailors like water leaving a showerhead.

"You bastards," Carson Braddock chuckled. "You sure know how to make a guy sweat."

"Consider it an object lesson," Gunny Mann suggested. "You will be chewing out enlisted ass and spreading terror through the ranks a lot sooner than you think."

"You got the terror right," Carson Braddock allowed. "I have never felt so out of place or wrongly dressed since I put on a uniform."

"Admiral Nimitz knows our names, rank, and serial numbers, for Christ's sake." Max Bryson insisted. "How the Hell can we face him in these monkey suits? Shit, even the shoes are the wrong color. Everybody knows that naval aviation officers are brown-shoe bastards."

"You just walk in there like you was born in them officer's duds," Corporal Vinnie Cantelmo advised. "Make him proud of you. We are, by God."

"Trust us," Corpsman Casey Dworkin urged. "Since you are regular navy and not reserves black shoes are preferred. We checked. Even though you fly you are still surface Navy."

The congratulations, questions, and the reassurances were taking too long. Determined to keep to a tight schedule, the colonel's niece spoke out with a vigor that shocked them all.

"For the sake of Mary, Joseph, and Jesus," Monica Ritter declared, "don't make them late."

The non-coms whisked the sailors through the double doors and the girls took them upstairs right past Mrs. MacArthur. After the heated trial and hurried restoration, the General's softly lit sitting room was a relief. The porch that surrounded the building on the second floor made it inviting, cool, and quiet. Even the girls welcomed the calm atmosphere. Still it did little to ease the stress brought on by the secret burden they bore.

CHAPTER SIXTEEN

*As administration is the art
Of action before conception
Every decision
Is an immaculate abortion.*

On closer inspection, the chalk on General MacArthur's well-scrubbed upstairs sitting room walls and the pale gold paint on the worn rattan furniture gave it a spare and scrimped look. The drapes and the cushions rescued from the basement by Mrs. MacArthur were faded and shabby enough to draw strength from the girls' attire. Shirley Hashimoto's pale green dress gave her skin an almond glow. That combination brought out the diluted bands of peacock ink and saffron in the bleach-dyed window drapes. Monica Ritter's pebble-brown shirtfront accented the touch of rust in her hair that matched the small purse that hung from her shoulder. Together, those soft hues coaxed life from the prints of large pink rhododendrons that covered the sofa cushions. Seated with their shapely legs crossed, the neatly groomed girls made even the streaks of henna in the homemade whitewash on the ceiling seem cozy. And the men responded to that, as well as the all too rare female presence, by exuding carefully measured warmth. The posture of the admiral, the general, and the President took on a supple and inviting bend as they welcomed the ladies. The air of congeniality extended to even their conversation with the sailors.

"You chaps have given us a bit of trouble," President Harry Truman snorted through a smile. "It is very rare that two enlisted men earn the same recognition at the highest of all levels."

The President's short sleeved shirt and neatly pressed gray slacks gave him a casual yet dapper appearance that drew attention to his quick and vigorous gestures. But the carefully combed salt and pepper hair and the steel rimmed eyeglasses suggested the merciless concentration of a poker-faced card shark. For all that, however, he welcomed being interrupted by his companion.

"But Colonel Jeffers would not have it any other way," Admiral Chester Nimitz explained. "He was most persuasive."

The admiral wore his sturdy white uniform and gold braid with an ease that gave the lines in his weather beaten face a certain natural authority. Despite the evidence of a lifetime of exposure to the elements, however, the pale blue eyes and the crooked teeth receded as he smiled. The hint of a younger and more forgiving man hovered just under the surface. But even the inner man knew that he would not have the last word.

"That is not quite right," General Douglas MacArthur insisted. "I resist the pleas of determined colonels every day. But when a Marine gunnery sergeant threatens to turn in his stripes if the recommendation is not approved, I know it is time to yield."

The ripple of mirth from the ladies brought a bow in their direction. Tall and arrayed with a chest full of ribbons, the general wore his tailored khaki dress uniform with a touch of majesty. Satisfied, he stepped back alongside the admiral and drew on his unlit corn-cob pipe as the President took charge of the ceremony.

"Gentlemen, and ladies too," President Harry Truman stated. "I do not know what makes two young men leap from the safety of their aircraft into a sea of total devastation and organize the rescue of what remained of an entire Marine division in the face of superior enemy forces. But I do know that you turned an American Dunkirk into a victory. And for that we all owe you a debt of gratitude that can never be fully paid. In honor of your courage, that magnificent deed, and your admirable devotion, it is my privilege to bestow on you the nation's highest award for valor."

The pause was filled with silence that was both profound and awkward. The men clasped their hands, shifted their feet, and lowered their eyes as they waited for the moment to pass. But a slight cough and the rustle of a long skirt drew an inquisitive frown from the man in charge. The recognition prompted the young lady on the sofa to lean forward as she spoke.

"I beg your pardon, Mister President," Shirley Hashimoto interposed. "As an applicant to join the women's branch of the Navy I feel it is my patriotic duty to speak up before it is too late."

The unexpected interruption broke the President's momentum and left him adrift with an unopened decoration box in each hand. The admiral took them from him before his irritation surfaced. Relieved and free to act, Harry S. Truman took off his steel rimmed eye glasses, steamed the circular lenses with hot breath, wiped them extra clean in his handkerchief, and put them back on for a fresh start. A quick nod from the general brought the admiral a step forward toward the girl since he knew her best. Shirley rose to her feet and stood as tall as the admiral. Feeling uncomfortable, Monica stood up and held her friend's hand.

"Yes, Shirley?" Admiral Nimitz asked. "What is troubling you?"

"Am I right, sir?" Miss Shirley Hashimoto inquired. "The Medal of Honor has never been awarded to a foreigner. Has it?"

"That is absolutely correct, young lady," President Harry Truman confirmed. "I dare say that Congress would commit collective suicide rather than let such a thing happen."

The question forced the general to give careful consideration to the President's facile reply. Seldom sensitive to the feelings of others, he could not stand to have any of the men who had served under his command overlooked. Least of all, a man who had received the nation's highest honors for his bravery during the enemy's long and bloody siege of Corregidor.

"What about Sergeant Jose Caluga, my Filipino mess cook?" General Douglas MacArthur demanded. "He fended off a Japanese advance single handedly by blasting them with an endless stream of howitzer shells? Hell, the order announcing his medal came along with Mister Roosevelt's insistence that I leave the Philippines to avoid capture by the enemy."

"Oh, come on, Doug. That doesn't count," President Harry Truman declared. "A Filipino is just as much an American as an Alaskan or a Hawaiian."

"Then I think there is something you ought to know," Shirley stated. "According to their service records both of these men are aliens."

The revelation made the President flinch as if a wasp had stung him. The admiral and the general grew pale and serious as they looked for un-American traits in the faces of the two handsome young men. And Shirley struggled to hold back the tears that flooded her eyes.

"That is true, Sirs," Carson Braddock affirmed. "We are Canadians."

"We hitchhiked down to Seattle from Vancouver, British Columbia, to enlist," Max explained. "Just three years ago."

"Ooohh," President Truman moaned. "I see."

The men in their dress uniforms and the girls in their colorful frocks stood in the center of the shabby room like parrots in a dingy zoo. For a short while the silence was opaque. As soon as the President began to move around, however, things seemed to improve.

"Problem solved," President Harry S. Truman declared. "I'll just make you boys American citizens by executive order."

"I am afraid it is not that simple, Mister President," General Douglas MacArthur offered. "You can commute the death sentence. You can pardon a traitor. You can even prevent another politician from being tried for his crimes. But only Congress can grant honorary citizenship."

"They will do it, Mister President. I guarantee it," Admiral Chester Nimitz insisted. "All these men have to do is to renounce their Canadian citizenship."

The strategy settled on the other Americans like a soft spring shower bringing smiles and moisture to parched lips. The President and the general thanked the admiral with knowing nods that anticipated grateful acceptance.

"With all due respect, sir," Max Bryson proclaimed. "We cannot do that."

"We will not. Not now, or ever," Carson declared. "We will not disavow King and country any more than we would turn our backs on our own fathers."

Even the oblique mention of Big Carson forced his son to swallow hard. The refusal of citizenship dashed spirits and camaraderie with the speed of a pail of ice water. President Harry Truman interlaced his fingers and bent both hands backwards until all the knuckles cracked like dry twigs. General Douglas MacArthur bit down on the stem of his corn cob pipe so hard puffs of dry ash shot up out of the bowl. Distressed, Admiral Chester Nimitz undid the brass button at the top of his tunic and wiped the sweat off the inside of his collar before buttoning it up again. They were stumped and their faces showed it. In turn their eyes sought out the Japanese-American girl with great intensity. True to her heritage she stood her ground despite the anguish she felt.

"We thought something like this might happen," Miss Shirley Hashimoto confessed. "So Monica and I took the matter to her uncle, Colonel Jeffers."

"Uncle Mikie can fix anything," Monica Ritter explained. "He sent his men around to every pawn shop in Manila looking for the right medals."

"They came up with two Navy Crosses in absolutely mint condition," Shirley reported. "I hope they will do."

Timid and slightly bent from her years in a prisoner of war camp, Monica bowed in the Japanese manner. Carefully, she took the small jewelry boxes out of her shoulder purse and handed one to the general and the other to the admiral. The deep hazel shades in her blonde hair and the collar of the tan shirt combined to frame her attractive face in a wreath of beauty. With each move her loose leg-length blouse fluffed out as if it were suddenly billowed by a light breeze. The natural tenderness and the womanly proportions she possessed were not lost on the older men.

"Thank you, child," the general stated. "Iron Mike knows his medals and his women."

"Excellent, ladies," the admiral said. "The Navy's highest medal for gallantry in action."

Bolstered and restored, General MacArthur and Admiral Nimitz decorated the sailors and gave them a firm handshake. Yet the ceremony had lost its luster. Uncomfortable, the two senior officers stepped back and turned to the President as their political spokesman. The closed circle of elders barred easy access and it fell to the girls to admire the newly conferred decorations. The burnished gold cross that hung from a dark blue ribbon marked with a silver stripe gave the crisp new uniforms a sober dignity. Impressed, Shirley Hashimoto fingered the thick wings of the Maltese Cross that decorated her friend's chest. Yet her words held a degree of concern that went far beyond congratulations.

"I am sorry, Carson dear," Shirley whispered. "Please forgive me. I could not let the President make such a mistake."

"You can't ask me for forgiveness," Carson said. "Indeed, it is not mine to give."

The young man spoke to the girl with the frankness and simplicity that made their conversation intimate. The things they said were shared by the other couple but none of it seemed to penetrate the circle of seniors.

"What do you mean?" Shirley inquired. "We all know you deserve The Medal of Honor."

The tears that clouded her vision brightened and smeared the narrow line of turquoise mascara that darkened the rim of her eyes. The tremble that invaded her lips and worked to the edges of her mouth made her cheeks quiver under Carson's level gaze. She was afraid that she had lost him and it stabbed at her heart.

"Medals like these are not really ours," Carson insisted. "They belong to far braver men resting in shallow graves or on the bottom of Shibushi Bay."

"If this award somehow reduced the measure of respect accorded to their sacrifice," Max Bryson explained, "they are the only ones who can forgive you."

"And I suspect they do," Carson assured her. "Real heroes don't put much stock in medals."

Shirley Hashimoto choked the flow of tears back until Carson stroked the nape of her neck and wiped her eyes with the tiny silk handkerchief she offered him. A tearful Monica Ritter stepped up to Max and gave him a gentle but affectionate kiss on the cheek. Undone, both girls retreated amid the soft murmur of their sobs as the President approached.

"There is nothing like a woman's tears," President Harry Truman observed, "to give weight and depth to a solemn occasion."

The President of the United States shook Carson Braddock's hand and looked the young sailor full in the face. The eyes behind the steel rimmed glasses were as firm and steady with genuine devotion as the rough grip was strong and callused from hard work. Moving on to Max, the President clapped him on the shoulder and pumped his hand with a mixture of small town sincerity and campaign vigor. It was a deep and moving experience for the sailors and for President Truman, but it did not last. The smile and bounce that invaded his face and step as he turned away from the hand-shake signaled a change of thought and mood.

"Let me see, now," Harry Truman chided. "About those uniforms."

"Oh, please forgive the impertinence, Mister President," Carson pleaded. "Things got a little out of hand downstairs."

"It was either this or nothing, sir," Max protested. "Literally, nothing but our skivvies."

"We will get rid of these outfits and put on our proper uniforms," Carson promised. "As soon as we recover our gear at the naval air station."

Max's apology and Carson's promise were delivered with Canadian deference to authority and a genuine desire to do the right thing. The slight bow and the nod of the head that accompanied each expression of remorse made the medals hang loose on their ribbons for a moment. Despite the genuine show of contrition, however, the senior officer seemed unmoved.

"It is not that simple, Mister," General MacArthur insisted. "It never is."

"Nonsense," Admiral Nimitz declared. "It is quite simple. And as usual, the ladies have the solution."

At the admiral's nod, Shirley Hashimoto and Monica Ritter finished drying their eyes and stepped forward. Blinking, squinting, and breathing through latent sobs, the two girls undid the small metal bars attached to the inside of their garments and pinned them on the sailors' uniforms. Much smaller than the medals, the blue and gold insignia of military rank gave the crisp white jackets with their rows of brass buttons and battle ribbons a finished elegance.

"Congratulations, gentlemen," President Harry S. Truman stated. "As the Navy's newest chief warrant officers you have all the privileges and responsibilities of that honorable station."

Only half recovered, Shirley Hashimoto sealed the promotion with a kiss that took Carson by surprise. The warmth of her lips and the trembling that her body projected into his threw them both slightly off balance. Reeling, his hands traced her hips and her waist along the flow of her silken gown until his arms held her steady in a firm embrace. Forewarned, Max took Monica's kiss and hug in stride even though her heart was only half in it. Her mouth vibrated with a mixture of impish delight and barely bridled passion. But her lithe body drew back with an awkwardness and a painful hesitation that made the President blush and clear his throat.

"Aagh—uuh—hem," President Harry S. Truman coughed. "With the formalities behind us, perhaps we should move on to the military business at hand."

The girls stepped away from the sailors and used the mirror over the fireplace to freshen up their faces. Instinctively, the new chief warrant officers stretched their necks to get their skin away from the collars that circled their throats. Familiar with the discomfort, the admiral smiled as he opened the discussion.

"We want to know anything you can tell us about the Japanese atom bomb," Admiral Nimitz explained. "It is of the utmost importance."

"Do you think the Japs used our bomb?" General MacArthur inquired. "Or was there something to suggest that it was a copy they made from ours."

"Our technical people are evenly divided on the question," President Truman stated. "Half of them think that the enemy had neither the time nor the resources to make copies. The other half insist that they would not have used their only bomb so early in the final phase of the war."

Chief Warrant Officer Carson Braddock and Chief Warrant Officer Max Bryson exchanged glances and then studied the men before them for clues as to how to start. The admiral watched their faces for a nervous twitch or a stammer that would reveal uncertainty. The general turned and stared out the window to take his eyes off the men and free his ears to pick up the timber of their voices. The President paced back and forth in front of the fireplace. Every few steps he scanned them from a different angle to focus on what their bodies said that words could not convey.

"The explosion demolished everything within a cubic mile and sank warships up to five miles away," Max indicated. "But a good copy would work as well as the original."

"Still, one thing was odd," Carson ventured. "The Japs were sure it would halt the invasion. They made no further provisions for attacking it. Even their inland defense force was minimal."

The young officers stood erect and addressed each of their seniors directly whether he was looking at them or not. To bolster themselves, they spoke rapidly in short bursts and passed the initiative back and forth like a relay-race baton.

"If they had bothered to put a back-up plan in place," Max declared, "our spontaneous rescue would have fallen apart at the seams."

"It wouldn't have taken much," Carson explained. "A few suicide planes. A couple of fresh artillery units. Even a few kamikaze motor boats could have blown us out of the water."

"For over two hours we were utterly defenseless," Max insisted. "There wasn't an American aircraft or a combat ready warship available to come to our aid."

The momentum that the two young aviators built up gradually animated the ladies. Listening with great interest, Shirley Hashimoto and Monica Ritter stepped away from the mirror and eased into the small discussion circle.

"That indicates that they used our bomb," Shirley said. "Their own untested copy would not have inspired that degree of confidence. The Japanese usually distrust their own technology."

"You know how much stock the enemy puts in elaborate diversions," Carson added. "If they had their own copies ready they would have set one off on some deserted island just to distract us from their main thrust."

"Oh, he is right," Monica announced to her own surprise. "They do it in the smallest things. The guards would set off firecrackers in the play-yard just before a gang rape. Believe me, they would never have missed such an opportunity."

The assurance and the revelation in the girl's words shocked the older men even more than her language. Their rigid posture and their frowns left Shirley embarrassed for her friend. Nevertheless, it seemed utterly correct to all concerned. Propelled by a surge of conviction, Max and Carson found themselves delving into the technical side of things. And that carried them far beyond their training or any sure knowledge. But their habit of reading technical manuals and entering serious discussions whenever they could gave them a certain measure of assurance.

"It seems that the only way to make fissionable uranium," Carson observed, "is to build a mass separator."

"That takes a tremendous industrial capacity," Max insisted. "And it is quite unlikely that the enemy could build one so quickly with most of their manufacturing centers in ruin."

The declaration startled the President and surprised the general. Even the admiral was distressed by the lapse in security the disclosure implied. But his secretary looked beyond such issues and addressed the heart of the claim.

"I am sorry to disagree, Maxie-san," Shirley replied. "They have a small reactor in Tokyo."

"If that is building forty-nine of the Riken Institute located in the Koishawa District," Monica ventured, "it was destroyed in an air raid some five months ago."

The inside information brought everyone else up short. The general took his pipe in hand and tapped out a thin spread of dry ash on the mantle of the fireplace. The admiral shifted the small gold charms he had on his key chain back and forth at a rapid rate usually reserved for Greek worry beads. And the President chewed on the mangled gold ear-stem of his metal rimmed glasses.

"How do you know that, young lady?" President Harry Truman demanded. "I have had three hundred men working on nothing but that for six months and they don't have a clue."

The President's blunt question and total amazement made Monica Ritter blush. Suddenly aware of her surroundings, she shrank down into her skimpy frock in an effort to hide. Despite her child-like fright, however, she was confident of her claim. Bolstered, she slowly emerged from her protective shell and met the President's flinty glare with a bold glance of her own.

"You would be surprised at what floats around a prison camp, Mister President," Monica explained, "especially when the guards don't know that you have learned their language."

"That just about clinches it," Carson concluded. "The enemy's supply of copper is particularly low and it takes a lot of tubing to re-build a generator."

Hearing a young girl dispense vital intelligence was bad enough. But the specter of a new junior officer assessing the enemy's atomic capabilities rubbed the general raw. Added to his ignorance of nuclear technology, it was like squeezing lemon juice into an open wound.

"For a couple of enlisted men fresh out of combat," General Douglas MacArthur noted, "you boys know an awful lot about top-secret matters."

"Oh, the information is out there, General, believe me," Carson replied. "It's just that most guys don't read enough of the right things to know what it means."

"We started with stray copies of the New York Times and technical articles in the Navy's All Hands magazine," Max explained. "Once we found out what questions to ask there was always an egg-head or some young brass only too eager to give us the answers."

For a moment, the swift exchange initiated a dialogue among equals. But the tilt of the general's head and a stiffening across his shoulders prompted the admiral to issue a warning.

"You may have an officer's privileges, gentlemen," Chester Nimitz admonished, "but you are still obliged to mind your manners."

"Aye, aye, sir," Max replied. "No offense intended."

"None taken, son," General MacArthur stated a bit too quickly. "Is there anything else?"

In the pause that followed everyone looked around. The twilight off the street filtered into the well-used sitting room as a cool tungsten glow that drew the last vestiges of color out of the pale walls and the faded cloth covering the cushions. Even in the still of early evening, the air that drifted in through the open windows benefited from the porch that surrounded the second floor.

"Just one more thing, General," Chief Warrant Officer Carson

Braddock said. "Why aren't we dropping an atom bomb on a different enemy city every odd numbered day?"

"And issuing an invitation for them to surrender," Chief Warrant Officer Max Bryson ventured, "on the even ones."

Admiral Chester Nimitz caught his breath and looked away like the captain of a ship gazing over the horizon. General Douglas MacArthur poked the pipe around in his mouth before he shook his head and stroked his crop of thinning hairs with his fingernails. President Harry S. Truman fixed the young warrant officers with a baleful stare over the top of his steel rimmed glasses and bared his teeth. In the silence, only the girls noticed how much the daylight had faded. Quietly, they walked around and turned on the lamps. As the artificial light gave a copper glow to the henna streaks that swirled across the crudely whitewashed ceiling Carson's cousin pressed his point.

"We do have more bombs," Max supposed. "Don't we?"

"Some, perhaps," the admiral hedged. "The question is whether or not to use them."

The dim current, the low wattage, and the dark shades on the lamps all combined to change the room by degrees. The high ceiling, the ruddy walls, and the leather bound books scattered around the room receded. And the warmth within the circle of yellow light deepened to amber.

"The Japs hit us with one, didn't they?" Carson demanded. "What are we waiting for, an engraved invitation?"

The discussion stopped as if no one dared speak. The President, the general, and the admiral all exchanged glances like unwilling conspirators. Each waited for the other to break the silence. Finally, the cousins could wait no longer. They were forced to break the spell by the torment that bubbled up from within.

"We were ready enough to drop ours on Hiroshima," Max insisted.

"What has changed?" Carson asked.

The direct challenges broke the deadlock. Speaking out in reverse order of authority, the three leaders swiftly staked out their positions.

"Almost everything," Admiral Nimitz indicated. "It's a whole new ball game."

"The drop on Hiroshima was a decision that President Roosevelt made before he died," General MacArthur insisted. "So it was easy enough to go along with it."

"That is not true, General, and you know it," Harry Truman protested. "I made that decision several months after I took office and don't let anyone tell you otherwise."

The dispute quickened the President's breath and brought a bright flush of color to his face. Unruffled by the correction, the general stifled a smirk and proceeded with the confidence of a lawyer who had been overruled by a judge but made his point nevertheless.

"My apologies, Mister President," General Douglas MacArthur stated. "Still, you must admit that even before you took over, the whole issue of using the bomb had the momentum of a steamroller charging down a mountainside."

The confrontation made the President strut and bristle like a bantam rooster. Content with the interchange, the general scraped the inside of his unlit pipe with a penknife and knocked the cold ash into the fireplace. The foul dust from the dry ash made Harry Truman wrinkle his nose.

"By unleashing the full fury of the first atom bomb on us," President Harry Truman explained, "the Japanese have provoked outraged editorials in every newspaper in the nation."

"Each day they are denounced as monsters, barbarians, savages, and animals of the worst kind," Admiral Nimitz reported. "Except for the Nazi Holocaust, there has not been such an outpouring of public hatred and private disgust since the Bataan Death March."

"Besides, some of our nuclear scientists and soft headed intellectuals are having second thoughts," the general added. "Suddenly, the whole issue of atomic warfare is a national dilemma."

Worked up at last, the President spoke with the ardor and conviction of a circus barker. The force of his delivery drove the girls back a few inches and had the sailors listening with care.

"By being the first to explode the world's most powerful weapon in anger the enemy has given us the moral high ground," President

Truman insisted. "And that will give us the upper hand when it comes to making the peace."

Short as it was, the tiny political speech hit the cousins like a body blow. Reeling at the thought of being pawns in a political game the new junior officers fought back.

"Meanwhile," Max Bryson said with a softness that raised a chill, "we could die defending your precious moral high ground."

"Is it worth another million Allied dead?" Carson Braddock demanded. "And an invasion of the enemy's homeland that will cost God knows how many Japanese lives?"

The challenge was a knife in the heart of everyone there. No one had an answer. But as the Commander-in-Chief, it fell to the President to give a reply.

"That is something I ponder every day," President Harry S. Truman confessed. "And again at three o'clock in the morning when I am waiting to go to sleep."

The weight of the President's burden brought nods of sympathy all around. But even the silence was clouded by the general's dark frown and scowl of grave dismay. The depth of disagreement between the General of the Army and the American Commander-in-Chief ran from the use of more atom bombs to the top-secret stockpiles of poison gas being rushed to Guam.

"Moral high ground be damned," General Douglas MacArthur muttered just loud enough to be heard. "Never mind how much the troops must pay."

Admiral Chester Nimitz set his finely chiseled jaw and cast a glance of sympathy and concern toward his friend, the Commander-in-Chief. President Harry Truman's entire body stiffened into a ramrod inches taller than his normal height but before his mouth opened the sailors intervened.

Acting in unison, Chief Warrant Officers Carson Braddock and Max Bryson came to attention. Each one took a short step toward the President. They undid the clasps that fastened the blue ribbon with the bold silver stripe to their chests. Together, they held their Navy Crosses out at arm's length and offered them back to the President. Shocked and undone, President Harry Truman let his face sag into a mask of regret. He reached out with both hands like a man in a dream and allowed the young chief warrant officers to place the medals in his upturned palms. The gasps of the girls rang through the silence as heart-felt sobs but the young sailors were unswayed.

"When you make up your mind, Mister President," Carson said, "please let us know."

"If you act in our favor, Sir," Max declared, "we will be proud to have those medals back."

"If not," Carson added, "please bury both crosses at Arlington Cemetery in honor of all who might have lived."

"Including us," Max added. "In all likelihood."

Tense in every muscle, both chief warrant officers put on their peak caps and gave a crisp hand-salute. In tandem, they did a precise about face and left the room. The mixture of dusk and lamplight they left behind them remained charged with their presence even after the double-doors closed. It took a full minute before anyone spoke.

"By all that is holy, Mister President," General Douglas MacArthur vowed. "You have just heard from a pair of the finest."

"If I didn't know better," Admiral Chester Nimitz mused, "I could easily be convinced that those boys are graduates of the MacArthur School of Dramatic Effect."

"Agreed, gentlemen. Agreed," President Truman replied. "But the decision is mine. And mine alone."

"We know, Mister President," Admiral Nimitz declared.

"More's the pity." General MacArthur sighed.

Infuriated, President Harry S. Truman clamped his fists closed over the pointed medals and trembled with rage. Seeing a chance to leave, Monica Ritter nudged her friend and started for the door. Shirley Hashimoto followed, then hesitated and returned. With a girlish step, she walked back across to where the Commander-in-Chief stood fuming over the general's remark. Sedately, the beautifully gowned young woman kissed the President on the cheek and waited for the film of tears that glazed his eyes to vanish. His face softened and he looked at the attractive young woman with the deep appreciation of someone who was unexpectedly relieved of a terrible burden. Gently, she pried the President's fists open and lifted the Navy Crosses from his blood streaked palms.

"You can leave these with us," Shirley promised. "Once the boys have calmed down we will have our own little investiture."

Her impish wink caught the President by surprise and completely short-circuited his reply. He sent her off with a hesitant smile and a fatherly but uncertain wave of the hand. Clearly, the girls were once again in charge. As the door closed and the last of the fading afternoon light played across the saffron window drapes and the gold rattan arm chairs the small sitting room seemed to shrink.

CHAPTER SEVENTEEN

Beauty is the lure
That will not endure
So a love beyond lust
Must stem from trust.

Miss Shirley Hashimoto followed Miss Monica Ritter out of the general's library with a quick step that gave a slight sway to her bottom and called attention to her trim figure. Arm in arm, the girls walked down the carpeted wooden stairs together. Shirley gave Max's medal to her friend and concealed Carson's in the palm of her hand. In step they strode along the thin reed matting that carpeted the corridor. The cadence of their high heels sent a staccato rap down the main floor's cathedral hall as they hurried to catch the fellows.

"Wait up," Shirley called out. "We have to get dressed for the Fox Company Ball."

"Shirley has a changing room," Monica said. "Right across the hall from my quarters."

The sailors stopped and waited for the girls to join them. Alone in the spacious foyer, the four young people stood apart from the classical pillars that reached up to the vaulted ceiling. Their attire was in bright contrast to the large burnt-orange Chinese urns against the walls. The crisp white officer's uniforms, Shirley's slick green shift, and Monica's revealing tan shirt made them look like tourists in an oriental museum.

"I don't know if I want to go to any dance," Carson Braddock disclosed. "Not after that snow job about occupying the moral high-ground."

"The President makes me wonder," Max Bryson ventured. "I'm

not sure he really knows what this war is all about."

A simple glance at the others assured Shirley that the mood was much too somber for what she had planned. Annoyance kept the newly appointed chief warrant officers pacing like animals in a cage. And for the moment even that was not enough to contain it.

"How stupid can people be?" Carson demanded. "Japan occupied Manchuria, conducted the rape of Nanking, attacked America without warning, carried out the Bataan Death March, massacred one hundred forty-six captured Canadian soldiers in Singapore, and God knows how many other prisoners of war. Who could think that such a barbaric nation would have held off using the atom bomb if they had developed it first?"

Wrath gave Carson's natural tan the heat and color of a severe sunburn. The veins in his neck stood out like the naked stalks of climbing vines fused to the trunk of a cedar tree. Outrage worked on them all as a perpetual irritant. Further condemnation of the enemy was the outlet that triggered a sympathetic response even from the former female prisoner of war.

"That's right," Monica concurred. "Wiping out Honolulu, San Francisco, and Los Angeles with their own nuclear weapons would have forced America to sue for peace."

The fury that coursed through the young girl's flesh made her cheeks swell with suddenly recalled prison camp abuses. Her fair skin took on a ruby glow that extended up into her scalp and gave her auburn hair pink overtones. Swaying back and forth, she almost danced with an aggravation that evoked spirited commentary from her newfound girlfriend.

"If the President really has the moral high-ground," Shirley proposed, "he should show us a list of all the women who are willing to sacrifice their husbands or sons rather than use the bomb to end the war one day sooner. That's where the moral center lies once battle is joined."

Even in agreement the young naval aviators were awash with disgust. The scar along Carson's jawbone stood out as a pale slash beneath his weathered tan. Max's eyes were flat with anger until he realized that their disapproval had driven Shirley to disavow her heritage. Relenting, he gave her a gentle smile that invited her to lead them beyond the condemnation of her parents' original homeland. Grateful, she steered their conversation away from the war.

"Each Japanese child memorizes this ancient Haiku early in life," Shirley said.

"In the peal of the bell
Echoes the impermanence of all things
Thus even the mighty become
No more than dust before the wind."

Slowly, the anger that filled the foyer slipped away. The men turned to the girls with renewed appreciation for their sweet smiles and smart figures. Soon all hands were ready to abandon the collective sulk. Satisfied, Shirley Hashimoto took Carson's arm and led him down the rattan-matted corridor to the anteroom next to the vestibule. Monica Ritter offered Max her hand and steered him toward the servant's suite she occupied. As the couples separated, the deep shade that the dusk cast on the gray walls softened the tensions of the day.

"Come in," Shirley said to Carson, "You must see the gown I borrowed for the dance."

Out of habit, Carson removed his peak-hat as he stepped inside her tiny bedroom suite. Unable to fold it and tuck it under his collar, he set the officer's cap down on the letter-opening table just beyond the entrance.

"After life aboard ship," Carson disclosed, "this is like the Ritz."

As the solid teak door closed, Shirley Hashimoto switched on the Tiffany lamp in the small waiting chamber and led her guest into the main room. It was a spacious bedroom with a screened off toilet and wash basin. The high ceiling was a forest green that vanished into endless darkness above the dim moonlight coming in through the vine-covered window. The multi-colored lamplight shining in from the antechamber was also weak. Nevertheless, the worn and heavily scrubbed rust that covered the unpainted tin walls picked up the rose colored border on the worn East-India carpet. Indeed, the faded western touches in the sparsely decorated suite fitted in well with the tropic decay. And over near the mirror that lined the wall the ankle-length skirt and narrow waist of a titian yellow-red gown dominated the room.

"Do you like my dress?" Shirley inquired. "Mrs. MacArthur wouldn't agree to look after me unless Admiral Nimitz found me a suitable gown."

"It's lovely," Carson declared. "You will be the regal princess of the ball."

The diaphanous silk gown trimmed below the neck in duchess lace was draped over a hassock across from the oxhide sofa. Behind it, an over-stuffed loveseat half hid the mirror that reflected the double bed. The carved corner posts that suspended the gossamer canopy high above the sheeted mattress added the spaciousness needed to complete the old-world quality.

"Before I get changed," Shirley said softly, "I have a small request to make."

The tremble in her chin, the tiny bead of moisture on her upper lip, the guarded look in her eyes, and the arched brow all signaled the depth of her concern. But Carson was too naive to read the clues. And the hunched shoulders as well as the slightly twisted torso that gave added anguish to her body language simply drove him to compound his error.

"I'm sorry," Carson said. "I cannot take that medal back. It is a matter of honor."

"Oh, no," Shirley sighed. "It has nothing to do with this trinket."

The young woman dropped the be-ribboned medal on the nightstand next to the bed and took Carson's hand in her own. She studied it until her shyness receded enough for her to scan his chiseled features. The rumpled black hair and the two day growth of shadow that spread unevenly over his scarred and wind-worn cheeks gave her the courage to go ahead.

"I know that we are practically strangers," Shirley said. "But I have heard so much about you from the Admiral I feel that you are someone I can trust."

"Well, I sure hope so," Carson replied. "What's troubling you?"

Shirley led the young chief warrant officer over to the sofa and sat down next to him. In the mottled light that seeped in from the street he searched her half hidden face for clues to her distress. They were there along with others that made him confused. The twilight gave her lips and cheeks a soft allure. She was a very attractive young woman. Yet, a tightness in her throat, a certain brittleness around the mouth, and a darkness that masked her eyes all warned of fears racing ahead of her thoughts. Caught up in her allure Carson felt the need to give her assurance.

"Don't worry about me," he said softly. "I won't take advantage of you."

"I know that," she granted. "That's why I want you to do me a very special favor."

Shaking her glistening black hair and leaning her shoulder against Carson's chest, Shirley Hashimoto waited for her tremors and stomach flutters to pass. As the inner tensions subsided, she bent forward and turned to look into his eyes. The openness and sincerity she saw in his glance and his smile turned her fears aside. The fresh color that her restored confidence fed into her cheeks warmed her face with an angelic glow he could not ignore.

"Anything," he promised. "If I can."

The pale light of an early moon filtering through the trees gave a silver glint to the carefully combed hair that framed Shirley's face. The burnt-almond skin and the soft green gown allowed her to blend into the shadows as though she had no solid substance at all.

"If you hadn't shown such incredible bravery in the face of almost certain death," Shirley whispered, "I don't think I could do this even though it is something I desperately want. Would you undress me? Please."

Instinctively, the young chief warrant officer drew his hand away in shock. Then he stretched his arm across her shoulder in a gentle hug of reassurance. The girl shuddered and dropped her head in a nod of embarrassment. The warmth and tenderness of his touch enabled her to lay her head on his shoulder and lean into his awkward embrace.

"It is all right if you would rather not," she ventured. "Even though I am soon to be a Yoeman First Class in the U.S. Navy my parents are still imprisoned as enemy aliens."

"You mustn't belittle your family," he admonished. "You are a most desirable girl."

The gentle reproof made his compliment all the more sincere. Still bashful, but not coy, she found the inner strength to open her heart further.

"I know it seems like I am pushing myself on you," Shirley confessed. "And I would hate for you to think of me as being brash or too forward."

"Goodness, no," Carson insisted. "But this only happens in my dreams."

A tingle raced through his veins and emerged as electricity in the touch that brushed away her tears, traced her cheeks, and lingered just a moment on her lips. His fingers undid the top buttons down the side of her sleek gown with a deftness that allowed her to continue.

"Ever since you saved me from the mob," Shirley whispered. "And held my breast with such tenderness. Something deep inside me has yearned for still more of your affection. Sometimes when I am alone I want your embrace so badly I whisper your name aloud."

Her outburst made him bend over and still her lips with a touch. The soft kisses he laid on her neck eased the stiffness in her shoulders and made him reflect. The confidences she disclosed acted as that rare kind of mirror that allows a man to see himself through a woman's eyes. Gradually he sensed how a flyer's dark tan and a starched white uniform can create a false impression of maturity as the dusk taking over the room bestows a steel-gray luster.

"Oohh?" Carson Braddock chortled. "Just how old do you think I am?"

Surprised, Shirley smiled and answered by reflex. It did not seem important.

"Pushing thirty," she surmised. "Give or take a year."

The thought amused him. Without thinking, he tucked in his chin and flexed the neck muscles that stiffened his throat. The artificial tension deepened and mellowed his voice.

"Try pushing twenty," Carson urged. "And then take a year and a bit away from that."

Shocked, Shirley sat up and swung her torso around to get a closer look at the new chief warrant officer's face. In the semi-darkness, the heel of her hand hit his chest with a thump. The unexpected jolt froze the weather lines and the heavily etched battle strain that hardened his cheeks and his mouth. A swift reflex, just as quickly suppressed, sent a brief flash of alarm across his face. The extra blood darkened the tender flesh around his almost healed facial scar. The new skin that stretched tightly across his jaw was crossed with creases like wrinkled wax paper. And her glance caught the strain her scrutiny added to his battle weariness with the speed of a flashbulb. In that search for the truth her mind struggled to over-ride her eyes.

"Still eighteen?" Shirley Hashamoto blurted. "I don't believe it."

Despite her disbelief, however, Carson's soft brown eyes, rumpled black hair, and eager look brought out the underlying youth that gave his smile a boyish charm. The man and the boy were so intermingled that neither he nor she could separate one from the other. Yet the unfamiliar mixture made her hesitate. Shirley's distress widened her eyes and brought a silent apology to her lips as she started to back away. Even so, her girlish face and almond eyes retained their childish eagerness. Slowly a thought running through her mind warmed her cheeks and curled her lips into a half turned-down smile barely able to contain her amusement.

"Eight—teen—and—and," Shirley gasped. "And —you're— you're innocent as well."

A flash of mutual recognition passed between them. The sight of each other's timidity creased their faces with smiles that bubbled up into gentle laughter.

"A couple of good feels," Carson confessed. "And some back seat necking with an older girl in high school. But I can talk a torrid seduction with the best of them."

Each time they looked at one another the laughter erupted again. The richness that the revelation and the merriment gave to the spreading darkness relaxed them both. Shirley felt quite at ease unbuttoning the rest of her long shift straight down to her thigh. Still a bit self-conscious, Carson unhooked her brassiere and watched the slope, curve, and lift of her handsome breasts emerge as she shrugged her shoulders and slipped out of the sleek garment.

"Even in my wildest fantasies," Carson divulged, "I never got this lucky."

The young warrant officer's hands slid gently over her bronzed shoulders and his palms brushed lightly across her nipples as his sensitive fingers enfolded suspended flesh. The breasts he fondled trembled like the bodies of frightened doves rescued from the hounds. His tender touch set up rapid tremors that squeezed her heart and spread electric currents through her limbs. The girl vibrated all over with half-smothered alarms.

"Your touch," Shirley disclosed, "is my refuge."

Their kiss was a soft and moist exploration filled with searches that evoked a summons. A strong embrace quickened the blood and brought their bodies into play as instruments of arousal. Stirred, Carson slipped his hands down along her ribs and stroked the tight flesh that rippled across her stomach. Quickly, the muscles throughout her abdomen tightened and her skin took on the tension of a drum as his ardor increased. And yet she had to stop him.

"Not in those pants," Shirley warned softly. "Not unless you want to go to the dance wearing a great wet stain that no one could miss."

Even so, the sensible caution managed to let loose Carson's fears. The rigid erection throbbing inside his pants began to subside and his tensed muscles relaxed. He softened his touch in embarrassment without actually lifting his hands from her warm and pliant flesh.

"Oh, I'm sorry," Carson apologized. "I got carried away."

"Don't be," Shirley insisted. "Just make sure you disrobe and take me with you."

Chief Warrant Officer Carson Braddock lifted the half-naked young woman up in his arms and laid her on the bed. The green shift and undone brassiere slipped off her shoulders and her arms to reveal a smoothly shaped torso dappled by moonlight. The press of his palms as he took down her panties sent a surge through her pelvis that made her long legs stretch.

"Oh my heavens," Carson extolled. "You are beautiful."

His voice evoked spasms of delight that continued to rack her body as she watched him undress. Even in the silver twilight, the dark chest hair brought out the power in his boxer's frame. Muscles filled out his thighs and tensed the calves until his legs were girded like twisted lengths of heavy hemp. Each glance added to the heat stirring in her loins.

"Thank you, dearest," Shirley said. "I have never felt anything so wonderful."

"I want to capture your loveliness in my mind," Carson declared. "Those slender legs rise in gorgeous lines I will recall when we are at sea. The flat planes that sweep across your waist and swell into sensuous curves as they enfold your breasts are beautiful to behold."

To embed the image, Carson traced the full length of her body with his fingers. The delicate collarbones led into tight breasts while the angular curve around her hips drew his attention to her well-tapered thighs. His mouth followed the same path and burned hot kisses into her stomach and nipples before he buried his face in her neck. And still he had to speak.

"Your lovely face and silky black hair present a beauty no portrait could capture."

The ease with which he played across her body and the pleasure in his lingering touch slowly opened new sensual reservoirs. Through them the hidden feelings Shirley had locked up tight inside her soul made their escape. Nevertheless, they could not rush out all at once. To give them time, she clasped his hands in hers and spread their arms in an open embrace that drew him to her all along their naked body length.

"I don't know which thrills me more," Shirley sighed. "Your words or your touch."

Lying on their sides pressed together from cheek to toe she let her hands stroke his hips while he cupped her breasts. The tears that filled her eyes and streaked her face carried off the inner yearning like dust washed down by a trickling stream.

"Adrift on a sea of fondness," Carson ventured, "the talk and the touch are adjacent shores washed by the same tide."

In the deepening darkness he kneaded and kissed her breasts until the nipples popped up hard and coarse in his mouth. The thrusts of his hips quickened and the hot and swollen member pressing hard against her inner flesh stiffened with a new intensity that made him tremble on the verge of an eruption.

"Aahh," the young sailor groaned. "You are a wonder."

Gradually, her cheeks and her jawbone set in firm lines as her eyes widened and her beautifully sculpted face became a mask of grinding passion. Gasps and sobs sprang from her throat and her head bent back to anchor an arch that curved up through her chest. Her hips rose as their bodies came together in a union that throbbed with a single pulse.

"This is more than pleasure," Shirley allowed. "This is Paradise."

A fresh sensitivity swept through Carson's swollen shaft as it felt the clasp of her softest flesh. In a sensual daze the sailor renewed his inner delight with each thrust. The blood that invaded his lips drove his mouth to find hers with a passion that melted barriers from the inside. Lips, tongues, and sobs mingled in a soulful caress that tightened the sinews of their loins.

"Nembutsu," Shirley Hashimoto sighed in Japanese. "Nem—bu—tsuuu."

Carried away, the girl was unaware of her lapse into the alien tongue. Still her urgent invocation in praise of the Amida Buddha melted the last of the reservations that quaked and throbbed throughout her being. Freed by her parent's language, the hidden ache still locked in the very marrow of her bones quietly slipped away.

"NEMBUTSU," she cried despite herself as tears flooded her eyes. "Nembutsu."

The mental images of cherished innocence crumbled like caked and yellowed winter ice yielding to a spring thaw. Deep breaths filled with the rasp of fresh hope accompanied the longing that the approach of orgasm swept away in the miracle of emotional rebirth.

"I am no longer an alien in a hostile world," Shirley sighed. "I am one with you."

The timber and the rumble of her throaty voice stirred the man's ardor. Each word touched off a tremor in his soul as her voice beat out a drum roll. The aroused young woman repeated the Buddhist prayer over and over again. The kisses she lavished on Carson's face and chest carried him over the edge of self-control. The sight of her and the liquid touch of her soft lips tortured his flesh with an ecstasy that sent hot embers of delight surging through his arms and legs. The climax that washed over him drew a shower of sparks from his brain that left him limp and breathless. And still she did not stop.

"Nembutsu," she whispered. "Nemm—booo—tsuuu."

Moving her hips from side-to-side she gradually revived her partner's erection. The strokes his shaft traced across her swollen organ made her legs spread and her stomach rise and fall until her body was pumping like a bellows. The second orgasm was slow and long in coming. But when it took hold every line and muscle in their bodies stiffened into a raised sculpture. Desire moved through her flesh like molten ore triggering fits and spasms wherever it settled. The twitches that tossed her head traveled down through her breasts as a swelling that puckered the dark disks around her nipples. Caught in the new tempo Carson felt the juices gathered in his groin begin to seethe. The sensitivity along his shaft induced subtle wrenches that inflamed the tip. Instinctively, her vaginal flesh stroked and squeezed him at an ever-quickening pace until the fever in his blood overflowed.

"Oh my dearest," Carson intoned. "You possess my soul."

His voice joined with hers in deep moans that swept them both beyond passion. The final thrusts set off minor quakes that tortured their flesh with the agony of tender delight. Climax spread through legs, arms, and up into the brain as liquid flashes scorching the flesh from within. Wrung out, exhausted, and limp, they surrendered in one extended gasp.

"Where true love abides," Carson sighed, "there is a wedding that knows no bounds."

Their tender and rocking union carried them both into a gentle sleep where they rested as one. The tropic night moved in on a dark blue blanket of fresh ocean air. The many shades and shadows that drifted over them soaked up the sweat from their moist bodies. Yet the traces of their spent thrills kept their blood just warm enough to hold the evening chill at bay. For an hour they felt nothing more than the paired heartbeats that pulsed through their veins.

All around them the room was filled with the clean darkness of early night. Gradually the tropic breeze woke them and they rolled apart. Shirley stretched out her free arm and picked up the Navy Cross from the end-table next to the bed. Making sure that the pin on the blue and silver ribbon was shut, she placed the burnished Maltese Cross on Carson's bare chest. For a moment he lay still and studied the outline of her impish smile. Even in the dark she saw him wink. The gentle laughter that burst from their throats rippled through the room as fresh and clear as Ifugao mountain rain. Barely acquainted and soon to part, the fortunate couple reveled in their momentary Eden.

ISBN 1412003&&-1